The Night My Husband Killed Me

by

Kathleen Hewtson

ISBN   1478231688
EAN   978-1478231684

All rights are reserved. No part of this book may be reproduced or transmitted in any form or by any means, electronic or mechanical, including photocopying, recording, or by any information storage and retrieval system, without permission in writing from the copyright owner.

'The Night My Husband Killed Me' is published by Taylor Street Publishing LLC, who can be contacted at:

http://www.taylorstreetbooks.com
http://ninwriters.ning.com

'The Night My Husband Killed Me' is the copyright of the author, Kathleen Hewtson, 2012. All rights are reserved.

Fact and Fiction

'The Night My Husband Killed Me' is a narrative fictional novel, told in the voices of four women who were murdered by their husbands.

All of the women were beautiful, and were either famous at the time of their deaths, or became famous for being the victims of the charismatic, disturbed, men who ended their lives.

Being dead doesn't end a woman's feelings, or her anger. There is Natalie, the international and revered movie star who died the death she had most feared all of her life. There is the beautiful, life-loving Nicole, who might just have gone back to the stunning athlete she loved, if only he hadn't killed her first. Then there is Sunny, heiress to one of America's greatest fortunes, sent into an irreversible coma for paying too much for all the wrong things. And finally, there is Colette, the high school sweetheart who married the golden boy and endured a marriage of increasing lies and disappointment, culminating in her death and that of her little girls shortly after Valentine's Day.

These four amazing women's lives were cut short, but each has a story to tell ... and now they have.

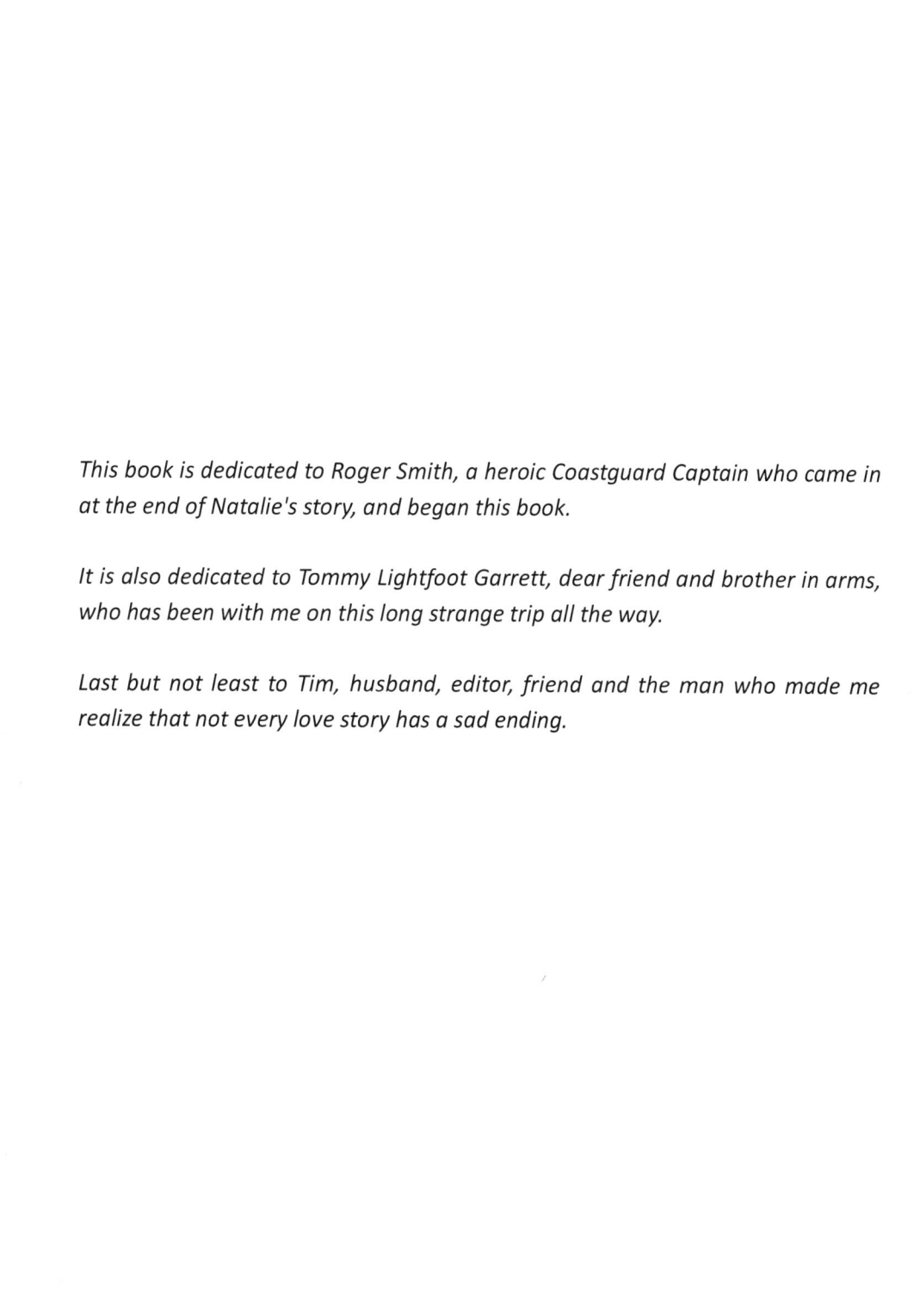

This book is dedicated to Roger Smith, a heroic Coastguard Captain who came in at the end of Natalie's story, and began this book.

It is also dedicated to Tommy Lightfoot Garrett, dear friend and brother in arms, who has been with me on this long strange trip all the way.

Last but not least to Tim, husband, editor, friend and the man who made me realize that not every love story has a sad ending.

The Ballad of Reading Gaol

Yet each man kills the thing he loves
By each let this be heard.
Some do it with a bitter look, some with a flattering word.
The coward does it with a kiss, the brave man with a sword!
Some kill their love when they are young and some when they are old;
Some strangle with the hands of lust, some with the hands of gold.
The kindest use a knife because the dead so soon grow cold.
Some love too little, some too long, some sell and others buy.
Some do the deed with many tears, and some without a sigh.
For each man kills the thing he loves, yet each man does not die.

Oscar Wilde

The First Death

Natalie

The Ghost of Isthmus Cove

Chapter 1

I didn't see this coming. Why, since I have been dead for ... for well a long time, apparently, why it is important to me to say that, I do not really know.

For nights without number the only sounds I could hear, here in the waters off Isthmus Cove, were my own cries. I cannot say exactly when I began to realize that the living - some of the living - could hear me too, and that I could hear them. It is always night here for me and I am always in water, drifting endlessly but never reaching the shore. The people who can hear me can do so only in darkness.

When I began to hear them talking was when I started to know that I had been dead for nearly thirty years. Very few of the people who drive their pleasure boats over my grave think or speak of me at all. But there are some, and from them I have learned what the world believes to be true about me.

> *It was right after Thanksgiving. She was out on her boat with her husband and Christopher Walken. They had been drinking all day long, and when they got back to the boat, there was some kind of fight or something.*
>
> *She was loaded, so maybe she wanted to go back and party on shore, or she was mad and she wanted to get away.*
>
> *Anyway, she went out for whatever reason and tried to get into the dinghy, and somehow she ended up in the water and she drowned.*
>
> *It was really sad. They found her the next morning, floating face down in the water. She wasn't very far from the shore but she had probably been dead for a long time before she got that close.*

There are sometimes variations on this story but overall it's pretty much the same.

And it was when I started to be able to hear them that I began to try and make them hear me. I would begin by talking in the same conversational tones they were using - and nothing. This frustrated me and made me cry, and I became angry. Then I noticed that my anger and my pain created some kind of trigger. Though to me my screams for attention and help were earsplitting, I could tell it was not the same for them and yet they could hear something. I understood that because sometimes they would get very quiet all of a sudden, then there would be a pause, and then, in uncertain voices, they would say to each other. "Did you hear that?"

Mostly it would just be one person, usually a woman, who would say that.

After a while I began to recognize one voice in particular. She began bringing out her boat alone and waiting, encouraging me to speak. She said her name was Marti. I wanted to talk to her. I tried harder to talk to her than I have tried anything since the night I was murdered, but all that she can hear are my wordless cries. I know this because she always ends up in tears herself. Sometimes she rows out here and scatters white gardenias around me. It was Marti who told me that I have been dead nearly thirty years; literally dead in the water.

When you are dead, time doesn't pass the way it does when you are living. Though I think I might be in a sort of hell, I am spared at least the minute-by-minute awareness of understanding time.

I do not know why I am still here in the cold dark waters where I died. My sole mourner, Marti, speaks out loud as though she were having a conversation with herself, but I think she is also trying to explain to me why I am here.

Once she said that she had read that a ghost cannot cross water. I thought that was funny. She is a very strange woman and not someone I would have known while I was alive. A ghost not being able to cross water seems like a silly thing to me, but then I am indeed a ghost and I am still in the water I died in so many years ago, so maybe that is as good a reason as any. But I don't think that is why I am still here. There are signs, faint but visible, that there is more than this.

Did you know that the night I died it was cloudy and rainy and there were no stars? I should know, it took me nearly five hours to die and I had ample time to study the sky. There are moments I have, or maybe there are decades - as I said, time is not the same to the dead - anyway there are moments I have when I almost think that I will begin to see the clouds move away in the night sky and there will be stars, a million, a billion stars stretching into infinity, and I think if I ever look up and can see the stars, my long night will finally end.

No, I believe that I am still here because I am still so confused by my death and by the life I led that brought me to this death. Maybe to truly die, to either have the endless sleep or the endless life of peace we all hope for, I have to go back to my murder and the times that brought it upon me. As I have said, I didn't see it coming. Is that why I am here, because in my own way I was as careless as he was?

When my husband put me into the Pacific, I still in no way foresaw the outcome of that argument. It was not our first, but as it happened, it was our last, ending in my death.

After he put me into the one place I had feared all my life, dark water, I was too angry to be frightened at first. I knew of course that I was actually in the water, but I thought - oh, it is hard to remember this - I guess I thought he would pull me out and we would continue to rip and tear at each other until one of us gave up or passed out, as we always had. I never thought, I never believed, that he meant for me to die. Even when he pried my hand off the swim step with his face twisted up in rage, no, even then I thought he would change his mind.

While I was still near enough to the boat, my boat, our very own boat, to hear him screaming abuse at me, I remained so certain of imminent rescue that I did not yet begin to dwell on anything besides the pain and indignity of the bruises his hands had put on me and on my sense of outraged injustice that I had been placed into the Pacific Ocean like a sack of garbage.

Understand that.

I never thought for a second that I would not be pulled back in to the warmth and safety and hostility of my very own boat. In those first few minutes in between calling me a whore and saying that he was so glad I was off of his fucking boat, he would lapse into drunken self-pitying whining and tell me to 'Hang onto your hat, I'm coming, I'm coming'.

I wasn't afraid yet. The coat he had forced onto me, my big winter coat, was acting as a surprising life vest. I wasn't sinking at all. I was buoyed up by my coat and warmed by my rage. I was not crying for help, not then. Instead I was, for the most part, quiet. He was talking incessantly and I was just listening, storing it away. Indeed I was already planning my retribution. I could see it so clearly: he, or one of the other men on board, would in seconds hoist me back over the side.

Why not? A strong man - and all three of them were strong men - had only to lean over and grasp my hands and pull. I weighed less than a hundred pounds. It would have been a hard tug but nowhere near impossible.

As soon I got back on board, though, I was going to unleash twenty different kinds of hell on him. Before I was through he would be the one spending some quality time in the water, swimming to the shore where, as far as I was concerned, he could spend the night wet and cold and miserable, waiting for the dull first light of morning and the shame to follow.

Would I have gone public with the things he had done to me? Would I have divorced him again? Yes, I think this time I would have. Our Second Act, which began as a glorious cinematic waltz with all the world watching and clapping from the sidelines, had degenerated into a bad remake of 'Who's Afraid of Virginia Woolf'. And he had hit me and he had put me into dark water, the one thing that he more than anyone knew I was truly afraid of.

So, no, I don't suppose there was any going back from that. He had crossed the Rubicon and had fatally destroyed what was left of our marriage. But this is also where I made a mistake, a fatal mistake as it happened.

I know now that he was sure he had gone too far to take any of it back; that he knew he could not un-ring the bell this time, but like other less extreme times, he was willing to be reassured, hoping to be told all was forgiven.

> "You are still my darling; we are still the world's darlings and will remain so, world without end, amen."

He had been my darling, or my love, for great swathes of time in my life, but, and this is hard to explain to anyone who is not an actor themselves, most of it was a play. When you are paid, and I was paid very well, to convince other people that the love and pain and happiness I displayed on the screen were valid and true, it can carry over to your personal life as well. And speaking of personal lives, the truly famous don't have much in the way of that. Does anyone still remember, I wonder, Liz Taylor and Richard Burton? They played great doomed lovers in 'Cleopatra', and failed hating lovers in 'Virginia Woolf', and on screen it was all an act, and yet the act carried over and became reality.

We, my husband and I, were not so evenly matched, not in our first marriage and much less so by our second try, but we might have imagined ourselves as the world's greatest romantic couple on-screen and off, and sometimes imagining a thing makes it so.

In our first failed union, I was already an enormous movie star and he was the very handsome not-so-leading man, but to me, at eighteen, he represented a romantic ideal, with champagne and big gestures, and a promise of not just adulthood but of glamorous movie star adulthood, where our perfect lives together would be played out in front of an adoring worldwide audience - not just when I was making movies but all the time.

I had to marry somebody. I wanted so badly to leave my mother's home, but I could not leave because she had filled me up with dozens of amorphous fears, fears which left permanent imprints and made me positive that if I was ever alone, they might all come true.

Chapter 2

I never could stand to be alone. I am alone now and have been so for nearly as long as I lived, but that was not my choice, it was his, and he knew I could not bear to be alone. He knew and he made me die alone anyway, and I think because I died alone, and died in the way I had feared above all else, he ensured my entrapment. My husband always needed me to stay in one place, to remain where he could easily find me. *Well, here I am, darling, come back and look down into the water. My arms will always be raised for you to join me.*

Our first marriage happened not because I felt the deep love and soul mate connection with him that I had displayed on screen when making 'Rebel', but because he said the magic words, "You will never be alone, my darling, I will always take care of you. We will live out everyone's dreams. It's just like a movie, Nat, but everybody lives happily ever after in this one." That seemed so safe and right to me then, because the only time I was ever truly sure of myself was when I had the cues and directions given to me on set.

The rest was all uncertainty, confusion, bad drama and fear. It is where I came from. I have had nearly three decades to run back the film of my own life out here, and what I think now is that part - not all, but part - of my mother's evil genius was to create a home atmosphere so toxic and unsafe that the only place I could ever be certain of the ground under my feet, and of a happy outcome, was while I was making movies.

I was a very different kind of mother to my own girls. I worked so hard to make sure that they knew their safety lay in home and family and friends, that the ordinary things I feared - had been taught to fear - were the very situations they could trust. I taught them this and then their father killed me, and I have no way of knowing that what they grew up believing was the safest route to take.

I'm sorry. I became lost again in my terrible loop of knowledge that I could have got it all so badly wrong. Perhaps, after all, my own crazed mother's lessons were the better ones: trust in the perception of happiness and never, ever, try to find the real thing, for in doing so you may be terribly harmed.

I am a good example of this maxim as I was murdered and am now nothing more than a sad shade that does not even have an old mansion to haunt like the

Captain in one of my early films, 'The Ghost and Mrs. Muir'. I have only this small forgotten slice of ocean. It doesn't help, this kind of thinking, it really doesn't, and it may be contributing to my continued presence here. I will try and stick to the facts of my situation and not speculate on what may or may not be true.

What is true is that I married my handsome actor, who was then also very young and hopeful, and may have loved the idea of us as a couple a great deal more than he ever loved me, or maybe I am wrong about that too because it is very hard for me to attribute any sincere motives at all to the man who eventually killed me.

We were very happy the day we married, I remember that. He was undeniably handsome and I know I looked unusually beautiful. We took a train for our honeymoon trip because I had convinced myself that I was afraid of flying, and in those days he liked to indulge my neuroses as long as they didn't inconvenience him in any significant way.

If I am going to talk about my honeymoon, I am going to have to talk about our sex life, and even here alone in my dark water, I do not enjoy doing this as it raises the inevitable question, 'How did you let yourself be led back into a second go round?'

I was not a virgin but I was an eighteen year old girl of very limited experience. In the beginning I thought it was romantic that he treated me like spun glass when he touched me. In the beginning I thought it was sweet that he almost always had to be at least a little bit high to touch me. I thought, and he helped me in this delusion, that he loved me so much that he was a bit intimidated by me. I thought he made love to me like a character in a Fifties love scene, complete with darkness and tentative brush strokes, because he thought I was nearly too precious to touch. I didn't know then, because how could I have known, that sexual love between a man and a woman can ignite and burn like a forest fire. I later learned what it should be like, with Warren, but I also learned - and I never forgot this lesson - that deep physical passion did not mean that you could not be left alone.

With my husband and me, at least the first time around, it was so wonderful after we made love. He would kiss me and stroke my hair, and tell me in his beautiful voice how much he loved me, and what I didn't hear, and I think I can excuse myself for this, is that he was always happier and more loving afterward.

I think it was relief but it didn't feel like relief to me; it felt like love and safety that stretched as far into the future as I could see. I need to explain again that I was an actress and had been an actress since I was five years old. When you grow up making believe, it's hard to draw the lines. He was not the only one who was acting; we were mutually guilty there.

And yet, because I related terms of emotion in my own life to movies, I could not help but compare our movie, the movie of our marriage, to a Doris Day, Rock Hudson film, and I wanted to be living out Scarlett O'Hara's passion with Rhett, but then too, I would remember that in the end he left her alone. I thought about that also in the years between Act I and Act II of our marriages. So, no, the sex was not great - it wasn't even significant - and I hardly ever let myself think about how he touched me more in public then he did in private, or how as soon as a camera appeared, he would pull me into his arms and kiss me deeply. I didn't allow myself to wish we had cameras rolling at home or to wonder what we would be like in private if we did.

Besides, we were almost never at home. He liked to be out, my husband, at Romanoff's, at Chasen's, at industry parties, and then, at eighteen, nineteen, twenty, twenty-one, so did I. It didn't seem unnatural to me that every single milestone in our lives together had to be celebrated under klieg lights. It was how my mother had insisted I live and now it made my husband happy, and I don't remember being unhappy myself. We both smiled a lot in the endless pile of scrapbooks he kept, so I guess we must have been terribly happy all the time. We might have gone on doing this for years, being Hollywood's young golden sweethearts, until I finally grew up and wanted more. I eventually did get more, much too late in the day, and that in turn caused him to kill me, but I am skipping ahead to our later marriage where the stakes became higher and so did the losses. This is about our relatively harmless first time. No-one dies in that movie.

Though to be fair to both of us, our first divorce did not seem relatively harmless at the time. I caught my husband with another man, one of our employees. I lost my mind and ran temporarily back home to the unsafe harbor of my mother, and we both imploded for a long time. I was too young and damaged and shocked and disgusted to be forgiving, or even willing to listen, and he was too young and humiliated and damaged to try to explain something to me that I don't think he understood himself. My husband was a prisoner of his time and his desire to see himself and, just as importantly, have the world see him, as the urbane leading man, our generation's Cary Grant, and you cannot be gay and be Cary Grant.

I believe he did not mean to deceive me. I believe he meant to marry a movie princess and insulate himself behind such iron walls of fame and privilege that he would create a life where it was almost impossible for anything unnatural or base to creep in. He found out that sometimes your true nature makes you do things you know are not the best or safest for you, they are just the things that have an inviolable pull. He found out, and so did I, I never could stand to be alone.

I left him, and a few months later I started a movie that would define me as an actress, and I started a relationship that would define for too long how I viewed men who were challenging and treated me as an equal and not a goddess. The movie, 'Splendour', made me an icon, and though I could not know it at the time, it created a burning hole in the psyche of my once and future husband that he could not exorcise until he put me into cold water.

It is one of the great misconceptions of the myth that our second marriage became, that it was I, and not him, who wanted to name our boat after my greatest screen triumph. When he suggested it, I remember hearing a tiny warning bell in the back of my head, a small cue to react. But then he was looking at me so earnestly, and his sweet eyes seemed to hold nothing but his apparently endless need to bring me pleasure, so I acquiesced. That was a mistake; I was letting him name my coffin.

When we purchased the dinghy on a windswept happy day at a boat dealer in Marina Del Ray, he laughingly asked me what we should call it. I was pregnant and edgy, I'm not sure why. It was one of those days when our relentless double-act was wearing on me. I should have said let's call it 'The Thief', darling. I knew how proud he was of that show, his bow to his adored Cary Grant. I didn't say that at all. What I said instead was, 'Oh let's call it 'The Prince Valiant', darling. That way both our boats will be named after our greatest triumphs on the screen.'

If his eyes flashed with the hurt or rage that he always concealed unless very drunk, I did not see it. He merely laughed as though I was the wittiest girl, instead of the bitchiest girl, and agreed to the name.

I believe now that he also heard a tiny cue begin for the scene he subconsciously wished to play. I think from that moment forward, every time he saw that poor black rubber vessel slapping incongruously alongside our movie star boat with its equally vicious name, he started to develop the determination that would grow into our final scene at sea.

Before I haplessly returned to him, I lived out what would unknowingly become the only adult and valid years of my life. During those years, which at the time I discounted because I was alone, I created both the finest body of my work as an actress and my first child. It was the only time in the forty-three years I was given that I lived on my terms. I had relationships with men who judged me on my merits as a woman and not as the great star. I bought and decorated my own beautiful home, I learned about money and how to make it grow, and in addition to being a movie star, I became a mini-mogul.

Yes, there was an in-between marriage for each of us, my husband and I. These marriages, both to kinder people than we possibly deserved, were unimportant previews for the upcoming event, except that without them our reunion special would never have been made. After several years on my own, trying and failing to play the carefree movie star, and usually instead being - as someone kind once wrote - 'the prettiest and loneliest girl in whatever room she was in', I became convinced that happiness, the imaginary movie set happiness I had always sought but failed to achieve in my off-screen life, lay in marriage and children, in being ordinary.

Don't judge me too harshly for wanting that. Everybody has different dreams at different times in their lives. Everybody is always trying to reinvent themselves. It is not just cats or movie stars who live nine lives.

I want to be honest; I want that so badly. I think I need complete honesty if I am ever going to see another thing beyond black water and this starless sky.

I went after a good man, a happily married man, because one night in Chasen's, when I was having a girls' dinner with my little sister, my husband came in. I hadn't seen him for years. He looked stunning and he looked different – manly, and flushed with some kind of inner pride and certainty that had not existed in him during our marriage.

He was passing out cigars and telling rapt diners that he had become a father - a *father!* I knew he had gotten married - it had been in all the trades - but when I read that she was a little older, British and had her own children, I remember nodding in understanding. People in my circle felt the same way I did, but he had fathered a child now and that made what I believed false. It made my leaving him seem wrongheaded. What if I had misunderstood? What if I had stayed? Then I would have had the child, I would have been the reason he looked so tantalizingly masculine and glowing with happiness.

I remember sitting in my booth waiting, with hopeless embarrassment, for his inevitable arrival at our table. I knew we would be the focus of every eye in the restaurant and the best of the evening's later gossip. I was all dressed up and I know I looked beautiful. I know he thought so too as admiration flashed in his eyes, admiration quickly drowned by pity and, yes, a little triumphant contempt, because at that moment, none of the rest of it mattered. My stardom, my money, my beauty, it was all ashes, because in his gaze I saw the truth.

I was a woman alone, all dressed up, sitting with her little sister, a woman who had no-one waiting for her and no-one to go home to.

I was alone and it was just as dreadful as I had always feared it would be.

Chapter 3

Shortly after that I met Richard. I wish he were more a part of my story, that there was more to say about him. He was a good, kind, talented, smart man who gave me one of the only two perfect unblemished accomplishments of my life. He gave me my first daughter, my Natasha, my love. But he didn't adore me, he didn't treat me as though I was more than human. He treated me like an equal, and after seeing my husband again, I compared him against the memories of that lost, now idealized, first union, and he couldn't win.

He was driven by my coldness to make a mistake, just once, and I knew even then it was unimportant and meaningless. To tell the truth, I was glad it had happened. I needed a way out of that marriage. I had what I wanted from him, my little girl, and I needed to be free of my hasty marital ties, not because I wanted to be alone again, no, I was never planning on being alone. I was planning on doing what can never, and should never, be done. I was planning a rewrite.

Seeing my husband that night at the restaurant three years before had resonated inside me. I could not get over the change in him. He had fathered a child and now, in this new, older incarnation of himself, he was everything I needed, both the lost fairytale prince to my princess of our first marriage and the strong hearty father figure I had been looking for all my life. Two great needs and dreams fused into one beautiful package. Could any woman resist a try for that?

There was another, darker reason, of course. There always is. I was the star, the prize; it could not be he who would go on in triumph and happiness after losing me, his erstwhile goddess. I knew that my leaving had left a gaping hole in him, a dream unfulfilled, that while he might be succeeding in his own way without me, I knew he was still secretly pining for the true stardom only an association with me could give him.

I was so right about that and so wrong about how either of us would feel when he resumed - as he had to by nature of my status - his old role as a supporting player. If I had not reached out my hand to him and offered both of us what seemed at the time a miraculous opportunity at not only a chance to roll back the film but a chance at perfect cinematic happiness, then he would have gone on to become a respected television actor and attained a level of stature and admiration in his own right. He might have married some understanding woman who knew the truth, but never showed by word or deed that she knew, and the cracks in his picture of himself might have become papered over.

Instead I made him Mr. Natalie Wood once more and the cracks became fissures, and then crevasses, and we both became victims of that, I more than he. If I had not reached out to him, I would have gone on to become a greater star, and instead of trying to make him feel secure, I would have gone on to play Daisy in 'Gatsby' and Sophie in 'Sophie's Choice', and become a respected scion of film greats instead of a cartoon caricature of myself who rode on Pasadena Parade floats.

I would be alive.

If I had not reached out then, of course, there would have been no magic little blond baby to love, and she was worth any price, although mine has been higher than that of ordinary women. It does not help to think like this. It does not help to say to myself that I did not see it coming. I am beginning to realize that I might have seen it coming.

In my final bid for freedom from him, I knew the ending would be catastrophic, that he could never let me go a second time, not when he was no longer young or able to start the long road back to becoming someone other than Mr. Wood again, not when he blamed me, and maybe with some justification, for turning him back into a supporting player, but promising in compensation that I would never leave him behind empty-handed.

He made renewed accommodations to being second. If he wasn't the star, then as part of a package he would have at least star power. Increasingly, in our second marriage, he saw us as something glorious and above the common, and I began to see us as a silly, somewhat shoddy, double-act, as slightly ridiculous.

He used to say to people when we were asked to parties - and everyone wanted us at their parties - 'We'll bring the glitz'. I was always vaguely annoyed by that; glitz, after all, is just cheap glitter and paste.

I know I am making it all sound very bad when it was not all very bad. As a matter of fact, in the beginning of our second marriage, and many times in between, I was happier than I have ever been. It is just hard to admit this to myself because it ended with me being murdered in the dark water I had feared all my life, and now I find that nearly thirty years have passed and here I remain, forever drowning.

But again, I have to mine this strain honestly or always remain here.

As I have said, it started out as close to perfect as any union could be. We were married off Catalina Island on a boat. My husband loved boats, and in spite of my fear of water, I wanted to please him, so we began again, and ended again, on a boat surrounded by friends. Naturally, on our wedding day, we had our girls beside us and no one in our small group, including me, saw anything ahead but clear sailing for us. My husband and I were both radiant with joy and anticipation, and I spent the entire day either under his arm or standing adoringly beside him while he toasted me, telling our guests that I took his breath away. I'm sure I can be pardoned for mentioning how well he returned that favor a few years later.

I was determined to make a success of this marriage, come hell or high water. Oh, there I go again - high water. I am not, or I should say I *was* not, overly given to sarcasm before I was murdered, and I do not wish to spend eternity as some kind of water witch, but it is really hard to escape all the sayings that I heard thrown around during my life, and now think about endlessly, wondering if they were messages of some kind.

What does an actor fear most - being washed up, having a movie that is dead in the water? I even know every word to a poem by Shakespeare that Larry Olivier recited one day when he was our guest on the 'Splendour'. At the time, a couple years before I died, I remember thinking how special it was, looking out over the water, listening to his beautiful old voice reciting the words. Beautiful? I should have known somehow that he was being prophetic, delivering my eulogy.

Full fathom five thy father lies;
Of his bones are coral made;
Those are pearls that were his eyes;
Nothing of him that does fade,
But doth suffer a sea-change
Into something rich and strange.
Sea-nymphs hourly ring his knell:
Ding-dong,

Hark! Now I hear them – Ding-dong, bell.

I never did forget a line. I remember so clearly when he said it, thinking, 'Yes, that is true death, the endless death of the sea'. I looked at my husband sitting beside me to see if he had been as affected as I was, but his eyes were unreadable to me, hidden behind his dark glasses.

However, our second marriage wasn't all portents and cliff hangers, far from it. We got married and after a few months I bought us my dream house on Canon Drive in Beverly Hills. When I say I 'bought', that is exactly what I meant. When we remarried, he didn't have a dime and I had lots of dimes. I had made a few million dollars on my last film and I dumped it immediately into L.A. real estate and invested with my old friend Aaron Spelling, a man who knew television and could predict what the American viewers wanted before they knew themselves. I shared what I had with my husband.

I was desperate to shore up his ego, to try as much as possible to keep that new swagger and confidence that had made me so determined to get him back that night in Chasen's. I asked for another baby and we got pregnant almost immediately. How we got pregnant, well, we did it the old-fashioned way, and I do mean the old-fashioned way, as in bed there wasn't much change from our first marriage, unless he was drunk, and increasingly that became a part of our lives. If he drank six Scotches on our rare at-home nights, I would have two, and then sometimes he would be less suave and tentative, but it was always there afterward, the relief.

By then I had convinced myself that you can't have everything, and I did have almost everything, so I let go permanently of the need for a perfect connection in bed, or so I thought at the time.

Oh, he could display huge amounts of passion towards me, my husband, at the Academy Awards, on the Pasadena float parade, in every interview he gave, at our parties and other people's parties. And every New Year's Eve, when we would have our black tie gala, he would start the evening by raising his champagne glass and toasting me with eyes that practically burned with passion. "I love you, my darling Natalie. You take my breath away." Passion has many different sides and outcomes.

We went along as married people do. If the kind of careless comfort and ease didn't exist when we were alone, then it was shielded for the most part behind our money and our glamor, and this kind of ceaseless busyness we had. Even before Aaron gave him his dream series, the one where he got to play him and me as he idealized it in front of a TV audience, we were very busy.

We went to Europe and Mexico, and spent weekends on our boat, and always there were people around us, and we played to them, and enough of our venerated public love story spilled over onto us that we believed it too, I think. But there were signs and stresses early, and he responded to them by drinking too much, and that scared me. We had the girls and I believed - needed so much to believe - in us as happily ever after, that I did whatever it took to keep an even keel.

My good friend Robert Redford offered me the part of Daisy in 'Gatsby' and I wanted it badly. I could have owned that part. My husband was not happy with the idea. He reminded me over and over how, after our baby girl was born, I had said, 'Who needs movies?'. My God, I couldn't believe it. Am I the only woman alive who ever said romantic things about new motherhood?

Maybe not, but he was going to hold me to it. He knew every button I had. All husbands know them, and mine more than most, because he had started with me during my great escape from my own mother. He used it then to ask me if I wanted my girls, our girls, to grow up believing as I did that movies mattered more than home, than them?

He had me. I was never secure in any role except as an actress and he was shaking out all my old fears that I could never be successful as anything other than an actress. 'Don't they matter more?' he asked me. Of course they mattered more. It wasn't even worth answering.

I turned the role down, and a few weeks later he was offered the role of Brick in 'Cat on a Hot Tin Roof' for a TV remake, but only if I would play Maggie. That was a different thing altogether. Then it was a chance for a family outing to England, a chance to practice our craft and be together with our girls while offering them a cultural experience.

I agreed. I missed acting and maybe this was the only way.

Chapter 4

I won an Emmy for Maggie and his Brick was savaged by the critics.

It didn't need to happen that way, but the character of Brick ran far too close to my husband's worst fears, so he sleepwalked through the role. The filming of 'Gatsby' only required three weeks on location, he wasn't working, and we could have taken the girls to Long Island more easily than to London. I didn't want to think about that.

I thought about that.

Soon afterward he started filming his first successful television series about a glamorous wealthy couple who spent an inordinate amount of time in cocktail attire and called each other 'darling' a lot. They even had a live-in butler. My husband had very much wanted us to have a live-in butler but I had drawn the line. In the series, my husband played the predominant role of the impossibly handsome and effortlessly successful Jonathon who was an adoring and indulgent husband to his beautiful trophy wife. At home this nonsense began to carry over in his increasing boasts to anyone who would listen.

Constantly, when we had friends to the house or on the boat, if they complimented our possessions, he would smile expansively and say, 'Television has been awfully good to Nat and me.' Or a variation of it might be, 'This is the boat [house, diamonds, etc. - you name it] that television bought.' Even the Blackglama mink I was given for that damn 'what becomes a legend most' ad, he claimed to admirers to have purchased from his T.V. success.

Maybe I should have laughed it all off and let him enjoy his time in the sun without casting any shadows, but I couldn't. I didn't. And it was after those God-awful award ceremonies started up that I began to become seriously unhappy, and he and I began our final descent, soon after my thirty-ninth birthday, that ended at Isthmus Cove one rainy night when all our home truths about each other came spilling out like the cold rain that had pelted us all weekend.

When I turned thirty-nine, I started to get nervous. I was decorating friends' houses, for Christ's sake. I was a typical Beverly Hills housewife with a closet filled with more clothes than ten women could wear, and I kept adding to it anyway because lunch and shopping is all that a Beverly Hills housewife does, and if I didn't buy a car-load of designer clothes after each lunch, then I didn't have anything to talk about the next day at the next lunch. The decorating thing came up because my own home had become decorated to the point where, near the end there, I was having fringes and ruffles removed off throw pillows in order to have them redone. Other wealthy women in Beverly Hills are constantly redecorating because you have to have something to do, and several of them admired our house on Canon and asked me for help, so for a couple years I would add to lunch and shopping by running around with material swatches, pretending to be frantically busy.

My husband, for the first time in his life, had a successful T.V. series and was working fourteen hours a day, so there were no drop-of-the-hat pick-up-and-go vacations. Natasha was seven and in school full time, and Courtney was four and spent most of the day following Willie Mae, our housekeeper, around. I was indeed another Beverly Hills housewife, with the tiny exception of having once in the not-so-distant past been considered one of the country's premier stars.

In those days, though, the only way anyone might have recognized my former status was because I was still approached by autograph seekers, but they were starting to get younger and they were starting to say unintentionally hurtful things to me like, 'Oh, Miss Wood, you were my mom's favorite actress'. For God's sake, I was thirty-nine years old, and I had become Bette Davis?

Then I was humiliated and honored simultaneously by a series of award ceremonies. The nail in the coffin of my faux complacency was a lifetime achievement award for the body of my work in films. Normally they hand those out when you are about eighty years old, but I hadn't made a film for nine years, since 'Bob and Carol', and in Hollywood time memories run in dog years, so by that standard I was almost exactly eighty. The 'what becomes a legend most' ad for my mink followed shortly after that and I remember sobbing all the way home from the shoot.

I might have pulled out of the downward emotional tailspin I was going into and gotten some perspective back, but when I walked into my house red-eyed, puffy-faced and draped in that ludicrous coat, I was greeted to my horror by the sight of a hundred of our closest friends, all beaming at me, all wearing cocktail attire though it was two in the afternoon, and front and center, dressed in a tux, was my triumphant grinning husband, the television star.

He said theatrically, "Here she is, ladies and gentleman, our very own legend, the love of my life, Miss Natalie Wood. Natalie, darling, you're the star. You take my breath away." I wanted to die or run back outside trailing my oversized coat. I wanted to hit him across his smug face. I don't usually use profanity but this was a mercy fuck of the first order and a very public one at that.

Instead, I reached down deep inside and pulled up the movie star inside me. I tilted my chin and gave a little spin to make the coat swing out, and then I shrugged it off and handed it to my husband and said. "Hang this up for me, won't you, darling? The legend needs a drink."

The room exploded into appreciative laughter; he couldn't quite manage much more than a death's head rictus of a grin. I watched him out of the corner of my eye as he dutifully left the room to do my bidding. His fingers were white as they clenched that coat.

Later, when I took it to storage, I could still see the imprints they had made against the black fur.

Chapter 5

I called my agent the next morning and dramatically announced to him that I was ready to work again. His silence spun out long enough for me to realize that, instead of being overwhelmed at my news, he was quite underwhelmed. I interjected nervously, asking him if he wasn't pleased. Thank God for the inbuilt hypocrisy in those who build their fortunes off others, because if it hadn't been for that, he might have been honest, and I think right then his honesty would have leveled me.

He began chattering away, telling me that of course this was the best news, the very best news imaginable, but we had to carefully consider the right comeback vehicle for me. Natalie Wood couldn't just be in anything, after all.

I agreed with him immediately and asked him what recent scripts and offers he had turned down on my behalf, since everyone knew I had taken some time off to raise my children. Again, I was met with silence, and then, "Well, nothing recent, per se, Natalie. Nothing for a couple years, actually. You know this town, memories are short. Maybe people start to see you as a relic from another time in Hollywood, but not to worry, you say you want to work, I say all we need is the right vehicle. I'll put the word out and I have no doubt that before the month is over we'll be swimming in scripts."

I wanted to tell him to go to hell. The word 'relic' had enraged me; the word 'relic' had terrified me.

It was October then. If by the following April we were swimming in scripts, it was in exceedingly shallow water indeed. I was offered two parts. One was in 'The Towering Inferno', playing a support role as drunken trophy wife; the other was at least a starring role in the movie 'Meteor', playing the love interest of another legend, Sean Connery.

I turned down the first and accepted the second. My husband, at first nasty and dismissive, perked up when I called the producers of 'Inferno' and asked that he be given a part. They agreed, and since both films were going to be shot in interior L.A. Studios, there were no negative discussions about me being away from the girls.

I should have seen what it is now obvious, that my husband had realized from reading the scripts that 'Inferno' was a box office smash. 'Meteor' just smashed altogether. Maybe my character's name, Tatiana Nikolavena Donskaya, should have tipped me off. It was humiliating and it was far from helpful that my husband patronized me in every way he could think of, and ended every criticism with the cloying sentiment that 'You're still a star here at home, darling.'

I called my agent and told him to take anything, anything at all that was well-written. He expressed surprise at my new openness to considering television. It paid off. Within a month, I had started work on 'The Cracker Factory', which was my first critical triumph in years. Close on the heels of that, I was offered the lead in the television mini-series remake of 'From Here to Eternity', and wonder of wonders, it was to be shot in Hawaii.

My husband's cardboard imitation series was also scheduled for an upcoming shoot in Hawaii. Two calls to my old friend Aaron and the schedules were aligned, and having no basis for even a flimsy argument against the project, my husband feigned enthusiasm.

So he and I and the girls took off for Hawaii.

Ten days into the shooting of my movie, he attempted to kill himself and was, as I now see it, unfortunately saved from doing so. 'Eternity' marked the beginning of homicidal rage in my marriage, and though I did not know it then, I had less than three years left to live.

My co-star was a man named William Devane. I had never worked with him before - of course, that is not saying much. In the years since I had disappeared, quite a few new actors had come onto the scene and become stars. Bill Devane was one of them. He was mesmerizingly attractive and that's the truth of it. He was also brilliant and one of those actors, like James Dean, whom I had always envied because they had come out of New York acting schools.

Bill was unashamedly masculine and comfortable in his own skin, and that very compelling skin was displayed amply during our filming because it was a beach shoot. Owing to my phobia about water, every scene that involved the ocean was filmed inside in a water tank, but I could manage the beach scenes since they never involved anything more than the filming of that iconic scene at the edge of the waves.

I had dieted and exercised to get ready for my first outdoor sunlit scenes in years, and every evening when I saw the dailies I knew it had been worth it. And, yes, I was thrilled to see genuine admiration, and maybe a little lust, in Bill's clear dark eyes. My husband's eyes were increasingly blood shot and swollen, and I think on his own shoot in Hawaii for 'Hart to Hart', the stores in Honolulu sold out on Visine.

In addition, he was now overweight enough that they had to film his scenes in tuxedos in Hawaii. I remember it so clearly, how on the afternoon of his suicide attempt, after he had finished his own shoot, he came down to watch Bill and me filming a fairly erotic love scene on the beach. Due to wind and sand, and the need for retouching, it took several hours, and through it all he just sat there beside the director, drinking from his flask.

When we were done, Bill and I, still in bathing suits, walked over to where he sat. Bill, relaxed and friendly, held out his hand to greet him. There was a long embarrassing pause before my husband reciprocated, and to make it perfectly awkward, he made a tasteless joke about water and shrinkage. Bill just smiled, but when he glanced at me, I saw pity in his eyes.

That is when I noticed the contrast between the two men. My husband was red-faced and sweating in this stupid tennis sweater and too-tight white slacks that he must have thought made him look movie star cool, but instead made him appear puffy and forced. Bill was hard-bodied and lean. He was also sober, while my husband was acting like a drunken ass already by five o'clock. I felt contempt and disenchantment and distance. I think I must not have been as good an actress as I thought, and he must not have been as drunk as he seemed, because he saw it. I declined Bill's polite but insincere invitation to dinner that night, though my husband protested noisily. I told my husband that I was exhausted and just wanted to have dinner sent up to our hotel suite, spend some time with the girls, and go to bed. I pointed out to him that if he needed to go out, he had not only the entire 'Hart to Hart' cast to choose from, but people available to him right in our own suite.

Like great vaudeville actors and celebrity morticians, my husband had a personal, and very favored, make-up man, Fred, whom he could hardly bear to be separated from under any conditions. Wherever he went, Fred went too, and that included Hawaii. In addition to Fred we had brought along my closest friend, Mart Crowley, whom I helped get a job as assistant producer on my husband's show. Whenever we traveled with Fred, I made sure to coerce Mart into coming. It tended to even things out. Fred was so blindly in love with my husband that he could finish his sentences. That was helpful for my husband, as when he became too drunk to articulate a point he wanted to make, Fred would do it for him, and Mart, loyal to me, would return the favor.

Sometimes, if my husband was very drunk and I was very tired, they would argue for us and save us the trouble of having to repeat the same worn insults and accusations we had used the night before. So we were for, the most part, one big happy family in the enormous suite the hotel had provided for us. Mart and Fred shared one bedroom, my husband and I the other, and Willie Mae, our nanny, slept in a third bedroom with the girls.

Chapter 6

That night we all had dinner together in the suite's living room and I curled up on the couch with the girls to read them stories. The three boys all clustered together around the big table by the windows, drinking and discussing the next day's shoot for 'Hart to Hart'.

Willie and I put the girls to bed about nine, and I went off to shower and get ready for bed. It was when I was changing into my pajamas that I heard the sounds of shouting and breaking glass. I yanked on my robe and went out to the living room.

My husband was outside on the balcony, bent over at the waist against the railings. He was shouting, "Let me die, just let me fucking die. She's done with me, can't you see it? She's fucking him, she's fucking him."

Fred had him around the waist and Mart was kneeling behind him, gripping both his legs. I remember being glad that we were on the thirtieth floor, as hopefully the people far below us walking around outside would not be able to understand what my husband was screaming.

It was only after Fred and Mart had hauled him back inside that I noticed one of the sliding glass doors was shattered. Mart told me later that my husband was very drunk, drunker than Mart had ever seen him, and that minutes after I had left the room, he had staggered up from the table and begun throwing glasses at the wall, screaming that he knew I was leaving him for Bill. Before Fred and Mart knew what was happening, my husband headed towards the balcony and smashed into, then through, the sliding glass doors onto the terrace. His momentum had carried him to the railing and they had rushed to save him from falling.

That is when I entered onto the scene. Mart said it was only when my husband heard my voice asking what the hell was going on that he began wailing about wanting to die, that it was only when I became part of the audience that my husband developed the face-saving idea of saying he wanted to kill himself.

I commented to Mart that if this was anyone's idea of saving face, we were in worse shape than I thought. We *were* in worse shape than anyone thought. We had an audience that night - Fred, Mart, Willie Mae and two terrified little girls who were both crying and asking me if Daddy was going to be okay. What else could I say but yes? To my husband I said only that he needed to come to bed.

The idea of having him in bed beside me, drunk, sweating, crying and needing reassurance was beyond disgusting, and yet I had no other choice. My husband was, and I imagine still is, that rare form of drinker who gets fired up and energetic from booze. He never used coke or amphetamines as far as I knew, maybe because he didn't have to; alcohol was enough for him.

Everyone else I knew who drank heavily, me included when I did it, would get high and then logy, and then either need to throw up or lay down, usually both. Not my husband. He would start happy, get morose and then argumentative. If he became damaging and made an ass out of himself instead of slinking off to sleep it off and try to fix it in the morning, he would rage and cry and insist on being made to believe it was all okay, that we were okay and all was forgiven.

I kid you not, if he did not hear what he needed from me, he would keep us both up all night. By the time Hawaii happened, I had this scene down cold and could play it with my eyes closed. Sometimes all he needed was for me, or another intimate, to make a joke about it. He would look at us suspiciously to make sure we were laughing with him and not at him, and if he felt reassured, he would calm down, laugh ruefully and go to bed. Other times, and that night was one of them, he could sense even through his drunken fog that he had gone too far for jokes. And at those times he needed me to hold him and stroke him and tell him that, 'It is all alright, darling. I know you didn't mean it. You just love me so much. I feel the same way.'

If I could pull it off, and let me say it required Academy standards of acting, he would sigh tearfully, curl up beside me and fall sleep. Ironically, it would usually take me hours to get to sleep myself after that. I would have to run over in excruciating detail, much as I have been doing since I died, the reasons I stayed with him - our girls, of course, the life we had created together, the security of not being alone - but each time it wore a little thinner and it took me a little longer to convince myself.

The next day he would typically go out and buy me an expensive piece of jewelry that ultimately I had to pay for, and I, in turn, would give him a love note. I cringe thinking about those notes. 'It's all clear sailing ahead now, darling. My darling, I love you more than love', whatever the hell that meant.

I think maybe these were lines from some of my more regretted movie roles which I simply regurgitated onto paper to keep up the appearance for him, for myself and for the watching world that we were still golden. We weren't golden, and I hope to God that since he had the bad manners to murder me, he at least burned those goddamned notes. It is a bit much to think of him proudly showing them off to people after killing me, but it's possible he has done just that.

My husband's view and mine of what was right were increasingly different, even before he became a murderer. I wonder how long it took Fred and the other sycophantic members of his little circle to comfort him down off his drunken emotional ledge after he did me in. I wonder if this is one of the things I need to stop caring about to leave my watery grave. But I do care. I find I still care a great deal about who exactly came to his rescue.

Who might have known what he did and still told him that it was alright, that I drove him to it, even? Who was the first who had the gall to tell him that I was in a better place now and wouldn't want him to feel guilty? Who would have said those things? Was it anyone I loved?

No, no, please no, and yet my blood was in that cabin, my broken things were everywhere, and I saw that boat still in the Isthmus the night after my death. So there was evidence, yes there was, and someone, someone who at least pretended to love me during my life, must have cleaned it up.

It wasn't him, he was gone, I know that because I drifted back to the boat the night after I died, looking for him, calling for him, and he was not there, and he has never come back here.

I would have sensed him in these waters if he had come back, and one way or another, I would have made him join me here in my black cold night. 'Darling,' I would have said, 'darling, it's more than love.'

Do I seek his death? Do I seek vengeance? It took me five hours to die. I spent those hours in a place of deep primal terror. There were no stars that night, only dark skies and darker water. It was very cold. I begged him for help and listened to him taunt me until the current carried me too far away to hear him any longer. I still cried out for help and thrashed violently trying to get back to the boat, but the current was too strong for me, and I could barely swim under the best of circumstances, and these were not the best.

Even if I had been a good enough swimmer to maneuver better, I would have been forced to remove my coat, and my coat was the only thing keeping me afloat. I stopped screaming when I knew I was too far from anyone to be heard. I stopped thrashing when I saw a dark fin cleave the black water nearby. I did not ever stop crying for my little girls, the salt from my eyes mixing with that of the surrounding ocean.

Do I seek vengeance?

Chapter 7

In the two years I had left to live, not much happened until my last six months.

Obviously I did not leave my husband. I thought about it. I even made a few tentative plans, moving a few thousand dollars into a new account I set up under the name Marjorie Morningstar. I think it was maybe ten thousand, and I imagine it's still sitting there today gathering a little interest. Money, unlike death, has a rate of growth.

We were held up and kept together for our remaining time by what I now see was a kind of inertia brought on by the things we owned and the people who knew us. My husband worked hard during the week, and I worked nearly as hard trying to look busy because, after the première of 'Meteor', the phone was only ringing with party invitations and luncheon calls. We entertained nearly every night of the week and attended black tie parties on weekends, or went onto the boat with friends, so the nights and free time went by and we could keep up our façade, still addressing each other as 'darling' in public, and even in private, although, fortunately, there wasn't much private.

If it was one of the rare guestless nights at home, we had the girls and Willie Mae there. I know he was watching me, watching me all the time, because he could sense rejection, my husband. He was very attuned to it. I was watching him too, not because I feared rejection - far from it - I was merely curious to see if he would address it, sit down across from me somewhere, anywhere, and ask me what we were doing.

I know I could have opened that scene too, that I had that option.

One night, right before events overtook us, we were up in our bedroom together before midnight, for a change. He had an early shoot the next morning and we had stayed home that night, pretending to be happy with each other for the girls. After they went to bed, he wandered off to his den to drink in front of the television and I just wandered, flicking fringes and moving small objects around on tables to better arrange the set where we filmed our roles.

I was very restless by then, restless all the time. I couldn't see another place or life to go towards, so I stayed where I was existing, with a kind of pent-up fury combined with the growing fear that where I was was where I would be staying.

To be honest, I see how unfair this time was to him. I wanted to be anywhere at all besides the house on Canon Drive, but since I didn't have a signpost telling me where to go, I stayed. I stayed and I resented the living hell out of him because I stayed. I can see so clearly now, with the marvelous hindsight of death, that if only I had taken the girls and moved away at that time, he would have let me go. I would have been leaving then in his mind to indulge a mid-life crisis, or to find myself, or any number of nonsensical phrases that he could have thrown around to our friends and the public.

If I had done that he could have saved face. He would still have been the handsome television star whose crazy middle-aged wife had inexplicably decided to leave. I know how he would have played it, a puzzled faux Cary Grant lift of the eyebrows and a humorous shrug. He would have quickly begun a public life of dating high profile women and possibly had a satisfying private life as well. We had not attempted sex for nearly two years.

But if I left him because I was a star and had a thousand exciting places to go, and new accomplishments and experiences to bask in, I was leaving him behind and that was a very different thing altogether. Leaving him for greener pastures would take him right back to the darkest days after our first marriage had ended. It might make people question exactly why he wasn't good enough, if there wasn't some other reason. We did live in Hollywood. People had heard rumors, old rumors, scotched rumors. Until he killed me, I never really understood what our marriage meant to him in terms of safety.

I thought I was the one seeking safety but he had too, and if a star left him again, there would be the scent of failure, and failure in our town brought scrutiny. If I had only left when I was in the shade, but I didn't, and he killed me, and in killing me he doubtless became the tragic, grieving widower which is a winning role any way you slice it, and as a side bonus he got to keep all my money.

When I delayed leaving for my own reasons, I unwittingly gave him time to start writing other possible scenarios, and from there it could only be a matter of time. It's not that simple, though; real life never is. By staying and letting him know how much I hated staying, I made him feel inadequate and unsure of himself, and at a loss for what role to play that would please me again. He didn't have a large repertoire. The role of young prince wouldn't play anymore, and if the tuxedoed suave television star wasn't cutting, what was left for him? What was left was nothing, and there is not a person alive who will thank you for showing them how to see an empty mirror when they gaze into it.

The night I am speaking of, I think for the first time I understood some of this. I took a break from my resentment and saw that I disliked and disdained him for being the only things he ever had been. He hadn't changed or moved on, he couldn't. I had, though, and it wasn't fair to scorn him for what he was. My God, if I hadn't known the first time around, I had certainly known the second.

It was in this frame of mind that I entered our bedroom that night and saw him sitting hunched over on the side of the bed, his head in his hands. From the doorway where I stood, he looked so old and defeated, I didn't want to apologize, because I had been through enough analysis to know you can't apologize for not loving someone, but I did want to try and somehow make my inevitable leaving okay for him.

I sat down beside him and put my hand against his back. He was sweating lightly. He was drinking too much and he had started to develop high blood pressure from it.

I moved my hand in a circle around his back and said his name. He jerked under my touch as though I had struck him. His face, when he looked at me, was twisted not with despair but with hatred. I recoiled and started to stand. He grabbed my wrist and pulled me back onto the mattress where he shoved me down flat. He loomed over me, his face red and swollen with anger and alcohol, and said, "Natalie Wood, what in the fuck do you want from me? What don't you have, you fucking bitch? Do I disgust you, Miss Wood? Have you figured out yet again that I'm not right for you? What exactly do you think I should be doing while you wander around looking at me out of the corner of your big black fucking eyes with that goddamned expression of yours, huh? What do you want from me?"

I turned my head to the side to avoid his eyes and his breath. I answered him in a faintly bored voice, bored because I realized that this man on top of me was not drawing down on some inner torment - inner was a concept he could never pull off - he was simply attempting to play Brick to my Maggie, because he was insightful enough to understand that the role of Jonathon Hart would be out of place at that moment. I told him as much and commented that if he hadn't learned by reading the critics' view of his acting in 'Cat', then I couldn't help him. I repeated to him that his rendition of Paul Newman's role was wooden then, and it was worse now.

I asked him icily if he wanted to carry it all the way through to the climax, displaying again his impotence. He, poor thing, was so devastated by my words that he could only roll over to his side and mutter that I was no Elizabeth Taylor either. I laughed and reminded him of how grateful he should be for that fact, since I had always heard that Liz worked Burton pretty hard at home. He began to cry. I didn't. I laid there for hours dry-eyed and staring at the ceiling, wondering how I had gotten here again.

The next morning my agent called to tell me that a Broadway producer wanted me for the role of Anastasia, interrupting my shrieks of glee only to ask if I would be willing to make a 'little blockbuster' first. It was a guaranteed winner this time, he said. Yes, it was science fiction again, like the disastrous 'Meteor', but it would be different with this film. They had a great script and the hottest young method actor alive, Christopher Walken, as my co-star.

It was a good day, a brilliant, wonderful day. I was even glad that I hadn't made a move. I told myself I had been right to wait, right to want a signpost to my new life.

For the next three months leading up to the Thanksgiving weekend when my husband killed me, I was busy with rehearsals, fittings and readings, and genuinely excited, planning with a clear directed vision for the first time in years how it would be for the girls and I when we got to New York and began our new lives.

Chapter 8

I want to dispel another myth about my death. My sweet friend, Marti, who brings her small boat out here to my grave sometimes, has informed me that half of the world thinks I was having an affair with Chris Walken when I died.

She said that my husband has recently gone so far as to pen a book wherein, amongst other statements, he claims I was being 'emotionally unfaithful and swishing my tail'. In my life I was considered a very beautiful woman and I never had to resort to, as he so elegantly put it, swishing my tail. Nor can you be emotionally unfaithful to a man you are long done with.

That said, I did indeed form a close bond of friendship with Chris Walken. Did I find him sexually attractive? Yes, I did. Would anything have come from it if I hadn't been murdered? Probably not. I was unlocking all the doors of my cages and busy planning a new life.

I had 'Brainstorm' to film, an apartment in New York to buy, my first play to begin, and another movie to start after that, starring Timothy Hutton. Did I enjoy flirting with him? No more than with any other attractive man.

Chris and I formed a connection based on our work, a shared sense of the ridiculous, and his understanding of my deep frustrations at letting go of my career for so long. He was married, and I was uninterested in the emotional morass that a relationship with a married man would cause me, not to mention the career-ending publicity that would ensue from such a liaison and the pain it would bring to my girls.

I knew they would go through a period of adjustment when I relocated them from their father, and a new man, a new married man, was not the right thing for them, or for me. I liked him - he was exciting - and of course I might have thought about sex with him, as contrary to popular belief during my lifetime, a woman in her forties might not seek a life of permanent celibacy.

But the reason he was on board the 'Splendour' that lost weekend was because I begged him to be there.

I need to explain this. The preceding three months had been some of the happiest and most miserable weeks of my life. On the one hand, I had a new movie, with a play to follow and another film coming after that. I had a stack of listings from a realtor in New York hidden at my lawyer's office, as well as brochures from various good schools there. I had a co-star whom I liked immensely, and a movie I was enjoying for the novelty, if nothing else. In my head I was running another movie called 'Natalie and her girls in New York', and it was a fine, vibrant script. Close enough now to taste was the new life I wanted. I knew there would be some adjustment bumps for all three of us, and I also knew we would be okay, more than okay.

I would show my girls that a woman could live quite a fine, satisfying life, whether married or not, and more, I was anxious to remove them from the increasingly rancid atmosphere that permeated Canon Drive, one of alcoholism and falseness. I hadn't told anyone what I was planning yet, as in Hollywood your own mother - particularly my mother - would have sold my personal secrets to the highest bidder without a second thought.

While I was doing the location shoot in North Carolina, my husband had shown up without warning on two separate weekends. Both times he got very drunk and it was all I could do to keep him from creating a scene that would have humiliated me in front of my co-workers. Both times he raged at me in my hotel room about the effect my prolonged absence was having on our girls. When I tried to point out to him, reasonably enough I thought, that the girls had Willie and that I talked to them both several times a day, and that most of all, if he was so worried about them, why was he here in North Carolina instead of home with them, he would hit a level of rage I had not seen in him before. His old song and emotional blackmail dance about my mothering skills wasn't working any longer and he could see that. It made him feel helpless, and being helpless made him feel homicidal, and I couldn't see that.

Obviously if I had perceived my husband's growing determination to either bring me to heel or kill me, I would not have agreed to the post-Thanksgiving days of wine and roses, 'Kill Natalie' cruise. I just thought he was drinking even more than usual, and that if I wanted to get through filming and what I knew - and I think he knew too - was going to be our last holiday season together, I needed to stay quiet about my plans and try valiantly to keep the peace.

He started bringing up the idea of a weekend on the boat around Thanksgiving. I couldn't understand it. We were, to all intents and purposes, estranged, and besides, we hardly ever used the boat in the winter. Moreover, I was in the middle of a film and he had been ranting for weeks about what a terrible mother I was for leaving the girls, so why would he want me to leave them again for one of my few weekends at home? It didn't make sense, and by the time I understood it, I was dead.

I begged Chris to accompany my husband and me on our stupid post-Thanksgiving boat trip because he was the only person I knew who might even consider coming with us as he was stuck in L.A. for the next three weeks for interior shots. Chris was a confirmed and permanent New Yorker whom I had decided was going to be my first new friend when I got there. Meantime, he was staying in town at the Château Marmont, and when I asked him on our last day before the holiday break what his plans were for the weekend, he shrugged and said he didn't have anything going on.

I jumped on it and asked him if he would join us on the 'Splendour' for two days after Thanksgiving. He wasn't enthusiastic but I was insistent.

Chris was a very perceptive man and he asked me why, since I was so obviously unhappy about being alone with my husband, was I going at all? It embarrassed me to admit to him that I was trying to keep the peace at any cost, if just for a little while longer. Chris ponderously lectured me on an actor's need to stay true to themselves in their personal lives if they were going to bring their best performances to the screen.

I agreed and told him I was working on it, but for the moment would he please promise to come and help me keep a calm front? Chris was a good friend and he agreed, though he cautioned me in advance that he was not a boat person and might end up spending the weekend flat on his back. He also warned me that he was not interested in playing referee if my husband and I got into a fight. "Natalie, if you two start beefing about shit that isn't my problem, don't expect me to get in the middle of it."

I assured him over and over that his presence alone would prevent anything like that from happening. I am not even going to address my mistaken thinking regarding that idea, since I am dead due to it, and so why point out the obvious?

Thanksgiving Day, my husband and I hosted our usual fifty or so for dinner. I was a tense wreck and drank too much, to get through the day. Later that night I asked him to reconsider our boat trip. It had rained and been unseasonably cold all week in L.A.. I had spoken to our captain, Dennis, that afternoon and he had gloomily predicted miserable weather.

My husband was adamant - we were going. He said we needed this time together, that it was very important to him, and besides, he said with a sneer, "You don't want to disappoint the great Christopher Walken, the Academy winner, do you, darling?"

I knew that at best I was facing an awkward time, and at worst a prolonged fiasco of a weekend, but I acquiesced. Funny thing, though, our girls were both set up to spend the weekend with friends, and that night, a few minutes before the mother of Natasha's best friend came to pick her up, Natasha became hysterical. She begged me either not to go on the boat or to take her along. I was torn. I had missed my babies for weeks, and now this. I remember holding her on my lap and looking up over her head pleadingly at my husband.

He shook his head tersely and reminded me that if we were taking Natasha, we would have to take Courtney as well, and she was just recovering from an ear infection. Did I want to make her sick?

The whole spin he put on it was ridiculous. Now I see so clearly the flashing red warning lights, 'danger, danger', nobody wanted to go, or wanted me to go, nobody but my husband. If anyone alive believes my death was accidental, I envy them their naiveté. Mine ended long ago in this water.

We arrived at Marina Del Rey on the afternoon of November twenty-seventh, 1981. We boarded the 'Splendour' and my husband joined our captain Dennis in the wheelhouse to take us to the tourist side of Catalina Island, a place called Avalon. I loved Avalon, a quaint quasi-Victorian island village that resembled an idealized little world, like Main Street on Disneyland. Avalon, even on a rainy winter weekend, was charming, and I started to perk up when we arrived there as I was looking forward to doing some Christmas shopping and to showing Chris around as well.

Poor Chris had spent the two hour ride over there mostly lying in his cabin, seasick and miserable. I could see how pleased my husband was at this turn of events, as though Christopher's illness made him look second-rate. It didn't. My husband's pleasure in our guest's illness only made *him* look second-rate.

Chapter 9

My husband, Chris and I all boarded the shore boat for the quick ride to Avalon. Dennis, our young captain, decided to stay on board.

Chris looked pretty green around the gills still and refused my husband's idea of heading to the nearest bar for a pick-me-up. He said humorously that it would turn into a throw-me-up and couldn't we just walk around and check out Avalon for a while?

I didn't particularly like the idea of walking around outside in the rain trying to keep a conversation going, but this wasn't one of those situations where I could say something like, 'Why don't you boys go off and explore while I do some early Christmas shopping.' I had brought poor Chris along and I needed to take care of him. What I would have loved to do was to have suggested to my husband that he go sit in a bar somewhere while Chris and I hung out, but I knew how that would go over.

So, instead, for an hour the three of us wandered sullenly around Avalon until I saw a little gold bear holding a parasol in the window of the local jewelry store. I knew Natasha would love it and I asked the men if they would mind if I went in for a minute and look at it. They both agreed, anxious I think, by that time, to get out of the rain and have something, anything, to do. The bear it turned out was only for display, but once inside the warm dry little store, the three of us wandered around curiously.

My husband pointed out a necklace which was an old barnacle with a diamond in the middle and I nodded politely at it, though inwardly I was wondering if the jewelry designer wasn't crazy for thinking that anyone would pay five thousand dollars for something so tacky. I found a pair of 'pieces of eight' earrings that I liked, and showed them to Chris who laughed and said I should get them and revamp my Gypsy Rose Lee days.

I thought that was funny and they didn't cost much, so I gestured to the clerk to put them on the counter. Then I noticed a man's 'pieces of eight' gold necklace. It was five or six hundred dollars but I knew suddenly that I wanted to buy it for our captain, Dennis. I had never given him an expensive gift before but I wanted to get him that necklace. Why, I'm still not sure.

I liked Dennis but that wasn't all of it. I was beginning to have a rising sense of growing menace. Maybe it was just the cold rain and the prospect of a long tense weekend that was the capper to a long tense marriage. Or, who knows, maybe it was a warning to run that I should have heeded, but instead I merely purchased the necklace for Dennis. I think now I bought it to show him that I did indeed like him, but more that I hoped he liked me and would stand up for me if I needed him to.

I don't know. I know he seemed really pleased about receiving the gift when I handed it to him. I imagine he has long since gotten rid of it; it would have been a terrible reminder, not so much of anything he did, but of what he failed to do.

Chris picked up a pretty little aquamarine ring for his wife, and my husband at the other end of the counter was ostentatiously trying to be secretive about having the second clerk wrap up something. I ignored him.

When we were done in the store, all of us were visibly cheered. Shopping can do that for people, and for the first time that day we were all fairly comfortable with each other. When my husband raised the idea again of going for a drink, Chris and I both agreed and we headed to an old favorite of ours, a cheerful Mexican restaurant.

Once inside and ensconced comfortably in a booth, our drinks arrived and Chris, raising his Margarita, grinned and said, "Here's to 'Meteor', the movie where the special effects have a better chance of taking home the Oscar than the actors do."

I met his toast and laughed. What it was about that simple, funny line that set my husband off, I will never understand. He didn't drink when we did. He sat there silently, fuming at us, and waited until he had made things awkward enough so that we had both turned to look at him.

When he had our full attention, he reached into his pocket and brought out a wrapped jewelry box which he shoved across the table towards me. I looked at him curiously and he said to open it. I did, and with Chris watching both of us with an unreadable expression, I saw that my husband had bought me the ridiculously overpriced, and very unwanted, five thousand dollar barnacle diamond necklace. I looked up, startled, and he smiled widely at me, his eyes dead, and raised his glass in his own toast, saying, "Merry early Christmas, my darling Natalie. You take my breath away."

God, it's hard to describe how inappropriate it was, how the very air of the little restaurant turned from warm and fragrant to cold and airless. I felt the room tilt and I might have curled up right there into the fetal position and begun keening if I hadn't felt Chris's hard fingers pinch my thigh tightly under the table.

It helped. I managed a smile and thanked my husband for the necklace. He did not smile back. He asked me tightly if I didn't want to put it on. I said, "Later, darling, it's too nice to wear with this ratty old sweater." I remember I placed it in the pocket of the down coat I was wearing. Maybe it's there now, or maybe it fell to the bottom of the ocean where it belonged.

I am still thinking about that terrible little gift after all these years because it was a final dramatic gesture. My husband adored ceremony and symbolic gestures, and so he presented me with a barnacle. A barnacle is a thing that boat owners scrape off the side of their crafts. Within twenty-four hours he would scrape my clinging hands off of the swim step.

It was close then, my murder. He meant me to die that very night but events forced him to postpone killing me for one more day.

When we got back to the boat, Dennis had prepared the steaks and fixings for my husband to grill. He did so and the four of us sat down to dinner.

I could see Dennis was visibly touched by my gift, but he was not himself that evening, either. Dennis was normally an extremely easy-going young man. That night he was by turns tense, chatty and silent. Chris was merely silent. He had no sooner chewed the last bite of his steak than he rose and announced to the air above our heads that the boat's rocking didn't agree with him and he was turning in.

My husband watched him go with a strange empty smile on his face, and suddenly he stood up and announced to Dennis and me that he was moving the boat 'right now' to Isthmus Cove.

Isthmus Cove, my long term grave, is located on the wild unspoiled side of Catalina Island. In the summer it's a sylvan paradise that both the girls and I had loved. In the winter it as bleak and lonely as a black and white lithograph. We never went to Isthmus in the winter.

I saved myself that night. With Dennis' help, I argued that it was pitch black and raining, and therefore dangerous to drive the boat as he might hit the shore given the zero visibility.

My husband was not deterred by our pleas. He was determined to move the boat to the more private waters off the Isthmus. I know it was supposed to be that night because he had screwed up his drunken courage to the sticking point, given me a barnacle, and made that skin crawler of a toast one last time. His scene was in place, as were the actors. It must have been a real shock to him when I threw up my hands and told him to move the boat if he wanted, but I was having Dennis take me to shore immediately.

Dennis seemed nervous but he knew I wasn't getting into that dinghy alone, and maybe he was relieved to have an excuse to escape what to him must have seemed an inexplicable plan. Dennis and I spent that night at a little motel in Avalon and the next morning I had decided to grab a seaplane and go home, putting an end to this farce, but I didn't know what to do about Chris.

I know, because Marti has told me so, that a million fantastic new things have been invented since my murder, including a device called the cell phone, but we didn't have them then. And so, reluctantly, I realized that I was going to have to have Dennis row me out to the 'Splendour' to go on board and ask Chris if he wanted to join me for a plane ride back to L.A.. I knew it would be an awkward and embarrassing scene for him. The boat was only sixty feet - about the size of a single wide mobile home - so it wasn't like we were going to be able to speak privately and escape without my husband noticing.

But when I got back on board, it seemed like maybe after all there was going to be no need to say anything at all to Chris. My husband was up and puttering around in the galley, Chris was still in his cabin, so it was just Dennis, my husband and I there for the moment. He smiled sheepishly at both of us and apologized for being an asshole the night before. He said that he didn't know what was wrong with him and please could we finish out the weekend and show the Isthmus to Chris.

He said he thought he would enjoy the wild rugged coast of the Island, that it would be interesting to see if it reminded him of Cape Cod.

Well, I was open to being civil and avoiding a hassle, so I pretended that I thought Chris would enjoy sitting on a boat in crappy weather and exploring Two Harbors, the tiny port of the Isthmus, in the rain.

After all, it would spare me an embarrassing scene, and in twenty-four hours Dennis would be steering us home to L.A. where I would resume work on 'Brainstorm' and finalize my plans for the move to New York.

The last morning of my life I played out the role of happy wife for my small audience of three men by making my so-called famous *'huevos rancheros'*. They were famous because it was the only thing I knew how to cook. In the crowd I lived in, any tiny domestic accomplishment was applauded. It annoys me to think about it now.

    We slowly made our way to Isthmus Cove, and upon arrival, my husband insisted that we bypass our usual mooring spot and stay out in the harbor. I didn't question it then. I was exhausted from lack of sleep the night before, and poor Chris was sick again from our one hour cruise. It was cold and rainy and miserable, and no one could come up with a single idea about what to do in Two Harbors, which is not hard to understand as the only business open that time of year was Doug's Harbor Reef, a bar and restaurant.

    Chris came outside to the railing when we moored and looked over the landscape, shooting me a puzzled look. I could only shrug in reply.

    He said, "You know you are really going to owe me when this weekend is over, Natalie, assuming it will ever be over, that is."

    I nodded apologetically and told him I was sorry, and that maybe he should spend this long gray day as I planned to, napping. I told him I would wake him later, we would go in for drinks and dinner, come back, sleep again and tomorrow this would all be over.

    He threw me a disgusted look and returned to his cabin, and I went down to mine.

    I was beat and hoping that my husband wouldn't follow me in and initiate a conversation that I knew we had to have. I just couldn't bear to have it right then.

    I woke up mercifully alone several hours later and looked out my porthole to catch dark gray skies and a thick drizzling rain. I gave serious consideration to taking a couple of sleeping pills and trying to stay asleep until the following morning, but again I thought of poor Chris, my virtual hostage to misfortune, and made myself get up.

    When I was dressed, I went up to the lounge and saw that all three men were sitting around, obviously uncomfortable. I could smell boredom and tension in the air like the scent of ozone. I drew down on my acting talent and greeted them all like *wasn't it the greatest thing in the world to be here trapped on a small stuffy boat in the middle of nowhere?* I suggested that we all head into Two Harbors and have a few drinks and an early dinner.

I remember wanting to call the shore boat because I knew we would be coming back in the dark and I never could stand to be that close to the water at night. I didn't even like to look at the ocean from our deck in the evenings, but my husband said it was a ridiculous idea and we would end up stuck at the Two Harbors dock after dinner, waiting in the rain, because it was off-season and there was only one shore boat.

I agreed only because it was suddenly much more important to me to get off that boat and be around lights and people than anything else. I kept saying to myself, 'Don't argue with him, not about anything, no matter what, and tomorrow this will be over. And if you want, you can just take the girls and check into a hotel for the next few weeks of filming in L.A.. Just a few more hours now.'

It was four thirty p.m..

Chapter 10

Marti has told me that a great deal of importance has been placed on those hours that our party of four spent at the restaurant. If I could communicate with her, or anyone at all, I would tell them they had gotten it terribly wrong as nothing happened at all there of interest, save two atypical small things. I drank far too much and my husband drank almost nothing.

The place was crowded with other cold, bored boaters who were glad to escape into the warmth and light of Doug's. It was a usual thing when people spotted me in public that they would send over drinks to our table, but that night I not only sampled everything they sent, I reciprocated by chatting away to any stranger with a friendly smile.

I had to: the atmosphere at our table was frankly weird. Chris was clearly bemused by my unusual social butterfly act, Dennis was also drunk and had withdrawn into morose silence, and as for my husband, he was vibrating with tension. Almost totally silent, he had picked at his dinner and spent the evening nursing two drinks. Aware of him, but trying to seem oblivious, I kept up my banter with people at adjoining tables. Periodically he would say that he wanted to leave and I would, with false gaiety, answer that so and so had just sent us a bottle of champagne and we couldn't go yet.

Finally he became visibly angry and stood up, saying he was going back to the boat, with or without us, Chris shrugged and stood up too, as did Dennis. I simply did not want to leave that warm restaurant, but I knew I was drunk, and that if I did not accompany them back, it would look odd to the other patrons. So I got up and shrugged into my coat. I remember on the way out the door I walked face first into this big Tiki statue near the entrance. I laughed, and so did Chris, but my husband was clearly unamused. He went so far as to cover my head with his own big coat and drag me down the steps with hard hands, whispering in my ear that I was drunk and making fools of all of us. Blinded, I was shoved roughly into the dinghy for our return journey.

It was ten-thirty p.m..

When we arrived back on board the 'Splendour', I asked Chris if he was tired. He said not very as he had been sleeping most of the weekend. I wanted to go to bed, but instead politely offered him a glass of wine in the lounge. To my dismay, he accepted, so within minutes he and I were facing each other over drinks on the big couches I had installed in there. The wine bottle was sitting on the table between us.

My husband came into the lounge and stared furiously at us, as though he had caught us in bed together.

We had been talking in a desultory fashion about the movie and he interrupted to ask Chris, seemingly out of the blue, if he thought that an acting career should come before anything else?

Chris shrugged and said maybe not for everyone, but it was certainly his priority at that time in his life.

My husband sneered and asked him if he thought it should be my priority as well. Should acting be the priority of a middle-aged woman with two small children and a husband to care for?

Chris, visibly uncomfortable, didn't answer, merely looking nervously at my husband.

His silence appeared to enrage my husband more, as he suddenly moved to the table between us, grabbed up the wine bottle and smashed it down hard on the surface, showering both Chris and me with wine and flying glass fragments.

He leaned into Chris's face and screamed, "Do you think you should fuck my wife? Do you want to fuck my wife?"

Chris rose shakily with his hands held up, edged around my husband, and headed for the balcony outside. I just sat there, wet with wine, and too shocked to move or speak.

Chris walked back inside a minute later and mumbled that he was going to bed. His entrance broke my torpor and I stood up. I didn't look at my husband as I passed him, although I did say when I reached the door of our stateroom, "Don't come near me tonight, or tomorrow either. We're done, you and me. Nobody treats me like this. Goodnight."

I walked into my little bathroom, stripped off my wet clothes and washed my face. In the bedroom I put on my favorite flannel nightgown and warm socks. My teeth were chattering as I slid under the covers but I wasn't crying, I felt no need for tears. It was finished.

It was ten fifty-four p.m..

We didn't have locks on any of the cabin doors on our boat. It isn't safe to do that with small children, and even if there had been a lock on my door, he would have broken it. I knew when I heard him come in that, drunk or sober, this was going to be one of those nights when he would demand reassurance.

I decided to play possum and ignore him.

He had other plans. He grabbed me by my right arm and yanked me out of the bed, flinging me into the wall. I tried to stand and he punched me hard in the stomach. I let out a scream and he socked me in the forehead. I fell down hard and he grabbed me by my hair and dragged me face forward across the carpet. I could only manage moans until I felt the cold night air against my exposed skin where my nightgown had ridden up around my waist.

He had opened the back door of our cabin which led out onto the swim step. I screamed loudly and tried to crawl past him towards the cabin. He reached down, grabbed both my ankles roughly, raised me up, and in one move, dropped me head-first into the cold water.

For a minute I struggled blindly before I came up to the surface, gasping for air.

I grabbed the swim step with both hands and looked up at him, stunned. He was crouching on the step, looking down at me with his face twisted in rage. "I want you off my fucking boat, you fucking bitch. You are gone, Natalie, all gone."

I gripped harder and screamed for Chris and Dennis both.

He didn't like that, and with an intent expression, stood up and raised his foot over my hands. "Let go of my fucking boat, bitch, or I will break your fucking fingers right now."

Scared, I turned and lunged for the dinghy. It was hard to scramble over the side in my wet nightgown, but I made it. I laid there on the bottom for a minute, panting and wheezing.

Before I had a chance to do more, I felt something soft thump down over me. I looked up. A foot away my husband was standing on the swim step, sweating and enraged. I sat up and reached for whatever it was he had tossed me. It was my red down coat.

I looked at him, confused. He smiled. "Put it on, darling. I don't want you to be cold for your trip to shore."

Freezing, I did what he said and watched, paralyzed with fear, as he untied both dinghy lines. I asked him what he was doing. Did he expect me to take the dinghy to shore, and do what when I got there?

I demanded he stop this shit and step aside and let me back on my boat.

He did not answer until he was done untying the ropes. Then he did the strangest thing. He pulled the dinghy right up to the swim step so that it was parallel to it. All I had to do was roll forward and I would have been back on board, but I didn't do that because I was afraid that he was setting me up for just such a move so he could kick me off the step and back into the water.

I looked at him in silence

He leaned forward. "You look like a drowned rat, Nat darling. Have a good swim."

Before I knew what he was doing, he yanked up the side hard, and I slid across the dinghy and flipped out into the water. This time, when I came up, I was too wary to go near him again, and finding my down coat surprisingly buoyant, I paddled slowly around to the front of the boat to scream for Dennis.

I heard my husband's running footsteps and a few muffled words, followed by a louder yell of, 'Turn on the fucking music.'

I spent what seemed to me a long time calling from the water and then there he was again, leaning over the railing with a smile. "Hang onto your hat, I'll get you, I'll come right now, as soon as you say the magic words."

I was beyond angry, far too angry to be as afraid as I should have been. I wouldn't say the magic words. I knew Dennis would rescue me, and if not him, then anyone from the dozens of nearby boats. As soon as Dennis told Chris, people would get called and I would be brought out of the water, and from that moment on my husband was going to learn the meaning of revenge, movie star style.

I should have been afraid. I should have said and promised whatever he wanted to hear. Maybe I could have changed his course, maybe …

Wondering if that could be true is I think one of the things that has kept me here trapped all these years, but sometimes I understand so clearly that none of it was spontaneous at all and that I could never have been saved.

There was a strong wind that night and it created a current which caught me and began dragging me from the area near the boats. I struggled and gave up when I saw that I was not being cast further out into the ocean but towards shore. Then, like a miracle, I saw the dinghy floating ahead of me just a few yards away. I swam towards it, which was not easy in my coat. I was closing in on it when I felt, and then heard, and then saw, that I was not after all completely alone in the ocean that night.

   I cannot say to this day with certainty that it was a shark. Maybe it was a helpful dolphin. I did not believe it was a dolphin. I knew enough about sharks to know that movement alerted them to the presence of prey in the water. 'Jaws' had come out a couple years before and I had made the mistake of going to see it. Every scene from that movie played out in my head. I hung motionless in the water and watched silently, the first tears of real terror sliding down my face as the dinghy moved further away.

   I felt something brush against my hanging legs, and who knows, maybe it was only the current, but after a few minutes of slowly, so slowly, trying not to make a ripple, I managed to draw my legs up towards my chest.

   As the water had drenched my coat it had also expanded it, and I found that I could keep my legs curled up inside it, and that created minimal warmth as well. With my body pulled close like that, I felt vulnerable clinging to the dinghy, of course, but less so than with exposed limbs. I was now floating in a ball, not really drifting much either, towards or away from the shore.

   I was afraid but not yet hopeless. That came later.

   Hours in, I still could not manage the courage to free my legs and try to swim for shore. I felt the murderous malice of my husband somewhere behind me on the boat and I felt the mindless malice of the shark lying in wait between me and the shore.

   Despite my coat, I was becoming colder, and while at first it was my enemy, that cold became my friend. It lessened the immediacy of my aching desperation to reach the distant lights of Isthmus Cove and safety. The cold distanced me from the thought of my little girls and my terrible fear and rage at the knowledge that, after all, despite all the odds against it, I was indeed going to be left out here in the dark water un-rescued.

   I looked up for guidance into that endless night, hoping to see the stars, but the sky was black and blank. I looked down at the water, inches from my face, and saw that I cast no reflection. I wondered if I was already dead and didn't know it. I murmured a prayer for help and laid my face against the water.

   Death came in minutes but not as people think of death, at least not for me. I awoke from what passes for sleep amongst my kind. It's really more of a time slip, I suppose, but to me it felt as though I awoke from what had been a long disorienting dream. I was still here, it was still night, and I was still in the water. It was only the slow realization that I was no longer cold, and no longer felt any fear of sharks, or of my husband, that made me realize the dream I had woken from was my life.

Nearly thirty years have passed and here I remain, forever waiting, forever drowning. And yet having now remembered my story - all of it - and told the truth to the best of my ability, I think maybe if I looked up again I might see a million stars above me and be able to see even further, and higher, beyond them to the place where all of us stars first came from.

The Second Death

Nicole

The Ghost of Brentwood

Chapter 11

I should have, but I didn't see this coming. I know that everyone thinks I knew that my husband was going to almost cut my head off and stab me a few dozen more times, but uhm, that is ridiculous. I attended all three of my husband's trials, and let me tell you, I heard a lot of stuff in the first two: the criminal trial where they said he didn't kill me or poor Ron, groupie assholes, and the civil trial where they said that he had caused our deaths. Thanks for that much anyway.

But what really burned me during both trials is that everyone who testified on my behalf said that I knew my husband was going to kill me and get away with it. Well, I'll tell ya, I wasn't Madam Nicole, Brentwood psychic, while I was alive, and whatever people think about ghosts, we can't see the future either.

We can see the past pretty damn clearly though.

I have been dead now for, well, I'm not totally positive. The last time I knew exactly how long I had been like this was when I first got to Las Vegas to attend my husband's last trial and heard the magic words, "We, the people, find you guilty." It was said a little late in the day, but hey, better late than never.

I haven't really kept track of time since then, to be honest. I haven't been able to pull the energy together. It took energy like you cannot imagine to be with those jurors, and I don't mean that I was just sitting beside them in their box. I was with all of them twenty-four/seven during his trial. If you think I'm lying, ask them about their dreams sometime.

Is there anyone alive who missed the better-late-than-never guilty verdict coming down thirteen years to the day he was acquitted for nearly cutting off my head and stabbing me a few dozen times? Sorry if I keep bringing that up, but I guess I'm having trouble letting go. Ha! I wasn't the only sad pissed-off ghost in Brentwood, and here in Vegas it's pretty much a damn crowd. Every casino is filled with a few dozen ghosts who came here and lost their shirts and then took a powder, or a gun, and called it a day. Ghosts don't really interact with each other that much. It's not a club anybody's looking to join or dying to get into - sorry. But yeah, sometimes we exchange a little information to be polite, like people do in prison. You know, 'Hey how'd ya die? Oh, that's too bad.

So why are you still here?' etc..

No one asks me how I died since it turns out my death was almost as well covered on this side as it was in the world of the living. But they all want to know why I'm still here. That's a tough one. I have to remember everything before I can answer, and I have to get it straight so I know what to do.

I mean I had my chances in the early days to cross into the light. People don't know this but there isn't a ghost alive - sorry - who doesn't attend their own funeral. Usually a lot of love and white light is generated at these events, and you hear some great stuff about yourself from the people you loved, and - **Boom!** - there it is, the white light and you are off to, well I don't know where, because my funeral was totally ruined by my poor body being groped by my husband.

So instead of peace and forgiveness, I felt rage and a desire to get even with him for my head nearly being cut off and stuff. My funeral is also the last time I saw my kids and that still hurts bad. I could have gone to see them during the year of my husband's first joke of a trial - they were just up the highway at my parents' - but being dead when you are young and beautiful and have loved life is hard enough without piling unnecessary grief on top of it.

I knew seeing my kids hurting and not being able to touch them would make an already pretty grim situation even worse, if that's possible. That's how I became a ghost in the first place instead of becoming a spirit of the light. It is because of all the bad feelings I got seeing him touching my hair and even trying to move the high collar of the ugly dress I was buried in. I mean what was he doing, looking to see how the mortician had managed to balance my head on my body?

It made me crazy and I kept trying to get at him and touch him and let him know I was right there, and I don't know, pretty soon the light faded and all the people whom I loved and who had said all the kind things about me were gone, and I was just standing alone beside my casket in the dark funeral parlor. Time passed, I have no clue how long. Pretty soon I got awfully sick of being in the mortuary and attending other people's funerals.

Like I said, ghosts always attend their own funerals, and in ninety percent of the cases I would watch a light appear for them and off they would go. Sometimes they saw me too, and a few even held out their hands, offering to share their doorways, but I always turned my head away. I hated the funeral parlor and the light looked pretty nice, but I was held here by some feeling that I had to stay for a while longer, get to the bottom of my murder, and then, sure, yeah, the light sounded good.

As I was saying, in ninety percent of cases a light would appear and the recently departed would head on over, but it was the other ten percent that interested me. Sometimes no light appeared, and after a while you could tell by the mourners, or lack of mourners, that no one was sitting there thinking what a great guy or gal the newly dead was, in fact quite the opposite.

And if there were no good words or thoughts, there was no light. Those ghosts gave me the creeps, and I made it a point never to make eye contact with them if I could avoid it. Then there were the others, ghosts that were like me, them I would try and approach. These ghosts looked like nice people and I saw the light come up for each one of them, and they could have gone too, but same as me they pulled back for their own reasons.

Usually when I watched them they would follow someone they were obviously close to out the door, and that would be it, but a few of them hung around for a while at the funeral parlor, like me. Some would talk to me but most were quiet, seemingly lost in their own grief and confusion at being dead. I never saw an old person or child stay around; maybe they were smarter than I was, I don't know. I did eventually learn from some of the others that I could leave anytime if I just thought hard enough about where it was I wanted to be.

Unless I wanted to cross water. They said none of us could cross water.

I didn't care about crossing water, not then. Why would I want to cross water? Later, of course, that was all I wanted to do, and I think it was my decade of terrible frustration about that unfair rule which gave me the energy and power to reach the jurors in Las Vegas.

But all that came a lot later. I know now that I stayed in the viewing room for so long because I didn't know where I wanted to go. I missed my kids like crazy and I could have gone home to Rockingham, but he was there and at that time I thought I never wanted to see my husband again. And the thought of seeing my kids living with my killer was too sickening. I missed my parents and my sisters a lot too, but I didn't feel drawn there.

I thought a lot about going back to my condo on Bundy. I had loved that place, and after all, it's where all my blood was spilled. We dead have a strong connection to our murder sites, so it was looking like Bundy for sure, and that is where I went eventually. But before I made it back to Bundy, a big funeral took place, and for some reason that day I listened more carefully to what some of the mourners were saying.

They weren't talking about their dearly departed, they were talking about me. I found out that day, amongst other news, that I had been dead almost a year, that my kids were living with my parents, and that my husband's murder trial was starting the next day in a downtown L.A. courtroom.

I was completely awakened by this news and I knew exactly where I wanted to go finally. My immediate problem was that I had no idea where the courthouse was, and I couldn't visualize it either, so I couldn't try one of those 'think and you'll be there' scenarios.

I was panicking a little and the funniest thing happened. When I got upset like that, I noticed some of the people around me started rubbing their arms and looking around. I liked it. I didn't mean I liked being a ghost - I hated it then and now - but I liked that it looked like I was still around in some way, that some part of me could reach out to the living.

That was the day I took a chance, not on moving through time and space with my thoughts, but by getting inside a car for the first time since the day I had been murdered. The reason all the mourners at this funeral were talking about me was because one of them was apparently a guard named Chip who worked at the downtown courthouse.

His job gave Chip a kind of celebrity status with the people there, and it occurred to me that he would have to go to work the next morning, so maybe I could try to follow him and catch a ride. I knew then where I belonged - at that trial.

I found out a couple things when I ran out of the mortuary after Chip. I found out that ghosts can follow anyone they want, but if ghosts can walk through doors, I wasn't one of them.

I ended up on the roof of his car, speeding down the 405 out of Laguna towards L.A., as my attempt to mist myself through his closed passenger door hadn't worked out too well. That's how I got back to L.A. to attend the trial of the century, and how I got to see my husband again for the first time since the night he killed me.

Chapter 12

That trial. I'm not sure what I can say about it that hasn't already been said. I mean, there are a few things that I guess no-one will ever know. Sure, it's true that I told a few people that I thought he was going to kill me and get away with it, and ya know, I think half those jurors bought that story, and maybe millions of other people did too. Okay, yeah, I said it, and I wrote out my will, and I kept some pictures of the worst beatings he gave me in a safe deposit box.

I did those things, and no, I never believed for one minute that my head would get nearly cut off, or my breasts, or that I would be slaughtered and that I would be the unknowing cause of the equally bad death of a sweet young guy.

I don't get why no one has ever just sat down for a second and thought about what's totally obvious. I loved my kids and my family and my friends. I loved my life. I loved him. I had always loved him, and yeah, we were in another one of our break-up cycles the night he killed me, but all I figured would happen from that was that we were either going to make up, like we always did, or - who knows - maybe start trying to be friends.

If I had thought my husband was going to kill me, would I have lived in a place with a broken gate, would I have opened the door and walked outside to argue with him, or told Ron to stop by?

God, if people believe that I knew my husband could turn into a homicidal maniac, it makes it look like I purposely put myself in harm's way, and worse, that I put Ron there, and that is so not true.

My husband had scared me, and he had hurt me, more times than I could count out loud, and I guess there were times when he was hurting me and screaming at me that I did believe that he might kill me or disfigure me so bad that my life would end.

There were times after I left him, and times when I went back to him before I tried to leave again, that I felt terrified. But mostly I don't think anyone, and for sure not me, ever really, truly believes they are going to be killed. If I had, I would have moved into a fortress apartment - it's not like Beverly Hills doesn't have any of those - or I could have taken the kids and gone to stay at my parents' for the summer.

The reason I didn't do either of those things was because most of the time I was just living my life in the sun, being with my kids and my friends, being alive. If I had a do-over, then sure, yeah, I would change things that last summer, or even further back to the year before when I asked him if I could go home. But what's the point of thinking that way? A lot of ghosts do think that way, and they are seriously crazed because of it - if, if, if. If is a stupid word. If I start using that word, where should I start? If I hadn't said yes to him the first time he asked me out a month after my eighteenth birthday? If I had said no when he wanted me to live with him, to marry him, to love only him forever and ever?

That's another stupid word. People use it a lot when they are alive - I know I did. Now I'm beginning to understand exactly what 'forever' means, and if ... - there I go again with that bad word - ... if I could live again, I would never use it.

'Never' is a good word, though. I will never be alive again and my husband was never convicted of my murder.

I saw that last one coming early on. When I rode to the courthouse with old Chip the first day of the trial, I avoided looking at my husband or going near him for a long time. I was afraid of what I might feel if I went too close or saw him. I studied the people in the courtroom instead, and right away I could see that those jurors were never going to find my husband guilty.

They were almost all black, and I could see that was what the trial for my murder was going to be about. I knew it from Day One. Am I being racist? I hope if anyone thinks that they are kidding.

I spent my whole adult life loving one man, a black man. My kids are black. I wasn't the one who hated his being black, *he* hated it. Come on, get real. My husband was a very famous man and he used that fame to try and do the impossible, and he almost made it. He was almost totally white when he killed me. There was the all-white neighborhood, and the white hobbies, and the white friends, and the white wife. Though when he was through with me, I was more a red wife.

Of course the minute he killed Ron and me, the entire white world saw him as coal black, and all the distance he had worked so hard to put between the man he was then and the skinny rickets-ridden little kid from the ghetto, disappeared with the stroke of a knife.

I don't think that was right, but I don't think it was right either that twelve people sat in a jury box and plugged up their ears so they didn't have to hear the evidence that proved far beyond even an unreasonable doubt that my husband had killed Ron and me.

Those people, those black people, looked at my husband and saw a poor jammed-up black guy being set up by the white power structure, a structure that had probably fucked with them all their lives. In freeing my so-guilty husband, they saw a chance to get back at that system. I get it, but what they never got was that he must have hated them seeing him as their brother almost as much as he feared spending the rest of his life in prison.

Maybe they even hoped that by doing this for him, letting him go on a charge they knew was true, he would feel so much gratitude towards his own people that he would finally become a part of the black community. I could have told them that was never going to happen.

I learned a few things about my so-called ghostly powers while sitting in the jury box; namely that I didn't have any. There was one thing, though: if I sat close enough to someone and laid my hands on them, I could occasionally, very occasionally, pick up some of their thoughts.

Hearing those thoughts made me feel pretty hopeless as regarded getting a guilty verdict, and so I tried to send them some of my thoughts back, and maybe I would get a little jump sometimes. It's hard to tell, but there were days that a few of the jurors couldn't look at my husband or the evidence. Instead, they would stare down at their locked hands and tell themselves very fiercely that it didn't matter what the prosecution or the witnesses said; this one black man whose destiny they could control was going to be set free.

I have been asked by other ghosts over the years where Ron was. He was there for most of the trial. Ron, I think, would have gone into the light the day of his funeral but - and this is just my theory, so take it or leave it - I think the intense grief of his dad and sister kept him around for a while. I saw him in that courtroom every day for months, and I know he saw me too, even though he never came over to me. He stayed right beside his family, patting them and trying so hard to reach through their grief, and let them know he was okay.

Ron was different than me. Even though he was only twenty-five when he died, he was an old soul kind of guy. Ron talked about eternity a lot. He was even going to open a restaurant named 'Ankh', which I think means 'forever' in Egyptian. So I know he wasn't at the trial looking to get my husband, or to try and change things. He was just there to be near his family to try and help them.

Ron figured out a long time before I did that we ghosts don't really help or change anything - we're just here. The trial was coming to an end and the last time I ever saw Ron was the day before my husband's stupid glove stunt. Ron had been sitting with his family, like always, trying to comfort them, when all of a sudden he stood up and walked away to the center of the courthouse aisle. I was watching as he gave his dad and sister the saddest look and waved his hand goodbye to them.

For the first time in all those months, he walked right over to where I was sitting in the jury box. He smiled at me and held out his hand, but I didn't. I couldn't give him mine. He gave me a sad little nod and turned for the doors of the courtroom. Before he got there, I saw Ron disappear. It was the light and Ron must have somehow known that there was no point in sticking around any longer. Like I said, he was a guy who understood eternity.

Watching Ron leave gave me the loneliest feeling I had yet experienced. It was the first time I ever felt how totally and completely alone I was. I stood up then too, and I swear if I had seen the light, I would have made a run for it, but there was no light waiting for me. I turned to look for my family. I wanted to at least be able to sit with them and feel their love for me the way Ron had from his family, but their seats were empty. They had mostly stopped coming.

I looked everywhere in that crowded courtroom, trying to see or feel one person who was crying for me, thinking about me, maybe missing me just a little, and that's when I really looked at my husband for the first time since the trial had started. He was staring straight ahead at a large photo of me the prosecutor had propped on an easel, and tears were running down his face. I moved closer to him and I could hear him whispering my name over and over.

"Nic, Nic, I love you, baby. I miss you so goddamn much. Where are you, Nic?"

When court adjourned, I followed him to his cell. Like so many times before, he ended up being the only person who really wanted me, who truly loved me and so I went back to him. To be fair to my husband, since I'm pretty sure he didn't realize I was there and that, I was expecting a solemn reunion. He didn't purposely try to anger or disgust me when I went to his cell, it just happened.

I was shaking with so many different feelings that are really hard to express. I mean, I was dead but some things never change, and during my life, whenever I left him, and I did it plenty, he could always get me back one way or another. I heard what people said after I was dead, that I had been a gold digger and a trophy wife, and wow, those were nice things to listen to, especially from people who I thought were my friends. I'm guessing that they probably said and thought that while I was alive too but were too afraid to say it out loud.

Once you are dead, let me tell you, it's open season on your reputation. Sure, he gave me stuff. He gave me everything at one time or another: amazing cars, furs, jewelry, a mansion, a marriage, my babies, black eyes and broken ribs, bad nights and angry days, and more love and attention than any ten women got.

Let me tell you, though, that the only reasons I kept going back to him over and over, the only reasons were because no matter what, I always loved him more than I hated him and I always wanted to be with him more than I wanted to get away from him.

So that day I might have been dead but some things hadn't changed a bit, and when I had seen him crying in the courtroom and heard him saying my name, I figured it was the same for him. I hadn't forgotten he had killed me, in case anyone is listening to me and rolling their eyes thinking, *wow, what a sap!*

Nope, I am not a sap and, yeah, I was pretty fucking aware that he had almost cut my head off and that I was dead. See, ghost or not, that is the kind of thing a person tends to remember. But I was already dead, and so the threat of killing me was pretty much off the table. I hadn't gone into the light and I had spent almost two years telling myself that it was because I wanted vengeance, and then I realized I had been lying to myself, trying to make myself believe that, because it was the way I was supposed to feel. But it was bullshit, because the first time I really let myself look at my husband, I understood that, same as always, I still loved him more than I hated him.

Besides, I figured our situations had changed pretty drastically. Since no matter what I felt for him, I thought that being dead, as I so clearly was, put me for once in the driver's seat. I could stay with him or leave as I felt like it, and the sight of him that day had made me think he was a broken man, a changed man. I know, I know, I know that's what every abused woman says and thinks, I know all the language.

I read every book on abuse I could get my hands on in the last couple years before I died, and yup, more than half of abused women either ended up going back to their bad men or ended up getting killed. I fell into both categories, which may be exceptional, or maybe not.

So what? I never claimed to be different than other women, or better than them. People thought because of how I looked, or because we were rich, or because he was famous, or whatever, that I didn't meet the profile of an abused woman. Don't make me laugh. I don't think I met the profile of an abused woman either. I didn't just sit there and take it like some pathetic coward.

I fought back every time and I did leave lots and lots of times. I went back to him because I loved him very much and I still think now that the only profile I ever met was the profile of a woman who loved her man like crazy, 'crazy' maybe being the big word here, but what exactly is the profile of a woman in love?

There are millions of women who are married to men they love a hell of a lot less than I loved mine, and who don't get one tenth of the love he gave me, and who stay in their marriages and no one judges them or says they fit some kind of stupid pattern.

But God help you if he hits you, because after that all you are as a woman anymore is a battered wife, and that's all he is then; a man who hits a woman. After that happens, your whole life together - everything you shared and built and all the thousands of good sweet memories - don't count anymore; it's just a disaster, and all you are is a disaster victim. It's not too different than being a murder victim, because no one is ever going to remember me for anything except the way I died. And there was a hell of lot more to Nicole Brown Simpson than that, and there was a hell of a lot more to me and him than just the violence.

Anyway, when I saw him all broken and lonely like that, my heart went out to him because I felt exactly the same, and obviously I knew he had brought this on both of us but it had already happened, and this is where we were, right then, and I was never much for looking back. Doing it now is a real first for me.

I hadn't looked at him, or gone near him, in the year I had spent in the courtroom because I was really angry that he was spending all that money trying to get out of killing Ron and me, but that day when I went back to his cell, I was already making excuses for him, heading towards forgiving him again.

He had killed us but it had been a crime of passion. Well that much I knew for sure was true, ha. He had horrible guilt and was totally sorry and knew he belonged in prison forever but was working to get free because he missed our kids and wanted to try and make up to them for killing their mom.

Jeez, I have to say that admitting I ever thought anything so pathetic makes me want to blush, which is something else ghosts can't do either. I got over my dumbass thinking pretty quick in his cell.

For one thing he didn't want to be alone, as I had hoped, to cry and think about me some more. As a matter of fact, no sooner did he get back there than he was ordering the guards around like he was at the Four Seasons, telling them to bring him a Pepsi and to get such and such into the visiting room right away.

I didn't like seeing this at all and I started to feel angry again, very angry. I was happy to see that, just like in the funeral parlor when I got upset, it changed things a little bit. He felt cold, I could tell. He even made a guard get him an extra sweatshirt because he said he was freezing. That was when I noticed his hands.

My husband has the biggest hands. They're like meat hooks. Those hands had served him really well in football and when he used them against me in either anger or love, but when I looked at them that day they were like cartoon hands, freakishly swollen. I didn't understand why until I followed him into the visitor's room and watched him sit down to talk with his sports agent, a sleazy guy I had always hated named Mike Gilbert.

The first thing Mike said to my husband is, "How are the hands doing, Juice?"

I still didn't get it. I looked at my husband and he grimaced before answering Mike.

"How do you think they're doing, motherfucker, they fucking hurt." He held up his weirdly swollen hands and waved them in Mike's face. Mike didn't look concerned, though, he looked happy. He grinned back at my husband, like seeing his hands all messed up like this was the best news ever, and said, "Then you did it or, excuse me, you didn't do it, right?"

I thought he was talking about me but that wasn't it.

My husband kind of grunted, saying. "Yeah, I didn't take anything for my arthritis last night or this morning. Fuck, my hands look like something out of horror movie. I had to keep them under the table all day in court, I was afraid somebody might ask me about them. I mean, Johnnie knows obviously. The whole stupid fucking stunt with the gloves is his so called brilliant fucking idea, so yeah, he knows I'm skipping my meds; he knows but doesn't want to know, you dig me?"

Mike nodded. "Yeah, I dig you Juice. It makes sense. He's an officer of the court."

My husband snorted. "An officer of the court, my ass. After how much money I've paid him, he's chairman of the fucking board, but not of the court of the get-me-the-fuck-out-of-here board. And it's easy for all you brilliant motherfuckers, isn't it? Sitting around on your asses, coming up with your little ideas, while my fucking life's on the line and this glove thing is gonna blow up in our faces. No-one's that fucking stupid, Mark. Besides my hands are fucking killing me."

His hands were killing him?

I wanted to scream and rip the visiting room apart. Killing *you*? I would have said, oh no, honey, you got that wrong. Those hands are killers all right, but it's me and Ron they killed, not you.

He and Mike went on talking for a while, but I was so upset that I couldn't stand to be near him anymore, and I made my way back to the courtroom.

I hadn't understood what they were plotting with his hands, or the glove, not until the next day. Time varies when you are dead. Sometimes you think only an hour has passed by and then you find out it was three years, or something crazy. But I felt every second of that long night in the darkened courtroom. I didn't want to be there. I didn't want to be anywhere at all. I didn't even want the light to come back. I just wanted to go to sleep and never wake up again.

Sleeping is another thing ghosts can't do. Instead, we sort of fade in and out of awareness sometimes, which I guess is what passes for sleep amongst my kind. And eventually that is what happened to me that night.

I was brought back to sharp awareness by the energy of those around me who had entered the courtroom during my lost hours. I had not felt anything like this during the trial.

The people in the spectators' benches all around me started standing up and craning their heads, even climbing onto the benches. I heard the bailiff scream for everyone to sit down and they all ignored him.

I couldn't see a thing, so I made my way through the people up to the defense table and that is how I got to hear Johnnie Cochran say, "If the glove doesn't fit, you must acquit."

I watched silent and unseen as my still-handsome husband played to the crowd, smiling apologetically as he struggled to pull a leather glove over his grotesquely swollen hand.

Chapter 13

I decided to haunt him. I made up my mind to do it after I heard the expected, but still hard to take, words, 'Not guilty', and after I had watched him manipulate the gloves and the jurors and the world at large. I decided to do it because when I looked at the expressions on the faces of Ron's dad and sister, it seemed like the right thing to do, the only thing I could do.

I didn't know if I could haunt him, or anyone, successfully. After all, I had been around hundreds of people in the last couple of years, and nothing I tried seemed to make anyone notice me, except for those few times when I had gotten really upset and it had seemed to make the people nearby cold. I hoped if being upset was what it took to make things happen, maybe I could bring the house down or at the least create some heating problems for him.

I followed my husband out to the limo, which was crowded with his hangers-on, but I was surprised to see that not even one of his eight or so attorneys was with him. A pretty blond paralegal did ride with him in the car, and he started coming on to her the second the doors closed. Seeing it pissed me off so bad that I gathered myself up, and to my surprise and happiness, managed to knock over a wine bottle onto his lap.

He jumped about a foot and yelled at the driver to take the turns more slowly. When he stepped out of the car to face his adoring, cheering section at Rockingham, he did it with a big wet stain on his crotch. I was starting to enjoy myself.

My good feelings didn't last past the first few minutes, though. I could not believe the people that had shown up to welcome the conquering killer home from his joke trial. Two of my so-called former best friends were waiting for him, holding out their arms for the chance to hug my husband. A couple dozen other people who I had always thought cared about me were standing around grinning and waving champagne bottles, and it made me feel like I did the night he stabbed me.

I didn't get it then, and I don't get it now. My husband basically slaughtered me in a jealous rage, and not just me, but a sweet innocent young guy who gives new meaning to the old saying 'being in the wrong place at the wrong time'.

What did they see when they looked at him?

As upset as I was by all of that crap, it was being back at my house again - Rockingham, the house he had brought me to live in when I was his totally infatuated nineteen year old girlfriend - that really did me in. It was the house that I had made my own over the next sixteen years. It was the place where we had gotten married and where I had brought my babies to home from the hospital, and where almost every good and bad thing I had experienced in my too-short life had gone down.

I left all of those disloyal groupie assholes out on the lawn and went back into my house.

It looked the same as it had the last time when I had been there a few days before the murders. I wandered into the big living room and sat down on one of the white couches. Those couches, they were the only original pieces of furniture, left in the house because they had been reupholstered so many times they basically stayed new.

Funny thing, those couches. I loved white furniture and he let me have it because he loved everything to look immaculate all the time. It didn't take me long to figure out that white was a bad color for us, but the color of the upholstery became one more twisted thing between us. He insisted that it be recovered in white each time.

I breastfed both my kids on them, and at the slightest drip, he'd go crazy and start frantically wiping them clean. When my son was four, he put a fingerprint on one of them, and I thought my husband was going to have a stroke. Later that year my little boy wrote his first letter. It was to his dad, apologizing for marring his stupid white couch. The paper showed his hand print and said, 'Dear Daddy, this is a piktur of my hand now bekuz I am very small. I am sorry I made a mark on the couch. I love you.'

I don't want to talk anymore about my kids. I can't do that. So back to the couches ... Whenever we made love in the living room, we always had to do it on the floor. Don't get me wrong, he loved sex with me. That was one of the few things we never disagreed on. But every damn time we would get romantic on the couch, he would roll me to the floor, reminding me of the potential for stains. I used to hate that.

Blood is, of course, impossible to get out of white linen, so at least ten times they had to be recovered because of stains from my nose or mouth. He would be watching one of the TVs, or all four of them at once, and I'd be sitting there, and I'd say something that pissed him off. I can't remember anything in particular I said to set him off. I mean, it's not like I used to lie around trying to come up with the perfect phrase so he would decide to kick my ass. If he got mad, for whatever reason he'd reach over without taking his eyes off the screen, and smash his hand into my face. Limited force from my husband's hands still felt about the same as a car hitting you. I'd bleed, and a few times that would make him even madder, and then like he did when we would make love, he would push me down onto the floor to finish what he started.

My trip down Memory Lane hadn't started so well, and I was starting to feel all my old hurts mixing with the new ones in a rising wave of anger.

I stared at the clean white upholstery and wished I had even a tiny portion of the blood he had spilled the night he killed me. I would have smeared it across the furniture until it was bright red.

While I was thinking about that, several of my husband's relatives walked into the living room and sat down. I didn't want to stay and listen to them talk about what a hero he was for beating a murder rap, so I left and headed up to my - to our - old bedroom.

While I was walking up the stairs, I saw one thing in the house that had changed big time. For all the years I lived at Rockingham, I had kept a gallery of pictures of my family, and later of the kids, on the staircase wall. Those pictures, like our upholstery, needed constant repair because every time I did anything that upset my husband, he would head just like clockwork to those pictures and, one-by-one, throw them down the stairs onto the foyer floor.

It hurt every time, and I guess that's why he did it. Why I kept having the glass and frames fixed, and re-hanging them, is hard to say. I mean, I'm no shrink but maybe it was because I knew that when he smashed those pictures, he was smashing me too. I kept trying to fix them the same way I covered up my bruises with make-up. It was like if I could make the signs of the bad times go away, if I could fix what he broke, then I didn't have to think about it till it happened again.

I got so good at that. I had to be good, because if I had left the bruises uncovered, or the pictures laying there smashed, I would have needed to do something. Not only that but other people would have seen, and they would have judged us, and gossiped about us, just like they have ever since the murders, and stuff like that doesn't help. Really, it just makes things a whole lot worse.

Besides, if I had let other people see, or even let myself see, I would have had to have gone away, and I didn't want to go anywhere. I just wanted to be treated better and not to be afraid so much of the time.

When I finally did go, I took the pictures with me, except for three or four of us with the kids that I thought he would like. I was pretty hurt when I went back the first time and saw he had taken them down and covered the wall with pictures of himself standing beside other celebrities. I have to mention this because it helps explain how pissed I was that day.

All those pictures of him, and the celebrities were white celebrities. Not one picture was hung with him and another black person - not his own mom, nor the kids.

So it was kind of the last straw for me when I saw, as he faced his trial, he had taken down all those photos of white celebrities and replaced them with a gallery that would have made Dr. King happy. I knew he had had someone buy and hang all those bullshit photos of famous black leaders to impress the jury who had gotten to tour the house, because he sure hadn't owned any of them before. While I was eying his wall of lies, I heard the front door open below me and watched my husband come inside, trailed by his little fan squad.

I don't know if it was me and the feelings I was sending out that made him look up, or just a coincidence, but I think he saw me. No, I *know* he saw me, because I felt this huge wave of fear come off of him and it hit me like a blast of energy. I was positive that if I tried at that moment, I could make something happen.

I smiled at him and grabbed the nearest picture. It's funny, I felt really strong, almost alive, so when I grabbed at it, I figured it would be yanked off the wall. It didn't happen that way but I did make it come loose and it fell to the carpet.

One small ghost step for me ... one giant jolt of fear for him.

I don't think anyone else noticed my little triumph but he did, and he knew exactly what it meant. His eyes widened and bulged, and he stepped back so fast he smashed into his sister. She looked at him funny and asked what was wrong with him, and he brushed her off and started to walk towards the stairs. Then he stopped and changed his mind.

I could tell he couldn't see me anymore and that he was already starting to tell himself he had imagined it. That was okay by me. We had years ahead of us to catch up and I was shocked by how much that one little move had taken out of me. I felt completely drained as I drifted towards our bedroom, drained but triumphant. After all, I was finally home.

Chapter 14

I can safely say that my husband's last year in L.A. was the worst year of his life so far. Everything that he foresaw for himself failed and the bad things came at him like the worst of the L.A. landslides.

I did my small part in keeping him shaky and sleep-deprived, but we ghosts just don't have as much power as horror films make out. For example, I had read 'The Amityville Horror' while I was alive and I had believed every word, so when I moved home to Rockingham that year, I kind of figured that I could do some pretty nasty stuff to him if I tried.

But I know now that book was a bunch of crap, because no matter how hard I worked at it, I couldn't make blood drip out of faucets or slime run down the walls, and I would have loved doing that stuff because my husband was so obsessed with the house being perfect all the time.

I can't remember how many times during my life he would come and find me, no matter what I was doing, and scream at me that I had left my shoes out, or even worse, left a glass on a table. If the glass was left on a table with no coaster underneath it, then I could pretty much plan on needing a lot of cover-up the next day.

I didn't do those things on purpose - big surprise. I didn't much enjoy getting hit or screamed at, but I had little kids, and sometimes I messed up, and my husband never let anything go.

He cheated on me and he hurt me, and he hit me, and I wasn't allowed to talk about it at all, but God help me - though he never did - if I left my shoes laying on the living room floor ...

It wasn't always like that with us, obviously, or I would have split years before. Most of the time, in fact, it was love, and us being happy together and with our kids, and good times with our families and friends and the most amazing trips. Really, it was the best life anyone ever had. But yeah, it could go bad, worse than bad, without warning, and of course he did kill me, so I guess that, after all, it ended up being more bad than good, and that year I was determined that was how it was going to go for him too.

I managed to do a lot of little things that kept him an off-balance wreck, the way I used to be. I learned how to make the toilet flush over and over at ten forty-five at night - that's the time it was when he killed me. I could knock his glasses off the reading table and pull the covers off of him as he slept.

But it was in his dreams that I had the most power, or juice, if you prefer. I found out that when someone close to a dead person dreams about us, we ghosts can get in on those dreams pretty easily, and it was in my husband's sleep that I came alive for him, so to speak.

My husband tried very hard that year not to have to sleep alone, but because of his increasing unpopularity, it happened more and more, and when he was alone he dreamed about me.

I didn't like those dreams as they were hard for me to watch. He dreamed of me and him at the beach, or at Christmas with the kids, and sometimes he dreamed of us making love.

I'd step in then and change the scenery around, and help him to dream of a hot July night, watching me run towards the front gate, already bleeding like crazy. I'd make him dream of catching me by pulling my hair until I stumbled and fell to my knees, and then of yanking me up again, pulling back my head and slitting my neck crossways. I didn't hesitate to add sound effects either.

The dreams I helped create of my death didn't bother me a bit. Once you're dead, knowing how you got to be that way isn't something you are sentimental about. What hurts us is remembering our lives, not our deaths, and I wanted him to remember too.

He'd wake up gasping and shaken, and grab for the light by his bed. Before he could pull himself together, I'd do some little thing like make his glasses or a book fall off his night table, and pretty much that would be the end of his sleep for the rest of the night.

That was too bad because if my husband had ever needed a full night of restful sleep, it was that year. He had enemies a lot scarier and more effective around him than one little blond ghost who could make toilets flush late at night.

Ron's father, Fred Goldman, must have loved his son so much. I have to admit it hurt when I found out that it was him alone who had filed a civil suit against my husband. Oh, my family ended up getting in on it later when it looked like there might be some money in the deal, but I knew from listening to my husband, and his new not-so-dream team of lawyers, that the force and the idea had all been Fred Goldman's.

I don't really want to talk about my family either, but during that year friends of my husband, the ones that were left, would stop by and show him things that my family was doing to express their grief and outrage. My father had sold my wedding video to a tabloid show. My little sister had sold pictures of me sunbathing topless in the privacy of my own home to the National Enquirer. Stuff like that. It hurt me then and it hurts me now. Ironically, the only person who seemed bothered by it was my husband, though as the civil suit heated up, he started leading the squad in the 'trash Nicole's memory' detail.

Before I get into the civil suit, I want to talk about the other stuff that was happening to him that year. You have to understand that nothing, and I mean nothing, meant more to him than how people, white people, important rich white people, saw him. He had spent his whole football and post-football career building this persona of the best guy you'd ever want to meet, just a regular guy who was also a football superstar, and it had worked out really good for him.

He had it all for a long time, the rich white friends who didn't just look at him as though he wasn't black, nope they looked at him like he was the Second Coming. He was, I think, the only black member at one time of the Riviera Country Club and he had some serious endorsement money coming in, and even that wasn't the best part of it.

The best part for him was that, no matter where he went or what he was doing, everybody looked at him and smiled. By the time he killed me and Ron, he had been famous and loved for so long that he had totally lost touch with the real world or the idea that not everybody might always believe it was raining just because he said it was.

After he got acquitted for killing us, and got acquitted for being the one thing he never wanted to be - a black man - well, he just couldn't, or wouldn't, see the writing on the wall, which is hilarious because he used to say to me all the time when we did it, 'Once you go black, you can never go back.' Alone in bed was the only time he ever joked about being black.

It wasn't a joke after the trial, though. He was willing to do anything, even play a nonexistent - in his case anyway - race card to get away with it, and nobody in the world he had lived in before was going to forgive him for that.

I was in the living room, sitting beside him a week after the trial, when he and his friends watched the Police Chief Darryl Gates say that, no, the L.A.P.D. would not be looking for the murderer of Nicole Brown Simpson and Ron Goldman. Everyone knew exactly what that meant, and when my husband looked around the room for reassurance, nobody would meet his eyes.

A week after that there were no more rich white important visitors to the house and there was no more Riviera Country Club either. People on TV and in the streets started saying openly what they had been thinking; that he had killed us and gotten away with it.

And there was a big white backlash. My husband's damned trial probably did more to hurt race relations in our country than anything since the shooting of Dr. King, but in a different way. This time nobody felt bad for him or for every other poor black person that got compared to him. This time it was 'The rich n....r bought his way out', and people were saying 'All those fucking athletes are steroid-enraged thugs', and just a ton of ugly stuff like that.

Overall the white world said to my husband, 'You wanted to be black? Well, go ahead, fella, you're black now and we'll hit you with every worst case black stereotype there is.'

Sometimes I even felt sorry for him, he was so shocked. It's like how he was when he had finally gone too far one too many times with me, and I left him. He could not, would not, believe it. So many people let him get away with so much for so long - and yeah, I'll admit that I was probably one of the worst - that when all his bad debts got called in, he never believed it was really payout time.

Well, after the trial, it all got called in at once, and instead of receiving forgiving looks, now there was no-one at all left who would meet his eyes, no-one but Fred Goldman, that is, and what my husband saw in his eyes must have looked like a lifetime's worth of judgment

Chapter 15

The civil trial was one of those deals that I could see from Day One was not going to go my husband's way. This time the case was being tried in Santa Monica by a jury of his white peers, which is pretty funny when you think about it. The criminal trial for killing me and Ron was in front of a black jury, and my husband was at that time white as rice to all intents and purposes. The second time around he had a white jury but he was finally a black man. I don't just mean that because people had turned against him and were seeing him as the worst stereotype of a black man; it was because he had snapped, or something, and actually turned into the worst stereotype of the angry black man who had never caught a break.

I watched it, I know how he changed; I was in the house with him. My husband had always had a pretty nasty mouth on him when he got pissed at me or anyone else he was close to, but the rest of the time, no way. Now it was all 'motherfucker this' and 'motherfucker that', and he didn't care who was listening. He was drinking every day and he was seriously deep into coke, thanks to his new girlfriend who was some nineteen year old whore he had picked up on the curb, and I mean that literally.

She and her girlfriends were amongst a growing crowd of weirdos that used to cruise by Rockingham and pose in front of the gates. She was pretty, I guess, in a kind of overweight hooker way. But the day he picked her up, it was because no-one would have missed her act. Instead of just standing out in front of the gates, like all the other Lookee Lous did for a picture, she took it up a notch and laid down in front of the gates and had her girlfriends shoot pictures of her.

They were all laughing and screaming like it was so freaking funny to imitate me. Here's the ugliest part: my husband was inside the gates watching them, and when he saw it, he laughed too and walked over and invited her and her trashy girlfriends inside our house.

The first words out of her mouth were, "Got any coke?" He didn't then, but by the next day when she came back around, he had plenty. Her name was Christy Prody.

When he started drinking and partying, his looks started to slide. He stopped working out and didn't dress nice anymore. For all those years when he played white boy, he dressed totally preppy all the time. Even when he wasn't golfing, he looked like he was either about to golf or just had. He had always looked amazing too, in his suits and tuxes, but when it was time for the trial, he had to have them all let out.

When he wasn't in court, he walked around in un-tucked black silk shirts and designer jeans to match his new slutty girlfriend. Eventually they both got identical gold chains. I wanted to throw up looking at them but that's another thing ghosts can't do.

So when the trial started, he had all these new habits and language, and no matter how hard his lawyers tried to make him shape up in the courtroom, he just wouldn't do it. He slumped in his chair and rolled his eyes and smirked all the time. And when he took the stand finally, which let me tell you was a last ditch effort to save himself, he offended everyone in the courtroom.

But me he did more than offend. He shredded me.

He sat up there on the stand with his yellow eyes and his 'bring it on, asshole' look on his face and he didn't answer the plaintiff's attorney's questions. Instead he told stories about me. Turns out I alone was responsible for getting me and Ron killed. I had been consorting with known Colombian drug dealers and had probably screwed them on a deal which led to … "Nicole's unfortunate death. But I'll tell you, we could all it see it coming. That girl was living on the edge and something bad was gonna go down. It's too bad about the young guy with her, but maybe he wasn't that innocent either, you know what I'm saying?"

Then he did this awful thing. He brought out a letter I had written him during the sad confused time when I thought maybe going back home to him was the right choice. He read it out loud in court for the world to hear:

> *I always knew that what was going on with us was about me - I just wasn't sure why it was about me, so I just blamed you. I'm the one who was controlling. I wanted you to be a perfect husband and father. I was not accepting of who you are because I didn't like myself anymore. I never stopped loving you - I stopped liking myself and lost total confidence in any relationship with you.*
>
> *I want to put our family back together! I want our kids to grow up*

with their parents. I thought I'd be happy raising Sydney and Justin by myself since we didn't see too much of you anyway. But now, I ... I want to be with you! I want to love and cherish you and make you smile. I want to wake up in the mornings and hold you at night. I want to hug and kiss you everyday. I want to be the way we used to be. There was no couple like us.

I don't know what I went through ... I didn't believe you loved me anymore and I couldn't handle it. But for the past month I've been looking at our wedding photos and our family movies and I can see that we truly loved each other. A love like I've never seen in any of our friends. Please look at the 2 tapes I'm sending over with this letter. Watch them alone & with your phone turned off - they're really fun to watch.

You will be my one and only "true love." I'm sorry for the pain I've caused you and I'm sorry we let it die. Please let us be a family again, and let me love you better than I ever have before.

I'll love you forever and always.

Me.

It was so humiliating listening to that. It was also one of the few times that I was glad I was already dead so that no one could stare at me with all the judgments and questions that were no-one's business.

Listening to him read out loud our most private things, I felt killed again. You can die a lot of times, I guess, and you can kill somebody in a lot of ways, and only sometimes leave a corpse.

I wanted to disappear from the courtroom but I was too sad to move, and I'm glad I stayed after all, because Fred Goldman's attorney saved me. He strode up to the stand and he was pissed. When he got to my husband he said in a voice that you could tell he was trying his best to control, "May I see the letter you have just read, sir?"

My husband, who was either pretending to cry or really was crying, I don't know which, kept his head down and passed it to him.

The attorney scanned it and then shoved it under my husband's nose. "What is this on the bottom of the letter, sir?"

My husband looked at it and answered all shaky. "It's a smiley face. Nic always used to draw smiley faces on things she wrote." Then he acted overcome with grief, ha, and buried his face in his hands.

The attorney stood silently, waiting him out. When my husband had collected himself, the attorney said sarcastically, "A smiley face at the end of a letter from a clearly tortured and confused young woman, who was so far gone in pain and desperation that she wrote a letter to you that began with an apology for her being angry at you for your cheating on her, sir? She drew a smiley face? Sir, do you see any contradictions in that action?"

My husband was too quickly back into his smirking 'fuck you' attitude, and like a moron he grinned when he answered. "No, I don't see any contradictions, sir. She put a smiley face on because she was happy that we were gonna get back together. And you can interpret that letter as confused if you want to, but I don't see where you're getting that. Nic wasn't confused about what she wanted. She wanted to come home to me." He finished his little speech by throwing his old football hero smile at the jury.

The attorney didn't smile back. He said: "Isn't it true, sir, that during this time Ms. Brown wrote you more than one letter? Isn't there another letter that may indeed show that this poor young woman was going through a very difficult time of finding her place in the world after years of your abuse and control? Is that not also true, sir?"

My husband, obviously sure he had scored a touchdown with my pathetic letter, grinned, shrugged and raised up his hands. "Not that I'm aware of. Again, as I said, there was no confusion in Mrs. Simpson. We were working on some stuff, like couples do. We had our ups and downs, sir, but I can assure you, if she had not been murdered, we would be together today, and she would be right here beside me telling you that you were barking up the wrong tree."

The attorney smiled. "I do indeed wish that Ms. Brown was here, sir, and able to tell us that very thing. Sidebar, please."

My husband's attorney knew what was coming - I could tell from the look on his face. My husband, of course, did not. He was always able to forget ugly things. He spent the time during the heated sidebar with the judge throwing flirtatious looks at the female jurors.

The judge quietly addressed the jury. "In view of the defendant's own choice to introduce an undated letter to the jury, I have ruled a second undated letter will be admissible." He nodded at Fred Goldman's lawyer who walked over to the podium and began to read another of my pathetic letters. It was painful and embarrassing to listen to that one as well, but I understood, even if my husband did not, what the lawyer was going for.

He read it in a hushed voice. I could tell he was trying to be as respectful of violating my deepest privacy as he could manage.

> *I think I have to put this all in a letter. A lot of years ago I used to do much better in a letter, I'm gonna try it again now. I'd like you to keep this letter if we split, so that you'll always know why we split. I'd also like you to keep it if we stay together, as a reminder.*
>
> *Right now I'm so angry! If I didn't know that the courts would take Sydney & Justin away from me if I did this, I would do every guy, including some that you know, just to let you know how it feels. I wish someone could explain all this to me. I see our marriage as a huge mistake, and you don't.*
>
> *I knew what went on in our relationship before we got married. I knew after six years that all the things I thought were going on were! All the things I gave into - all the "I'm sorry for thinking that", "I'm sorry for not believing you", "I'm sorry for not trusting you".*
>
> *I made up with you all the time & even took the blame many times for your cheating. I know this took place because we fought about it a lot & even discussed it before we got married with my family & a minister.*
>
> *OK, before the marriage I lived with it & dealt with it, mainly because you finally said we weren't married at the time. I assumed your recurring and nasty attitude & mean streak were to*

cover up your cheating & general disrespect for women & a lack of manners!

I remember a long time ago a girlfriend of yours wrote you a letter, she said well you aren't married yet so let's get together. Even she had the same idea of marriage as me. She believed that when you marry you wouldn't be going out anymore. Adultery is a very important thing to many people.

It's one of the first ten things I learned at Sunday school. You said it when you told me some things you learn at school stick and the Ten Commandments did! I wanted to be a wonderful wife!

I believed you that it would finally be "you and me against the world." That people would be envious or in awe of us because we stuck through it & finally became one, a real couple, I let my guard down. I thought it was finally gonna be you & me - you wanted a baby or so you said & I wanted a baby. Then with each pound you were terrible. You gave me dirty looks and looks of disgust & said mean things to me at times about my appearance, walked out on me & lied to me. I remember one day my mom said, "He actually thinks you can have a baby & not get fat."

I gained ten to fifteen pounds more than I should have with Sydney. Well that's by the book. Most women gain twice that. It's not like it was that much but you made me feel so ugly! I've battled ten pounds up and down the scale since I was fifteen. It was no more extra weight than was normal for me to be up. I believe my mom. You thought if a baby weighs seven pounds, the woman should gain seven pounds. I'd like to finally tell you that that's not the way it is. And if you had read those books I got you on pregnancy you may have known that. Talk about feeling alone.

In between Sydney & Justin you say my clothes bothered you, that my shoes were on the floor, that I bugged you. Wow, that's so terrible! Try I had low self esteem because since we got married I felt like the paragraph above. There was also that time before Justin & after a few months of Sydney, I felt really good about how I got back into shape and we made out. You beat the holy hell out of me & we lied at the x-ray lab & said I fell off a bike ... Remember!?? Great for my self-esteem.

There are a number of other instances that I could talk about that made marriage so wonderful ... like the televised Clippers game & you beating me and locking me in the wine cellar before the game, & your fortieth birthday party & the week leading up to it. But I don't like talking about the past, it depresses me.

Then came the pregnancy with Justin & oh how wonderful you treated me again. I remember swearing to God & myself that under no circumstances would I let you be in that delivery room. I hated you so much.

And since Justin's birth and the mad New Year's Eve beat up, I just don't see how our stories compare. I was so bad because I wore sweats & left shoes lying around & didn't keep a perfect house or comb my hair the way you liked it. Or because I didn't have dinner ready at the precise moment you walked through the door or that I just plain got on your nerves sometimes. I just don't see how that compares to infidelity, wife beating and verbal abuse. I just don't think everybody goes through this.

And if I had wanted to hurt you or had it in me to be anything like the person you are, I would have done it after the New Year's Eve incident. But I didn't do it even then. I called the cops that night to save my life whether you believe it or not. But I didn't pursue anything after that. I didn't prosecute. I didn't call the press & I didn't make a big charade out of it. I waited for it to die down and I asked for it to. But I've never loved you since or been the same.

It made me take a look at my life with you, my wonderful life with the superstar, that wonderful man the football hero, everybody's favorite guy ... the father of my kids, that husband of the terribly insecure blond girl, the girl with no self esteem or sense of worth. She must be all those things if she is with a guy like that.

It certainly doesn't take a strong person to be with a guy like that and certainly no-one would be envious of that life. I agree after we married things changed. We couldn't have the housefuls of people like I used to have over & barbecue for because I had other responsibilities. I didn't want to go to a lot of events & I'd back down at the last minute on functions & trips I admit & I'm sorry.

I just believe that a relationship is based on trust and the last time I trusted you was at our wedding ceremony. It's just so hard for me to trust you again. Even though you say you are a different guy, that guy I married brought me a lot of pain & heartache. I tried so hard with him. I wanted so to be a good wife but he never gave me a chance.

When the attorney finished reading, the only dry eye in the courtroom was my husband's. He was even smiling a little.

Mr. Goldman's attorney walked to the stand and showed him the letter. "Will you agree, sir, that this is a letter written by your late wife, Nicole Brown Simpson?"

My husband shrugged and raised his eyebrows, and he looked at the jury when he said, "If you say so, sir."

The attorney bristled and said, "Are you implying, sir, that this letter is authored by anyone other than your deceased wife?"

My husband yawned and said, "I don't know ... that's what you say, so it must be true, though Detective Fuhrman is a good looking guy and all that stuff in there about weight gain, who knows, maybe he wrote it."

The attorney was starting to lose it. "Are you saying to this court, sir, that we have falsified evidence, and further are you implying that former L.A.P.D. Detective Mark Fuhrman was involved in this elaborate plot of yours?"

My husband sighed as though it was so boring for him to be there and raised up his hands. I knew what he was going to say ... 'If the glove fits', etc. He loved that line. His attorney knew he was going to say it too and shouted objection, but it didn't matter. It was all over anyway.

Lucky for me, the jury did know exactly what he was saying and awarded a thirty-three million dollar settlement to the victims' families. It was lucky for my husband, too, because when he was on the stand desecrating Ron and my memories, I looked at Ron's dad and I know for sure that if the second jury had said not guilty like the first one did, he would have killed my husband himself.

I thought it would feel so wonderful to hear him finally blamed in public for our deaths but it didn't feel wonderful, and it didn't change anything except to make things worse.

In the year between the first trial and the second, he had left my kids alone. The civil trial ended that. The kids were living with my parents and he hadn't tried once to change that. He had his new girlfriend and his new loser friends, and two sad little kids didn't fit in. But that night, back at Rockingham, he was in a rage. Nothing new to me but I could tell that his new girlfriend was a tad nervous. That much I liked seeing, but then he said, "Those motherfucking Browns, those assholes, getting cozy with that Kike motherfucker Goldman, going after my fucking money. They didn't give a fuck about Nicole when she was alive and they don't give a fuck now, but since I ain't been keeping up their handouts, they jumped in on Goldman's little dog and pony show. Well, I ain't playin'. I'm taking my fucking kids back from them right the fuck now."

I was more frightened right then than I have ever been before, and it created energy in that room - all his rage mixed with the threats against my kids and the bad memories in there, the goddamned horrible injustice of me being dead and my kids being left to this monster who had killed me and ignored them during the worst year of their lives. And he was now standing there, threatening them to get even with my family over money?

I exploded, and in the next few minutes I tore the living room apart like the best special effects big budget horror flick ghost you have ever seen. I ripped down the curtains and blew all their lines of coke to the ground. I made the wine bottles fly and smash against the TV sets and, for my grand finale, threw a glass full of Scotch in his face, which splattered onto her. And when it was over, he started to laugh. He put his arm around his shaken slut, and sat there and laughed - at me.

"Well, lookee there. I knew that sad bitch was still around. I've been telling you there was some weird shit going on around her. Fuck, don't be scared of her, baby, she's dead. This is the biggest show I've seen all year. She can't do shit except mess up my house, and that's not much different than how she was when she was alive."

In a shaking voice Christy asked him, "Well, honey, why would she still be here? I mean, why is she here and so mad at you?"

My husband stood her up and began walking her towards the stairs. "Oh, who knows about shit like that? She's probably just jealous of you, is why she's mad. And the being a ghost shit, well, Nicole was no fucking angel. I guess heaven didn't want her ..." he laughed, "... and I don't either. Come on, baby, let's go upstairs and get freaky. Forget about her."

Christy started to pull away from him and I wondered if she was finally growing a brain, but no. "No, I don't want to stay here in this house with you tonight. I am totally freaked out. That's just gross, thinking about your old dead wife wandering around here looking at us, doing stuff to us. She scares me." She finished speaking on a high whine and headed towards the front door.

Frantic to not be alone, he raced after her with me on their heels. "No, come on, baby, don't go, please. Nothing else is going to happen tonight. She's shot her wad."

I wondered how he knew that. It was true, but how did he know? As far as I had known, my husband had never studied ghosts.

She was shaking her head 'No', and she yanked her arm away from him and walked outside.

I could recognize so well in his eyes the rage, and knew that he was thinking hard about running after her and forcing her to stay, but he didn't know this girl well enough yet to see what she might take from him and what she might sell to the newspapers. He let her go and closed the doors, slumping against them and looking around as though trying to figure out where I was.

I don't think even a psychic would have been able to spot me. I had indeed shot my wad and I was drifting limply near the bottom of the stairs. He looked toward the living room and spoke. "Nicole, if you're still here, do something to prove it."

I couldn't have made a feather move by then, I was so weak. After a minute he shook his head in disgust and walked up the stairs, right through me. After a while I managed to make it to the bedroom, and when I got there, I was surprised to see him slumped on the side of the bed holding a picture of me in my wedding dress in his hands.

I wafted over and sat down beside him. He was speaking in such a low voice I could barely hear him. His thumb stroked my paper image and he said, "Look at you, sweets. You were so beautiful, the most beautiful girl in the world. I always thought that. I loved you, Nic. Every fucking day I loved you, baby. I don't think there's a guy on earth who loved his woman half as much as I loved you. I didn't do it to you alone, baby. You knew, you fucking knew what might happen."

He started to cry and I wanted to give him a sign of my presence but I was too weak.

He went on speaking to my picture. "I did love you, baby, and I am sorry, Nic, so fucking sorry, but you're dead now, girl, and I'm not. It doesn't work anymore, Nic, this house, this town, us. I gotta take care of myself now, sweets, and you gotta let go."

I was too sad and tired to understand what he meant, though within days I got it. A month after the civil trial, my husband declared bankruptcy. He asked for, and was awarded, custody of our kids, and in addition kept his huge pension and his horrible new girlfriend.

He left behind Rockingham and Los Angeles, and the shattered dreams of being the white hero. He moved to Florida, and when I tried to follow, telling myself that it was only for my kids that I needed to stay near them, to protect them from him, I found out that it was true, that old story I had been told by the ghosts in the mortuary - we cannot cross water. I don't know if, or how, my husband knew that, but I do know that he had meant what he said to me that sad night in his bedroom, that after all our fights and reconciliations, after killing me rather than letting me go, this time it was him leaving me.

Chapter 16

Surprisingly, there is not that much to say about the next ten years of my afterlife. I stayed on in emptied out Rockingham and gradually I became less and less of a presence. With nothing to fight for, and no one to love - or hate - I think I might have just disappeared altogether. I know I was very nearly gone when the first bulldozers came.

I guess the house had been sold to people who did not want to live in a house known around the world for being our home. There's celebrity and then there is just notoriety, and Rockingham attracted the wrong kind of attention, so they decided to raze it to the ground. A few months more and I don't think there would have been enough left of whatever I still was for me to notice.

Take note, ghost hunters. If you are looking for us, you had better do it where there are still people, because without the energy people give off, and without anyone around to make us notice the world is still there, we disappear. I'm not talking about going into the light; I'm talking about those of us who stay here. After a while we become less a thinking, feeling, wanting thing, and more of a memory. This is a sad state of affairs, even for a ghost, and our state is pretty sad to begin with.

I was saved, if that's the right way to think of it, by the walls of the house coming down suddenly around me. Without warning, I was in sunlight and drifting over the rubble that had been my home for so long.

It made me aware again, aware and scared. I didn't want to spend eternity alone in some stranger's back yard, and so I began drifting down familiar streets to the last place I had lived. It was unbelievable, once I started moving towards Bundy, how strong the pull was.

That was when I found out some of my own ghost lore. The place our blood is spilled has a really strong pull for us. I guess that would mean that it's a pretty strong bet that most murder houses have one of my kind in them.

When I got back to Bundy, I felt a kind of happiness for the first time in who knows how long. It looked just the same as when I had lived there, and when I drifted through the open front gate and saw a man sitting outside in my old courtyard with three beautiful husky dogs, I knew I had made the right decision.

It took a while for the dogs to become used to me. They saw me right away that first day and nearly went crazy. Their poor owner, whom I later found out was a sweet man named Steve, had wasted his time looking everywhere for what he was sure must be a hidden cat to make his normally mellow dogs act so crazy.

I had always loved dogs, and while it might not have made them happy to see me, I was thrilled to be seen. Being noticed by the dogs, and eventually accepted, made me feel real again.

Steve was a harder deal to figure out than the dogs. He sure never acted like he could sense me, and he seemed like one of those practical people who was never going to believe in anything he couldn't see and touch, yet it wasn't like he didn't know who I was or whose house he was living in. He had even named one of the huskies after me. It was nice hearing somebody say my name again, even if it was just a guy calling his dog.

I never haunted Steve; I just stayed there at Bundy with him, hanging out, watching his life, not bothering anybody, and sometimes I was really present and other times I kind of drifted, like I had back at Rockingham.

I didn't know, or care, how much time had passed until one night, when I was in the living room with Steve who was watching TV, I noticed he was really into the program and I didn't mean to scare him, but I was just curious, so I hit the volume on the remote and the sound boomed out into the room.

Steve jumped about a foot and the dogs started barking, and he reached for the remote and sat back with this funny look on his face, and said, 'Okay', in this nervous way. Maybe he knew for sure then something he had suspected in the back of his brain for years, or maybe he just thought his remote was shorting out and he didn't want to get a bad shock.

Either way, that was how Steve and I ended up watching the story of my husband's dramatic return to the same side of the country I was on, and how I found out that he had messed up in a big way, and how I decided I wanted in on it.

I repeat that I never haunted Steve, but I did begin to influence him. I found out that we ghosts can creep into the consciousness of the living, not just in their dreams but while they are awake, but only if they are thinking about us. And after the news show about my husband's arrest in Las Vegas, Steve was thinking about me a lot.

He even began speaking out loud when he was alone. Maybe he told himself he was only talking to himself, but I knew better and I think he did too. He started mentioning something that had happened the year before, a book my husband had written with a ghostwriter, which was not me; though I think, all things considered, I would have been the best choice.

After I heard about that book, I had to have it, but we ghosts don't have credit cards and I wasn't a thief, so I just laid hard on Steve's consciousness until he went out and bought the book. I could tell by his expression when he came home with it that he was puzzled and embarrassed to have purchased something like that.

I could tell that he was also beginning to understand why he had bought it, because that night, before he went up to bed, he lit some white candles and put the book down between them on the coffee table, leaving it opened to the chapter on my murder. The book was called 'If I Did It', and it was about my husband and me, and I don't know if people thought it was fiction or the truth - it was a little bit of both.

When I was done reading, I sat there not really thinking or feeling much of anything, but as I stared at the candlelight, I remembered and it was as though I was there again.

The night I was murdered was June 12th, 1994. I was thirty-five, Sydney was nine and Justin was only five. We had had a good day, one of the few in that last season of fear.

I call it that because during the first part of my last year I had spent all my energy trying to reclaim my life with my husband, and except for a few slips on my part, I had spent the last part of it trying to break with him for good. I did still love him but I had finally realized that I feared and hated him even more than I needed him. Sometimes I thought I would be able to get away and other times I thought he might kill me first.

And in those emotion-charged last months, my feelings shifted like sand. On the one hand, he had let me go once. He hadn't wanted us to separate or divorce, but he did let me go. I know a lot of it was the leverage I had from the big New Year's Eve beat down two years before, but it worked for me. Weirdly, our divorce was pretty friendly once he realized I was serious.

Before that, he had stalked me and spied on me and tried every trick in the book to get me back, but once the divorce was finalized he completely let go of me, and instead of flying, I went into free fall.

I had been a kid when we got together and he had been an older, powerful guy who molded me into what his version of the perfect woman was; which unfortunately for both of us was somebody who remained a girl. So when I left him, I was thirty-three, but only in years. Inside, where it counts, I was still eighteen and I acted like it.

I got involved with a lot of guys all younger than me. I hit the club scene hard and made a new group of friends who were all women like me, pretending that they were still twenty. I'm not gonna lie and say it wasn't fun at first, it was, it was fun right up until the time that it wasn't.

And then I started missing him bad, or maybe I just missed us, the way we had been, because when there weren't fights and bad beat downs, there had been a million good days with the kids and our friends and Christmas.

It was my first Christmas alone that made me sort of start rewriting our history together. Suddenly all I could remember was how beautiful and happy and secure it had all been with us. I missed my house too. I missed being part of a big circle of friends. I missed him, and so I put out feelers and I got the shock of my life. He was fine. As a matter of fact, his life was pretty much still our old life, except that instead of a beautiful but miserable wife and two little kids he had to take care of, he had a beautiful happy girlfriend, and other than the switch up in partners, everything was going on like the old days.

I stopped feeling like an escapee and started feeling lonely and shut out. I got jealous and insecure and I started calling him, and he wouldn't take my calls, and I'll admit it, at that point I would have done anything to be number one to him again and to get to go home.

There's no point trying to explain this to anyone. If you have never walked out on someone and then found out that they were doing better without you than with you, if you have never had second thoughts, then good for you. It wasn't that way for me, that's all.

I guess I went a little crazy and started kind of stalking him for a change. I called all the time and tried to drop by when he had the kids, and finally I got really stupid and sent him a package that had a copy of our wedding video and some home movies in it, and that first letter. An hour after I dropped it off, when I still hadn't heard from him, I went over there in person and I talked to him through the gates, and finally he agreed to take a walk with me.

The stuff we talked about isn't important, except that he said something to me that I wish I had listened to more. The thing is I wasn't really hearing anything he was trying to get across. I was just pushing hard for what I wanted, but I do remember this. He asked me, in a kind of desperate way, why I had to do this now when he was finally happy, when he had put us behind him. Maybe it's not what he said but the way he said it. There was this look of semi-desperate old love in his eyes and a little bit of triumph too. I understood, because it has to feel good to have the ex that ran away come running back, but his eyes also had real fear in them, fear that if he did this, gave into me, let me back in and opened his life and heart up again, he would be making himself vulnerable in a huge way.

I knew him so well and I saw it, but I pushed past any fears I had too, because I was totally single-minded that day. The phrase, 'I want to go home', was beating in my ears and it was all I could hear.

I knew that if we started over, this time we'd get everything right. I was so stupid. You can love someone more than anything else in the world, and you can want every bad thing that either of you has ever done to each other to just, poof, go away, but at the end of the day you're still the same messed-up two people who split up in the first place, and the destination that you are running toward is still the same place you ran from.

My husband was a very proud man and I should have known that you can leave a man like him once but not twice.

So, of course, our reconciliation was a fucked-up make-up-and-break-up mess, and after a few months I was done, no big reveal or anything, I was just done, and this time I knew I wouldn't want to ever try again. He's no dummy, my husband. If I knew him well, he knew me just as well, and when I told him in May of my last year that it was over, he believed me.

I get now, obviously, that I was on borrowed time from that day forward, as the saying goes, but no, back then, I did not understand that I was a walking corpse. I should have. The stalking and the endless phone calls started up again. Wherever I was, when I'd look up, there he would be, and in his eyes I saw all his broken love, and maybe worse, I saw his broken pride.

You don't embarrass a proud man like my husband twice and live to tell your story. The night he killed me, though, I wasn't feeling his pain or trying for the ten millionth time to soothe his huge ego - I was trying to move on with my life.

It was my little girls' first dance recital, and sure I noticed him sulking at the show, but like I said, I was done and that night all I felt was disgusted that he was using what should have been our daughters' night to make it about him, just like always.

I purposely excluded him from the family dinner afterwards and I did it in front of people - only my family - but I should have been thinking of his dangerous pride and his volatile temper. The stupid thing is I had spent seventeen years thinking about both those things almost obsessively every day to keep things smooth. I forgot once, one lousy fucking night, and I ended up dead.

Chapter 17

We had a nice time that night at dinner - no big deal, just me and my kids and my family. It was peaceful because nobody mentioned my husband for a change. The kids and I took off a little after nine and stopped in at Ben and Jerry's on the way home. They were so beat by then, though, that they didn't even finish their ice creams. I had to undress Justin because he was falling asleep on his little feet. I rushed through getting them down for the night because I was looking forward to some me time.

If only I'd known but I'm not gonna go there.

A few minutes later, my mom called and asked me if I would mind calling the restaurant where we'd eaten and ask them if they'd seen her sunglasses. She was really into her labels; it was kind of cute. I didn't ask her why she didn't call herself, I just did what she asked, and the hostess put me on hold while one of the waiters went and looked. It was the waiter, a super cute guy whom I knew from the gym, Ron, who came back to the phone and told me he had them, and that if I wanted him to, he would drop them off after work.

I know that everyone is going to wonder how he knew where I lived, so I'll say it: I liked hanging out with cute young guys, and I had had Ron and some of his buddies over a couple of times. Big deal!

After I hung up the phone, I went upstairs and started pulling my big 'relax Nicole' scene together. This was a little ritual I went through to unwind and not some big stupid seduction scene dealio, like my husband's creepy lawyers made it sound in that first trial.

I liked baths and candles and music - a lot of women do. I wasn't gonna yank Ron through the door and jump his bones. I was tired, and at most I would have asked him if he wanted to come in for a glass of wine as a way of saying thank you. But it's true that I had also used candles and music in the past when I wanted to get ready for romance, and my husband knew that, so I think when he came in the back gate and saw candle light flickering through the windows, it sent his already crazy head straight off.

I don't know. I only know for sure what happened to me. I was hanging out downstairs because I knew Ron would be bringing mom's glasses back any minute. I had already gone outside and unlatched the front gate for him, and a few minutes later I heard shouting.

What I think happened is that my husband came through the back gate planning to surprise me and either beat my ass or try to talk some sense into me, and when he saw Ron coming through the front gate, he added up one and one and saw me being with another guy.

That's what I think, but maybe I'm wrong, because when I heard the shouting, I ran right outside to tell him to get the hell out of there, and when I saw him, he was wearing a cap and gloves, so maybe he had come over to kill me that night. I hate thinking that way. It's easier to believe that he just snapped suddenly, but those clothes ... and, of course, as I was to find out seconds later, he had brought a knife with him, so it looks planned, I don't know.

When I got outside, I saw that my husband had poor Ron cornered in my courtyard and was blocking him from getting out the gate. It's a really small area. I ran over and grabbed my husband's arm, and he punched me in the shoulder and down I went, smashing the side of my head into the bottom step. I know in the couple minutes I was out that Ron must have tried to defend me and that my husband basically slaughtered him, and that still hurts me more to think about than even my own death.

I came to and saw the back of my husband. He was bent over Ron who was already down. I had a hard time standing up because I was so dizzy, but I made it on pure adrenaline and I ran for the open front gate. He caught me by my hair and jerked me back against his chest. He reeked of Ron's blood. I got my hands up in between his arms and my neck, and clawed at his hands, screaming. His glove fell off and he shoved his hand into my mouth to shut me up. I bit down hard and his last words to me were, "You fucking bitch, shut the fuck up."

Then he yanked back my head and slit my throat so hard, and with so much force, I was dying before he dropped me. Already rising up out of my body, I looked back down to see him kneel down beside me and shove down the top of my dress to try to saw off my breasts. He must have heard a noise from the street, because he stood up suddenly and looked around with this crazy expression. The last thing he did, before turning and running out the back gate, was to lean down over my body and wipe his knife off against my dress.

I guess that's all there is to tell about the night I died. When I was done reading his lying book and remembering bad things, I remained where I was in

Steve's living room and waited for the morning light.

I blew out the candles Steve had left me, not to scare him, just because I didn't want him or the dogs to have a fire. When he came down that morning, I stayed very close to him and made sure he understood what I wanted. It was time for me to leave Bundy again, time for me to try for justice. Reliving my death had made that much clear to me.

Two days later, after Steve had made a lot of phone calls asking the other vets for coverage and putting his dogs in a kennel, he loaded up his car and stood by the passenger door for a minute with a funny look on his face. Kind of laughing at himself, he opened the door of his Jeep and said out loud, "After you, Madam."

Steve was a nice man.

He drove us to Las Vegas in silence, and when we pulled into town, he started talking to himself again so I could hear him.

He said, "I think I'll drive by the courthouse, maybe take a look at it. Then I'm gonna go check into the Bellagio. Nice place. That hotel has a garden right inside. Hell, that's the kind of place I might stay forever if I could afford it. God knows, there's worse places."

I knew what he was doing and I was so grateful. I wanted to show him but I didn't, because it seems no matter what we ghosts are trying to say, people end up taking it the wrong way and get scared instead.

Steve drove right up to the front of the Las Vegas courthouse. It was getting dark and he reached through me and opened the passenger door. He stared right at me when he said, "This is it, Nicole. In the morning all the jurors and lawyers, and your husband too, will show up here en masse. I hope this is what you wanted. Most of all, I hope it gives you whatever it is you need. I'm guessing I won't be seeing - or not seeing you - again, so in whatever way there is for you to take care of yourself, I hope to God you do. You're a nice lady, Nicole Brown Simpson. You hold onto that wherever you are going, okay?"

I was crying, but of course he couldn't see that, or me, as he drove off. It's funny, but the best friend I ever had only came to me after I was dead. I wonder what that says about my life.

Chapter 18

I pretty much got the shock of my afterlife when I saw my husband again for the first time in more than ten years. Here in the land of the dead, we don't age. In fact, sometimes it's the reverse. While I've been in Las Vegas which, like I said, is a town loaded with dead people, some of them I've met have told me that when they died they were really old, but that is not how they looked as ghosts.

Of course there are exceptions to every rule. Some of them look exactly like they must have done when they crossed over, and I think that is where the people who can see us get their ideas for horror movies. For example, sure I'm dead, but you couldn't get me into Bally's Casino - formerly the M.G.M. - again, no matter what. Fire is a bad way to go and that is all I'm going to say about that.

Anyway, my husband looked like he'd aged about thirty years in ten. He was really overweight and his hair had receded, but the worst were his sagging face and his eyes.

He used to have the most amazing eyes, huge brown eyes that showed his every feeling in them. Now they were dulled and yellowed from what I am guessing was a combination of time, drug use and depression. His eyes were the only golden thing left about him and not in a good way either.

I might have even started to feel sorry for him, because I am a huge patsy that way, except I saw he had brought that horrible trashy slut with him. I could not believe he was still with her, though it did help to explain his pathetic appearance.

It scared me thinking about what the last ten years had been like for my kids growing up with this pair. I decided I had to go through with my plan, if for no other reason than to get my kids away from them.

I moved into the jury box and spent time with each juror, and my nearness created for them a sort of thought vortex where they began to look at my husband and dwell on me. The more they thought about me, the more I used it. I followed each and every one of them into sleep at one time or another during that trial, and though I knew they were good people and it was unfair to them to have the dreams I was giving them, I felt I had to do it.

The actual case which was before the jurors would have made a pretty funny film if it had been any other defendant. Apparently my husband was so far gone into drugs and the low life that he had lost any perspective on not only what was right and wrong but on how people saw things. To the best of my understanding, he was pretty much broke, except for his pension, and he had, to all intents and purposes, been hiding out in Florida to cheat Fred Goldman of the civil judgment.

But with the help of his slimy sports agent, Mike, he had over the years occasionally snuck into Vegas, and in private rooms signed sports memorabilia for the kind of weirdos who wanted to collect signatures from him.

It looked like sleazy Mike had been keeping a few items off to the side for a rainy day. The most bizarre of these was my husband's so-called lucky suit. That was the suit he was wearing on October 3rd, 1995, the day he was acquitted of killing me and Ron.

It turns out that my husband had either given the suit to Mike, or Mike had stolen it, and who cares anyway because it's disgusting, but it seems that my husband, down on his luck and maybe getting hard up to pay for his sleazy young girlfriend's who knows how many thousands of dollars a week coke habit, had decided he wanted all the stuff Mike, and Mike's associates, had kept back.

He flew into Vegas with three loser friends of his and burst into some poor sports collector's hotel room. They had guns, and even looking at this crew with or without guns would have given anyone a heart attack, which is exactly what happened to the victim.

The trial had its up and downs, but since this time, unlike when he killed me and Ron, my husband hadn't acted alone, he was vulnerable to how his co-defendants would stand up under pressure. No-one, except him, was shocked when one by one they all caved and cut deals, which maybe he could have seen coming because that old saying, 'There is no honor amongst thieves', is a pretty truthful one. Well there is no honor amongst killers either.

During the trial he got out on bail, and he took off like a bat out of hell back to Florida. While he was there, he tried to lean on one of his co-defendants who recorded the event, and the judge put a warrant out for my husband, forcing him to return to Vegas.

He was only there one night before posting bail and flying back again to Miami. I didn't have time to keep up with him. It was just me and the jurors, and

I needed to stay close.

By the end of the trial, they were drained from memories and dreams that were not their own, and on October 3rd, 2008, thirteen years to the day after he was acquitted of the murders of Nicole Brown and Ron Goldman, my husband was found guilty of criminal conspiracy, assault, kidnapping, robbery and using a deadly weapon.

I found that I could live with that, so to speak. After all, two of those charges would have applied to Ron and me as well. So I had it - a long-delayed, battered, twisted version of justice, and yes, it felt right.

I didn't have any sense of triumph when I drifted out of the courtroom that day. I was still pretty damn dead, as was Ron. And there were still devastated, wrecked families, and two kids who now had a new horror to deal with in a life I'm pretty sure was already filled with horror, but I did feel a sense of rightness about his sentence and I'm not gonna lie about that.

I drifted around outside the courthouse for a few days after the sentence, just hanging out outside in the sun, wishing I could feel it and wondering what I should do next. I decided to go and see him in prison. It would be the first time I had a chance to see him in years.

I wasn't looking for closure, or a chance to gloat or anything like that, I just wanted to get close enough to him to know what he felt now. I had gotten pretty good at hitching rides by then, so I caught one to the prison on another convicted felon's drive out with two deputies. Surprisingly or not, all they were talking about was my husband's recent sentence. One of the deputies said that the prison officials had kept him on suicide watch for an entire week, and that now he was in the medical wing because every con in the place wanted a shot at the very infamous former superstar.

Being a ghost has very few advantages over being alive, and I don't know that I would call being able to pass through prison security without being strip-searched an advantage exactly, but at least this was one experience of living I was glad to miss out on. I found his cell without too much trouble and drifted inside and sat down beside him on the bunk. I wasn't looking for intimacy; it's just the only other place available to perch was the toilet.

He looked horrible, sick, ashy and beaten - finally and totally beaten. All of a sudden I needed him to know that I was there, that I was seeing him like this. I had gotten a lot better at the whole ghost thing since the old days at

Rockingham, so it was nothing for me to make some of the stacks of legal papers he had in there fly up in a miniature hurricane. He didn't scream or jump up or anything, he just nodded and looked over beside him, as if he knew exactly where I was sitting.

"So you're still around, huh, sweets? This must be a good day for you, then." If he was waiting for an answer, he figured out pretty quickly he was out of luck, so he started talking again. He gestured around the cell. "Is this what you needed, Nic, you needed to see me in a stinking goddamned cage for some bullshit charge? Is this your idea of justice?"

Since it pretty much was, I made the toilet flush as an affirmation. He leaned back on his bunk and stared up at the ceiling. Tears began leaking out of his eyes. "Okay, then, girl. Here I am. You know I'll get out of here, though, you know I will."

I didn't know any such thing, and watching him, I could see he didn't really know it either.

After a while he said in a weaker voice, "So, I guess when I die, you'll be standing right there, waiting. We don't go anywhere after all, huh? This is it. You just spend fucking eternity wandering around looking, watching other people, fucking with them if you can? So when my day comes, you'll be there, and it'll be just like the old days, huh, Nick, you and me back together again after everything?" He sat up on the bed and smiled. "Well, you know what, girl, I'm okay with that. That's not nearly as bad as where I've thought I might end up, ya know? I gotta know, though, is that little shit Ron still with you, too? Are you guys tag-teaming me?"

When he asked me that, his fists clenched, I realized that he was still jealous of me. All of this, the time, the downfall of his life, the prison sentence, and he hadn't moved on one step, and neither had I.

The shock of understanding that moved me with sudden force out of his cell and out of the prison, and as I drifted back along that long black highway towards the nighttime lights of the neon city, I realized that the last thing, the very last thing in the world, I wanted was to be reunited yet again with my husband.

I've been in Vegas now for a while. The casinos have a lot of energy in them and I found other ghosts to talk with, some better than the others.

Yesterday, though, I finally landed here at the Bellagio. Steve was right. There is a beautiful white garden right inside the hotel. Above the garden is a glass roof that lets in a bright, diffused sunlight.

It's funny, but looking up now, it seems brighter than any sunlight I can ever remember seeing before, and I think maybe if I just reached up my arms a little bit, I might be met halfway by the light coming through and that this time, for the first time since I died, I would be able to feel the light's warmth against my skin.

The Third Death

Sunny

The Ghost of Clarendon Court

Chapter 19

I can say with some certainty that I did not see this coming. In the blissful year since I was finally released by death from my body coffin and have been able to roam freely once again, I have assured myself that I did not know my husband spent the last waking year of my life trying to murder me.

Sadly, during the preceding twenty-eight years, while I was trapped in my hospital bed, I may have viewed the situation quite differently, having been influenced by the ceaseless speculative chatter of my nurses. I might have hoped that if I were to be put into a permanent - and I do hate this phrase - vegetative state and consigned to bed for nearly three decades, I might at least have been accorded the luxury of being left alone in that twilight world to think and reason out how I came to be in such desperate straits.

I can say without a doubt that was not my situation. Owing to the endless resources my money provided, I was never left alone. Not for one minute, not for one second, in twenty-eight years was I left in peace. The irony of that is almost incalculable. I know that over time my husband, whom I hear lives a joyous existence in London, must have laughed heartily at my lack of privacy, since he knew that privacy was one of the many luxuries I afforded myself while I was a conscious member of the living race.

I shouldn't begrudge him his little inside joke. After all, he hadn't planned for me to spend twenty-eight years in a hospital bed, being turned like a baking potato every few hours to avoid the onset of bed sores. No, he had planned for me to die, and I am certain that by this time he has managed to blame my failure to do so upon me. He always blamed his failures upon me.

I doubt he wishes any less fervently than I that he hadn't botched it so badly. His terrible incompetence in killing me, not once but twice, led him to lose my money and led me to ... how can I begin to describe where it led me to?

Try to imagine, if you will, the worst and most frightening nightmare you have ever had, and imagine as well yourself at your most sick and helpless. Imagine the deepest moments of loneliness and regret and frustration you have experienced. Imagine all of that and you will still not begin to touch where I have been.

Maybe it would be better if I asked you to wake from a nightmare to find you have been buried alive in a tight, dark coffin. But in this coffin the air never completely runs out and you cannot even raise your hands to claw against the top in the hope that you can free yourself. Over your head you can hear the endless noises of people nearby, talking, talking talking. You are right there, inches beneath their feet, but you have no way of making yourself heard or noticed.

Slowly and inexorably, over hours and days that turn into months and years, you begin to realize that there will be no release from your prison. You scream but no one hears you. You pray and beg and debase yourself with promises to your creator, at first asking to be let out - 'Let me out, let me out, please. I will do anything, be anything you want' - later begging for death with every detested continuing beating of your heart, knowing it is the only escape you can hope for, but death is as elusive as the light and freedom of the earth just inches above your tomb.

Imagine all of this and you will begin to understand the very special living hell my husband gave me. I hope it is unnecessary for me to tell you to imagine my feelings towards the man who put me there.

Over time, and God knows I have had time, I began to speculate, even fantasize over, all the effective methods of killing someone that he hadn't chosen: the gun, the knife, a tiny push from a high place, the use of poison, methods that would actually have killed me, not send me to the one place he consigned me to. Is cyanide, for example, so much more difficult to obtain than insulin? And he certainly did not have the excuse of ignorance, as he had attempted this before and I had awakened.

He knew that insulin injected into a perfectly healthy body might not cause the death he felt he so badly needed, and that I would come to need as well. Many years before I was put into this state, another couple nearly as wealthy – oh, I hate that nonsense - nearly as ludicrously rich as we were, had run into marital difficulties and the wife had simply picked up a loaded shotgun and emptied it into her husband's face. She claimed that she had thought he was an intruder. No charges were brought and she went on to live out a rather grand life on his money.

In that case, as in my marriage, the killer was the arriviste, the one who married into our world. And those who are not born to stultifying privilege are rather more possessive of it than those of us who know nothing else. It is dangerous to try to remove hands that are grasping tightly to a treasure; you can get cut up pretty badly in the struggle.

My husband, of course, had assumed so many airs and graces by the time he first attempted to murder me that he must have immediately discounted such violent, if efficacious, methods when he decided to do away with me.

No doubt he will have decided that the inescapable mess left behind by such straightforward violence was beneath him. Also, as a former man of business, he must have calculated out the odds of failing the job a second time and convinced himself that he would, and could, murder me effectively. He must have reminded himself of the errors and variables that had let me pull through the first time around. He will have shored up his self-confidence until he believed he could succeed if only he used certain precautions that he had failed to think of in his first attempt.

And I'm sure that he felt a 'painless' slide into unconsciousness and death was the sort of well-bred demise I would have preferred if I could only have been consulted, which naturally I wasn't.

I imagine he was as surprised by himself as I was that night when I managed to anger him enough that he struck me. It is a well known fact that murdering someone takes nerves of steel, and his were a bit on the shaky side. I suppose the saying, 'There is no perfect murder', exists for a reason. I do think, though, that his assault on me was particularly cruel and inept, but then I imagine anyone in my position would feel this way.

Maybe he even justified killing me by telling himself that Sunny was such a miserable creature that she wouldn't much mind being dead.

In reality, I minded terribly. I happened to love my life a great deal. I adored my children and my mother and my dogs. I quite liked living in the gracious and beautiful homes I had created. If my idea of a happy life was so very different than his, did it mean I no longer deserved to live at all?

The answer, I know, is somewhat redundant, since he obviously did indeed come to that conclusion. I will grant that in the year between his first attempt and his second, I was not as happy as I had been previously.

Having gone to sleep one night at home in my bed at Clarendon Court, and awoken three days later in a hospital room in New York with no memory of any of it happening, disturbed my equilibrium and my certainty of the world around me. It did not, however, lead me to understand that my husband had attempted to kill me. I learned later, far too late for it to be of any use to me whatsoever, that many around me were suspicious, but they did not share their suspicions with me and that is why I can say with full truth that I did not see it coming.

For years and years, endless years, as I lay in my coma coffin, I listened, having no other choice, to my family members and attorneys and doctors discussing my condition. They were all in firm agreement that my present miserable state could have been avoided if only I had awoken the first time and screamed murder most foul, and ejected my fortune-hunting incompetent would-be killer of a husband onto the street. I learned over time that each one of them - my doctors, my attorneys, even my own children and mother, as well as my loyal maid, Maria - had believed he had engineered my first illness. That none of them had grasped me by the hand and sat me down in the intervening twelve months, and stated as much to me was not truly any of their faults.

Chapter 20

I was christened Martha but have always been called Sunny. I don't think it's because I had an unusually sunny nature, but in the tiny rarefied world into which I came into existence, the smallest gift is magnified a thousand fold, and the ugliest things are made to go away, or, if that is not possible, are ignored completely.

For example, I had always been a pretty girl, and later a pretty woman. It is possible that if I had been born on a farm in Iowa, I would have gone on to become a homecoming queen, and maybe the wife of the town football hero, but I was born on my father's private train car and was always referred to as radiant and ethereally lovely. And instead of marrying a football hero, I married a prince, a real one, and it didn't surprise anyone, least of all me.

America has its royalty too, you can't fool yourself about that sort of thing, and the day I was born my family fortune was valued at more than seven hundred million dollars, and I was an only child.

I had a rare life, it's true - limitless wealth and security, and opportunities that I understand are not available to other people.

I won't indulge in one of the pastimes of my peer group, which is to create problems that don't exist in the lives of the rich. If rich people have problems, they are unfortunately mostly self-created to give us something to talk about. I never did that while I was alive and I won't waste my lack of breath doing it now.

In the end, of course, I did have very real problems, and if they were self-created, I am having trouble seeing it, but maybe that is the point of my remembering now. I need to see my life as though watching a film and give it the same sort of uncritical appraisal I used to give movies and books.

I do understand quite clearly that one of the issues that might have brought me to my un-pretty pass was that for most of my life I felt like I was in a film, or a book, or a painting. If I had any strong characteristic, it was that I was always, to some degree, very removed.

My childhood was by any standards rather magical and it continued a bit longer than perhaps it should have done. Born into wealth, I was also fortunate, or not, depending on one's viewpoint, to be the adoring focus of my mother and grandmother's unwavering attentions. My mother, still spectacularly beautiful and quite young when widowed, created a dream life centered on me.

She bought a great estate in Connecticut, Tamerlane, and it was there that I spent the summers and holidays of my girlhood, riding, swimming and attending the small rigorously-vetted parties of the children who were allowed into my life.

Winters were spent in the apartment my mother shared with my grandmother at 950 Fifth Avenue. The term 'apartment' might imply a somewhat cozy generational family setting, but as the apartment stretched up over three stories and had ten principal bedrooms as well as another twelve or so for staff, that would be an erroneous assumption.

I was their primary interest and their darling. I learned to skate at Rockefeller Center with a private instructor and two bodyguards, and was driven to the Chapin School during the week in the chauffeured family Rolls Royce. I did not excel academically, nor was it expected of me; what was expected of me was that I remain at all times gracious, that I keep a well-modulated voice and expression, and that I presented well. I think I mastered these things competently by the time I was six or seven, and after that I had merely to exist to be in the world that had been prepared for me.

If I had any true interests or ambitions even in my youth, I cannot recall what they may have been. There are social expectations in my world that can be somewhat daunting, though I did not find them so until later.

During the gentle years of my childhood and early womanhood, my mother made certain that I was surrounded only by those I had known since birth. If I didn't have a great deal to say, or much to contribute to conversations around me, I was not thought odd, merely quiet and decorative. As I observed earlier, every virtue is magnified in my world. Of course, so are the failings, but at the time I did not worry about the future.

Actually I *never* worried about the future. Thoughts like that are the preoccupation of those who are expected to accomplish something one day, and as nearly as I could tell, all I had to accomplish was to be.

And so I remained placid, untroubled and a little removed.

I graduated from a small preparatory school in Maryland and came back to Tamerlane for my debut. It was a lovely occasion. My mother had all of the wall hangings and curtains on the lower floors changed to ice blue satin to match the interior satin of the tents. Surrounded by old friends, I enjoyed the evening greatly.

I chose not to attend college as I had no plans for a career, and instead spent the next years attending small parties and taking the occasional art tour of Europe, accompanied by my mother and Nana, who stayed with me until I married.

It was in my twenty-third year of life that mother insisted I accompany her and her fiancé, Mr. Aitken, to Austria to attend a round of shooting parties and balls at the famed Schloss Mitersall. It was there, on my second night in residence, when I walked into the ballroom, that I first saw Prince Alfie Von Auersperg. He was the most beautiful man I had ever beheld, truly beautiful in the sense that when I looked into his hooded blue eyes topped by gleaming blond hair, I felt his face resembled that of something painted by the Old Masters I loved.

Alfie was only a boy, really, just twenty on that gleaming night. I did not think of myself as an older woman, though. As I said, my girlhood was rather protracted. I fell in love in a cinematic setting and believed that at last I could see the direction of my future perfectly on that night.

We were married several months later in a lovely ceremony at Schloss Miterasall where we had met. I loved him very much, and when I took those vows, I meant them, and did sincerely plan to remain with him forever. Alfie was the complete European male and could never have lived anywhere but in the old world, so that was where I too would live. Alfie, like a character in a novel, was a little removed and unreal, like me.

His family money had disappeared after World War II, seized by the terrible Communists, but God knows, money was not an issue for us. Upon my marriage, my mother turned over the hundred million dollar trust that my father had set up for me at my birth. I am, or I should say I was, very uncomfortable discussing money. It was a thing people like me never discussed, however I feel that since it was money that dominated my life, as well as both my deaths - my coma coffin years and the final one where I was at last a recognized corpse - it needs to be discussed openly.

Alfie and I built our wonderful chalet in Kitzbuhel, and for a few years I was marvelously contented. I had two perfect babies, a boy and a girl, Alexander and Ala (whose full name was Annie Laurie, after mother, but was always known as

Ala). Alfie and I traveled and golfed, and even went on safari to Africa together; something it must be said that he enjoyed a great deal more than I did. Then, with our home done and our children born, we began to lead the life that would become our true marriage and I became unhappy.

Unhappiness was novel to me, as was the sense of not being right. I had never experienced either feeling, and being unused to any sense of responsibility for myself, I could only blame Alfie. Alfie, unlike me, enjoyed making new friends and meeting new people. As soon as our home was completed, he began hosting weekend house and shooting parties, every weekend.

I was unaccustomed to being continually around people who expected me to be both charming and entertaining. I found, to my dismay, that I was neither. I could hold my own in small gatherings of trusted old friends, but faced with these hardened glittering people who had lived out one dramatic escapade after another, I was left wordless and floundering. Since no one had ever asked anything of me before, and I had never been expected to do anything at which I might fail, I could only blame my discomfort on these people.

Like the worst insular American, I became nation-centered and judgmental. Privately I began to refer to them by the then popular name 'Euro trash'. I decided that if I bored them, then by God they bored me too.

My attitude and subsequent withdrawal from all social events bothered my gregarious husband a good deal and he began criticizing me. This, too, was an unpleasant novel event, and in short order I allocated him in my mind to the category of Euro trash as well.

Since I had not been raised to be introspective or self-critical, or have a moments discontent, I became obsessed with the idea of going home to America and my mother, and resuming an existence where I was understood. That I never once considered that the life my husband expected us to lead was indeed the life of the grown-up rich, I imagined that once back in America … no, that's wrong too, I did not imagine the future at all.

I was in a snit, a rather grandiose tantrum. I was spoiled and ridiculous, and faced for the first time in my life with disapproval, I ran instead of staying and trying to compromise. I did not stop to consider that my husband was very young and that he truly loved me and our children. I did not consider my children's feelings at all.

I adored my children and was very possessive of them. I had been raised as my own mother's favored possession and knew of no other way to look at my own children. My mother had not had to share me, as my father was dead, and since I had never had to share anything, I did not once consider the lifetime of hurt I would cause my son and daughter by taking them from their father. I wanted to go home, so that is what we did.

I realize that anyone observing my silly self-absorbed existence might well think, 'Ah, she got what she deserved.' I would find that a curious viewpoint. I was born with no expectations but pleasure. I lived a grand existence for forty-five years, during which, if I indulged myself, I also tried to do so without ever causing harm to another person. I did not ask for the great wealth I had - it was given to me. That I had it caused me to be buried alive for twenty-eight years by the man I loved and trusted.

Having money canceled out anything else that I was, including being a human being. I didn't choose that any more than I chose my birth. I had forty-five years to live my life and twenty-eight years of being blind and unable to move, blind but able to hear quite keenly those around me discussing me as some inanimate thing, which indeed is exactly what I had become; twenty-eight years of diapers and catheters and feeding tubes, and being touched by paid strangers to roll me and wash me and move my limbs around; twenty-eight years of wanting death like a regular person wants air.

I do not believe that my former life of privilege was one so vile and offensive as to have deserved this sentence. I do not feel that my life can be considered an enviable one by even the most desperate of standards.

Chapter 21

I returned to New York with my children and moved into the Stanhope Hotel. Within the week I had finalized the purchase of a nine million dollar apartment in one of New York's great pre-war buildings.

The place was a wreck and it needed extensive repairs before I could even begin to consider the interior décor, and before I ever chose a brush stroke, I had married my second husband and the place in Manhattan became our joint project.

I was desperate to be remarried almost before my divorce came through. What I had imagined coming home to be, and what it was, were terrifyingly opposite. When I had left America for my grand marriage, I had left as my mother and grandmother's adored child, the entire focus of their lives. I had never been alone; indeed my nanny stayed with me until my wedding day. When I returned, both my grandmother and nanny were long dead. My mother had remarried and had built this staggeringly busy social life in which she not only shone but thrived.

All of my girlhood friends were living out their busy adult socialite lives, and everyone, my beloved mother included, seemed to take it for granted that I would do the same. I did not want any of that. I wanted to stay home and play board games and eat cozy dinners, surrounded by people who adored and understood me, and treated me as important for just being Sunny.

That this is a strange, childish, even bizarre, lifestyle by most standards, I did not see. Until I was near dead, and then finally dead, I did not ever step back and examine myself critically.

I never bothered to consider that other people had needs too, and if they didn't mesh with mine, then maybe I needed to make more of an effort. I didn't learn a thing from my careless destruction of my first marriage. And later in my second, when my husband's misery became palpable enough to force itself to even my notice from my removed self-absorption, I wouldn't meet him halfway. I told myself that I had not been raised to compromise. I told myself that he had understood the life I had expected him to lead, and that if it was a cell, as he called it, it was certainly one of vast luxury. I wouldn't listen to him and I would not attempt any sort of change that might bring me the slightest discomfort.

I told him to go if he was so unhappy, but now I understand that was not fair either. My husband had by then become crippled in his own way, crippled by his love of the incalculable beauty and pleasures of great wealth. He was afraid to be without it, and so he stayed on and lived by my rules. That he would hate and blame me even for his own weakness, I now understand was inevitable. It would have taken some effort on my part for us both to have not all, but some, of what we each wanted. Sadly, I had never been raised for effort.

I met him at a dinner party that some of my old friends had forced me to attend. I did not yet know, and certainly he had no inkling, that I had reached the beginning of the end as far as any effort or ability to socialize. It was an utterly typical Manhattan dinner party; in other words it was resplendent with great couturier dresses worn by women who had little other purpose to their days but the purchase of these gowns which they would then wear in front of the only other two hundred and fifty same people they met in varying incarnations every night of the year.

I did enjoy buying beautiful clothes. I even enjoyed the process of dressing up and appearing in them. My problem, as others saw it, though I did not, was that once I had appeared, I immediately wanted to go home. That night was no exception. The dinner was at my old friend Peggy Bedford's new place. She had just separated from her third husband, which seemed to be the bleak prospect for women like ourselves - Doris Duke, Barbara Hutton, me as well I imagine, though to my credit I only married twice. I suppose if I had not been buried alive, the number might have crept higher over time. At any rate, as always, I was seated between the sort of overly gregarious types of dinner guests who could converse at length on anything from fine French furnishings, or F.F.F. as we called it, to the latest scandalous divorce in our set.

I wanted to leave, or better yet, I wanted to be somehow miraculously transported home without having to finish the tiresome dinner and negotiate my excuses for an early evening until I was safely into the back of my limo, the party behind me.

I know exactly what I thought when I noticed the tall, striking man with the intense dark eyes studying me from further down the table. I thought, 'Oh he is bored with this silly pointless evening as well, and wishes he were home alone.' Then, when I studied the depth of interest and intensity in his eyes, it was but a short step in my mind to deluding myself that he wished he were alone with me.

I knew I looked beautiful that evening, and I fancied that I appeared something apart to him, and that he was gazing at me and hoping to whisk me off to a room and say everything to me without ever having to speak aloud. As I have said, my overriding trait was how removed I felt from life. Remembering now my thoughts on that evening, I see that I was also vastly removed from reality itself.

I understand, with the specious gift of hindsight, which is the only real sight we dead have, that what he saw that evening was a discontented, lonely woman, pretty enough, but made extremely beautiful by her aura of vast wealth. He knew who I was, of course, and he must have spent the evening studying my ignominious failures at providing even the minimum of polite conversation to those around me. He must have seen my deep isolation and known that I would respond eagerly to someone who offered romance and companionship without me having to do more than just to be, which sadly, except for my ability to love my children, is really all I could do, or no, let me be honest, is all I *would* do.

Our courtship was brief and impassioned, and when he asked me to marry him, of course I said yes. I knew I had to be married or else face a most terrible solitary life. I had found, since leaving Alfie and returning to New York, that I despised being alone and left to my own devices. In fact, before meeting my husband, I had taken to spending most of my day in bed, rising only to dine with my children.

I despised socializing and being around strangers but I had very much liked the companionship part of marriage, including, though not limited to, the sexual partnership. I knew when I married my second husband exactly how to keep our union happy. I decided we would center our entire lives on our homes and our children, and create my ideal of the perfect life - *my* ideal.

I believed that in order to cement our family life, I should give him his own child. I was not particularly anxious for maternity again, but I did adore and enjoy my children absolutely, and having a child of our own seemed to me the perfect way of creating a blended family circle.

Within a year I had given birth to our daughter, Cosima, and unlike other choices I made regarding our marital state, the decision to have Cosima brought us both unclouded joy.

He didn't know, my husband, not in the first years, exactly what he had done to himself, or, as he saw it, what I had done to him. For the first couple of years I was uncharacteristically busy with the new baby, the Manhattan apartment and the purchase and reconstruction of our Newport cottage, Clarendon Court.

The houses required weeks and months of meetings with architects and interior design teams, as well as lavish buying trips all throughout Europe. Never having been begrudged anything myself, I certainly was not begrudging when it came to indulging those I loved.

When my husband asked, with what I considered gruff hopefulness, if we might do over his old apartment in the Belgravia section of London, I agreed immediately. I am amazed now that the considerable work and money spent on the Belgravia apartment didn't alert me that we were on opposing tracks.

That neither of us could see the other's direction is astounding in hindsight. I thought we were redoing the London apartment as a sentimental, if costly, gesture to a place where we would stay as a family during our annual trip abroad; he thought it was going to be our home for a great bulk of the year. My husband had no money of his own when he married me. What he did have was a promising, and according to him, fascinating and fast track position as an assistant to J. Paul Getty, headquartered out of London.

Through careful overspending, he had managed to build a reasonably glamorous life for himself, with an apartment in one of London's finest neighborhoods, extensive travel all around the world, and thanks to his own charm and intellect, an enormous roster of interesting friends, most of whom came from the same world that I did, thus our initial meeting.

Unfortunately for both of us, while my husband thoroughly enjoyed his career and his busy social life, he had begun increasingly to feel like a child with his nose pressed against the candy store window. He was invited to fabulous homes and glittering social occasions, but he could never reciprocate his hosts' hospitality. And though he shone brilliantly at these occasions, he felt he appeared more as the entertainment than as himself.

In that he was right. There is only one coin of the realm granting access to the world of the very rich, and that is to be very rich. All the rest of it, a person's intellect and joie de vivre, their charm and warmth and accomplishments, do not matter one iota if they cannot back it up with an enormous personal fortune.

Is this fair? Of course not, it's ridiculous, as are so many things in life. Indeed, because the rich value only money for the most part, we are an ill-educated group of crashing bores with little to say or even think about. We are largely desperate for entertainment and novelty, so often we *surround* ourselves with those who have accomplished great things by virtue of something other than being born wealthy. We surround ourselves with them, but we do not *include* them as equals. To be included you must have the wealth. Though the wealth does not make you more interesting or special, it is a non-negotiable rule of inclusion.

My husband did not understand that the price of finally becoming one of those on the inside might be that he had to let go of everything about himself that had made both he and his life very special. He did not understand until too late how empty the vast rooms of privilege can be.

Chapter 22

Immediately after I died, I rose up from that bed and blasted through the door of my coffin room with such force that I knocked over a nurse standing in the doorway. For me, death created an instant and exhilarating liberation. I could see again. The insulin had created instantaneous blindness and paralysis; it was all gone now.

Dead I might be, but I had never felt more alive. While I was living, before the coma coffin, I had never particularly wanted to be anywhere, or do anything. Indeed, for me, it was always more a matter of not wanting to do anything or be anywhere.

Maybe I hadn't valued my life a great deal. I hesitate to think that, because in some dreadful way, that thought helps me to understand my husband's mindset, and that I will not, cannot, do, not after the last twenty-eight years.

I liken the expectations put upon me to the same unrealistic projections put upon the very beautiful: people see them, and they are so pleasing to look at, that fantasies are projected onto them. Because they are so wonderful to gaze upon, one might assume that they are also special in other ways. No man looking at a truly beautiful woman could ever imagine that she has to clip her toenails, or that she is stupid, or that she has never had a kind word or deed for anyone. No, they reason out that if she is lovely on the outside. she must be very interesting as well.

It is exactly the same for those of us born to great wealth. People who do not possess it might walk by the outsides of our special homes and gaze with great longing at them. I imagine they stop and stare admiringly and imagine that if only they could be surrounded with such beauty and opulence that they would be completely happy in every way. What I wish more people could understand, what I wish with every remnant of my soul that my husband had tried to understand, was that to me, and the few like me, these apparent palaces of pleasure are only dwellings, no different to us than a small modest apartment is to those who live there. You only know what you are used to. Whether you are born in a trailer or a palace, it is the only life you understand. You don't spend your life thinking I *must* act this way, and say this, and do that because I live here. No, it's just your life and your home, and you live it out, as do those close to you. It isn't special, it just *is*.

There is, of course, one crucial difference, and in my case it led to my being buried alive.

If you are not born to great wealth, nobody thinks it odd if you love your children more than your money, or if you like hamburgers and ice cream better than foie gras and chocolate truffles. For the rich it is different, and my husband began increasingly to complain that I had the tastes of the lower classes.

At first I was amused and would happily engage in discussions with him when he would accuse me of playing Marie Antoinette at her Trianon. I would shake my head and laugh at him, disagreeing. I would remind him that if he must insist on comparing me to some historical figure instead of simply seeing me as I was, a terribly ordinary person, he should correctly compare me to Empress Alexandra. Like me, she had suffered from the great sin of being a home-oriented, child-loving woman who had despaired of social occasions. I reminded my husband that Alexandra too had been mocked for her lack of witty conversation at functions and that we even shared the embarrassing habit of breaking out in blotches when we realized how harshly we were judged for our lack of ability to shine in public. What I didn't add was that, unlike me, Empress Alexandra had been loved and appreciated by her husband for the things she was and not scorned for what she was not.

In the beginning I did not take his complaints and discontents so seriously. I believed we had the issue of perspective working against us. I saw our lovely homes, which I had filled with great art and furniture and daily with flowers, as just that, our homes. He saw them as empty stage settings, where if only I would come to life, they could be filled on a nightly basis with the great and good of the land. He wanted to act out the part of the social grandee, and to him there was no point whatsoever to having a Gainsborough if he could not show it to an admiring throng. To me, great art as well as living out our lives in great rooms, was merely one of the pleasures my wealth afforded me. I did not need the admiration of strangers for our possessions in order to enjoy them. He did. I did not need, nor indeed did I wish, to be surrounded by others to validate my existence. He did.

Unused to conflict, I at first deflected, then tried to avoid, what seemed to me nonsensical conversations. What I didn't see, what I refused to see, was his very real growing sense of desperation, his feeling that he had lost his center. I understand now that I handled him in the worst possible ways. Instead of listening to him and trying to understand, to compromise, I would become exasperated and tired, and usually ended our conversations by suggesting that if he was so terribly bored and restless, he should run out and fetch me a pack of cigarettes or restock our ice cream supply, suggestions that make me cringe now.

He had given up the position at Getty Oil he loved shortly after our marriage, and never having had a job, I failed to understand that they might provide one with more than simply the money needed to survive. Unused to having to be anywhere or do anything, I assumed, based on my own languid experience, that everyone else wished to lead a life removed from the day-to-day business and pressure caused by career and money troubles. What was money for, I reasoned, if not to enable you to do whatever you wanted? My husband found this attitude maddening and would, with increasing ire, remind me that I didn't do anything at all.

"For the love of God, Sunny, you lay about all week long in the city. For all the use we get out of the apartment, we might as well turn it into an enormous bedroom with a television. When we come up here, *here*, to this magnificent house, I spend the summers and weekends watching you do more of the same, which is nothing."

I watched him curiously as he seemed about to throw his drink against the fireplace, so great was his frustration, but he caught himself when he realized he was holding a Baccarat tumbler in his hand and set it down carefully on the table. I wish he had thrown it. *I* would have thrown the glass in anger, but you see *he* couldn't smash a Baccarat glass, and to me it was merely a glass used for drinking. It is a small thing but so illustrative of our differences.

He sighed and sat down heavily, his head in his hands, and groaned despairingly. "This life we lead, or don't lead as the case may be, it isn't what I thought it would be, Sunny. It's so ..."

I wanted him to be cheerful again and play Backgammon with me, so I tried to rouse myself to interest in his plight. "So what, darling, *what* is it you see as the great lack in our lives that causes you to be so unhappy, or at least to perceive yourself as so unhappy? Calm down, darling, and freshen our drinks. Come, have a game with me." He stared at me rather wildly, so I felt the need to temporize my comments. "Darling, I do understand that as a man you might wish to be more …" I struggled a bit trying to think what exactly it was that he might want more of, and then feeling I had hit upon a solution I said triumphantly, "… that you might wish to be more active in the world outside the house. I do understand, darling. It isn't me, of course, but I am quite supportive if you would wish to, say, join the Board of the Historical Preservation Society here in Newport. I'm certain that a small well-placed donation would earn you a spot right away, and then you could -"

He cut me off. "A small well-placed donation could earn me a spot? Do you hear yourself at all when you speak, Sunny? Might it ever penetrate the fog of your lassitude-filled self-absorption to imagine that, before marrying you, I never needed anyone to give donations to earn me a spot anywhere? Can you just for a moment imagine that I might be suffocating in all this empty luxury? You say that my desire to attend dinners and parties is silly, and perhaps you are correct, but unlike you, I find the endless prospect of days and days of never having anywhere to go, anything to do, not to be comforting but rather the opposite. Frankly, when I consider that vista, I feel a bit like opening the doors and throwing myself off the cliff walk at the prospect of it."

I shrugged, bored by his theatrics. "Well, that's one activity you could do, I suppose. Meantime, do you mind terribly making me another drink and then we might have a game while you consider the most appropriate attire for your final escapade."

He stared at me blankly for a moment, then he laughed and rose obediently to mix my drink.

I thought I had handled the whole thing rather well and I didn't think of it again until the next time he raised the subject. On that occasion I rather more tartly reminded him that it was he, not I, who had insisted on hanging a sign in our downstairs bath that read, 'Fuck Communism'. I asked him was he now so disenchanted with wealth that he wished to join the Bolshevik party?

He sourly answered that he didn't think he was quite there yet but he was beginning to sympathize with some of their viewpoints.

Odd how I forgot that the Bolsheviks had imprisoned and slaughtered Empress Alexandra with whom I had unwisely compared myself during a previous disagreement. I did, however, write a healthy check to the Historic Society, and my husband at first enthusiastically, and then later dutifully, attended the bi-annual meetings. I believe he even ended up placing a plaque somewhere.

Over time he seemed to accept and settle into the bargain he had made. If he appeared less lively, and stopped constantly raising ideas and suggestions of places we could go and people we could see, I felt it was all to the good. From my viewpoint, we were quite happy, the children were doing splendidly, we were in lovely surroundings, and I loved my husband and enjoyed his company.

Though, though it is true that, after the first few years, when he appeared to resign himself to living in all ways to my needs, I grew ever more filled with lassitude, as he had put it. You see, I loved him and he was the first person I had ever loved who had looked at me long and hard, and found me wanting. He had expectations of me. He needed me to be more than what I was. No-one I had ever loved, or let close to me before, had ever made me feel lacking. I had no inner resources to justify myself or my way of life, since I had never been judged before, at least not outside of the dreaded social evenings. So, in time, I became in my home as uncertain as I had once been outside of it.

I did not know when his moods of discontent and judgment would strike, so I became fearful and unsure of how to act around him. In the past, whenever I had felt judged, I had withdrawn further into my home. Now he had breached my final defenses and his silly statement about living in my bedroom became a self-fulfilling prophecy.

I think - no, I know - but only know now, that I became sad and self-conscious. My husband had brought into the safety of my private life the unwanted knowledge that I wasn't quite up to par, and unlike the looks of boredom I had received from strangers, his disappointment in me hurt acutely.

There were days when I became so listless that I would find myself in bed by three in the afternoon, and I would remain there until noon the following day, unless I had a hair appointment.

To think that I voluntarily spent hours of my waking life in bed, considering what later befell me, is too awful to contemplate, even now when I am dead. It is sad that only in death am I excited and interested in the world around me. Dead, I am filled with a lightness and enthusiasm that I can never remember experiencing while I was alive.

When my heart at last stopped beating, I drifted joyously out of the rest home, which had held me for so long, and down the coast, returning to my beloved Clarendon Court. I was achingly aware of every beauty and enchantment of the living world, the world which I had been kept by my condition from seeing for nearly three decades, and which, before that, I had never bothered to see at all.

With my newly-gained clarity of vision and thought, I can now grasp so clearly that while I spent those last sad years of consciousness lying in bed and smoking, staring blankly at the walls of my room, wondering what, if anything, I should do, my husband, former man of business that he was, had decided on exactly what to do.

It was time to put both of us out of our misery.

Chapter 23

Twelve years into our marriage we had come to an impasse. I thought we might have to break it through divorce, which was something I dreaded a great deal. Divorce would mean Cosima losing her father and it would mean me losing my companion, a companion I still loved, though it is possible by then I feared him more. Not that he ever hit me. He never laid a finger on me in violence until that last night, but I am skipping ahead of my story.

I feared his increasing distance and his disapproval, which depressed and angered me. I did not like it one bit. But I disliked the idea of being left alone even more. Divorce and the inevitable procedures that I would have to take to go about finding another husband, and one who might lack the very things I loved about the one I had, was a daunting prospect. Ironically, the intellect, wit, drive and energy he possessed, and which had initially attracted me, still did so. But the characteristics I loved in him made his life with me seem impossible to him.

I spoke at length to my mother about my fears and dissatisfaction, and she crisply advised me to end my marriage, stating, "Darling Sunny, I am somewhat surprised it has lasted this long. After all, he did marry you for your money and the advantages that your money could bring him. It seems he has now weighed the advantages against time and attrition, and found them rather lacking. I always felt he was too much of the world and a rather commercial person. Of course, that's very entertaining over dinner but can become a bit wearying in private. What you need, darling, is a nice compliant companion, not necessarily a husband, who will keep you company at the few pursuits you do enjoy. Really, darling, I think it would be for the best to give him a reasonable sum of money and move forward. An unhappy man can be a terrible bore, and besides, darling, this marriage is becoming a bit embarrassing for me as well as for you."

I was flabbergasted and, moreover, terribly hurt. She had not said one thing I was hoping to hear. I had wanted her to tell me how to fix things, not how to end them, and besides, some of what she said frightened me.

I asked her what she had meant by my not necessarily needing a husband, and worse, why had she used the word 'embarrassing'?

There was a protracted silence during which I heard her call her butler for an unprecedented morning cocktail. When she spoke, her voice was subdued. "Sunny, when I mentioned a companion, I was not speaking of a nurse, for heaven's sake. I was thinking more along the lines of a servant with whom you could have a simpatico understanding. You know, darling, like Queen Victoria did with that nice Mr. Brown, her estate manager. It seems to me that the interests you pursue could be easily accommodated by nearly anyone of a pleasant and retiring disposition."

I interjected angrily. "Mother, you make it sound as though I have no interests at all."

I heard her exhale smoke against the earpiece. "Sunny, at least amongst ourselves, let us be frank with each other. You don't go anywhere but to your hairdressers and you don't see anyone. Even Russell and I are only graced by your company if we promise a dinner in with no one but you and the children, and have it served on trays in front or the television. I have asked you dozens of times to join the board of the Met, or the ballet, or at the very least to accompany me on occasion. You consistently refuse, and, darling, I suppose if I don't ask you, no-one will. What exactly is it you do with your time?"

I sputtered, "You know I have the children and -"

"Oh don't, Sunny, not with me. The children, as you call them, have their own lives now. Ala is newly married, Alex is away at school, and -"

"There is still little Cosima," I interjected desperately.

"Yes, of course there is, but Cosima is in school and quite occupied with her little friends and activities, and at any rate, darling, I don't wish to quarrel with you about how you choose to spend your time. It's your own affair. We were speaking of your husband, who it seems is also involved in his own affairs, and rather public affairs they are, and *that* I do feel you will have to address."

It was my turn to be silent until I could bring myself to ask her what she meant. "What have you heard, mother? Ridiculous gossip, no doubt. People will always -"

"Indeed they will, Sunny. People will always comment when the very married husband of a very rich woman is seen out and about in all the right places with his very beautiful mistress."

I lit my thirtieth cigarette of the morning and strove for a tone of casual amusement. "Oh, mother, really. If my husband has decided to take up with some poor girl as a temporary diversion and seduce her with the high life, he certainly wouldn't be the first, and I am not going to accord this any false importance. I'm surprised that you would."

"An interesting turn of phrase, darling, but Alexandra Isles is hardly some poor girl who needs your husband to entertain her on your money. In fact, it appears that the two of you have nearly everything in common, including a rather specious taste in men. Of course, unlike you, she is very social. She even has some sort of silly career on television, I hear."

Naturally, I knew immediately who Alexandra was; she was the daughter of an old family friend, Count Bobby Moltke, and the television career my mother was referring to was a rather well-known one, although it was the custom of our kind to pretend that we did not know a thing about television.

I felt sick and shaken, and began making noises about being late for something in an effort to end the phone call. My mother understood me better than anyone and played along, but only after adding a final coda to hammer down her points. "Darling, it is best in these situations not to allow this sort of thing to drag out unnecessarily. You have to understand that wide latitude is given to people like us. At this time your lifestyle may only be considered eccentric, and eccentricity is certainly allowed, but if you were not to act quickly and decisively in ending either the affair or your marriage, you might begin to be viewed as somewhat pathetic, and that behavior is not so quickly forgiven."

I knew she was absolutely correct, and rather than succumb to my customary sense of helpless depression, I was uncharacteristically galvanized by this discussion. Looking back on that brief flurry of activity, I wonder what I might have become if only I had channeled it into more productive actions than the ones I undertook.

It's impossible to predict any outcome once you are dead, but I do think that if I had chosen a different road, I would not have been subjected to twenty-eight years of soundless screams and equally unheard prayers for death. It's all too late now, of course.

What I did do was to rise up from my bed and demand that my maid, Maria, get my doctor on the phone immediately. When she did so, I curtly instructed him to find me the finest plastic surgeon in the city and arrange for a face lift and some minor liposuction as quickly as possible. Then I instructed Maria to pack several weeks' worth of nightwear and robes, as well as two day dresses.

After that I rang my butler to arrange for the car to be brought around and to inform my husband when he returned that I had had a sudden emergency and been forced to leave town without notice. Cosima was in school, so I left her a letter telling her that Mummy was off to Europe for a few weeks unexpectedly and to be a good girl, and that I would see her soon.

Following the surgery on my face and neck, I demanded to be moved to Essex House for my recuperation. I kept Maria with me as she understood my needs and could handle the hotel staff. Three weeks later I felt and looked sufficiently well enough to contact my husband.

I reached him at our Manhattan apartment. When he came to the phone and spoke, I was stunned at how glad I was to hear his beautiful voice. I was certain that my sacrifice had been more than worth it, if it meant keeping him with me.

He quickly disabused me of that notion. At times my husband used an exaggerated British drawl to show his deep disdain of people or situations, and he chose to address me, his own wife, in that very annoying tone. "My prodigal at last calls from her overseas adventures. Tell me, darling, was your crossing arduous. I know that personally I have always found the drive across the East River tedious in the extreme. I know you must be quite nearby. After all, you wouldn't deign to travel as far as California, would you? No, what was it you said about Los Angeles when you refused to move there so I could continue my position with Getty? As I recall you said it was a cultural wasteland, which is still amusing in retrospect, Sunny, as I'm quite certain they have televisions and beds in California."

I ignored his remark about Los Angeles, and at first I tried to pretend confusion, but he merely laughed and told me that if I was trying to pass off my sojourn as a last minute run to Europe, I should not have left my passport behind in the safe.

Furious at Maria for this oversight, I tried to make the whole episode seem rather a lark. "You've caught me, darling. I'm just up the street. You're quite right. At the Essex, actually. I had a bit of tucking done here and there. I think you'll be pleased with the results. Would you like to come up? I can have dinner brought in. I want to stay a few more days, until the last of the swelling disappears, before I see Cosima."

There was a long hesitation before he spoke again. By the time he did, my hand was wet against the phone. He sighed before answering. "Sunny, I'm glad for you if having surgery has made you happier. I've been doing a bit of surgery on my own life as well, a bit of tucking and tightening, as you would say -"

I interrupted him, speaking with forced gaiety. "Wonderful. darling, you can tell me all about it over dinner, then."

I heard him breathe in and out deeply before saying, "I'm sorry, Sunny, this evening just will not work. I have promised Cosima that we would dine out together. I'm taking her to Caravelle."

I answered him icily. "*Cosima*?"

He laughed a little. "Yes, Cosima, our daughter. But I gather from your tone that you are aware that on a different given night it may be otherwise. I am happy to discuss Alexandra with you, but not now and not on the phone. I'll tell you what I think would be the best. You rest up and finish out the week at The Essex, and have John drive you up to Clarendon from there. Cosima and I will meet you in Newport Friday evening and you can tell her you came there directly from the airport. We'll have dinner together, we three, and after she goes to bed, we can talk." His voice lightened perceptibly. "I will be so glad to talk all this over with you, Sunny. I do care about you deeply and have despised these secrets, truly I have. I hope you will believe that."

I said coldly, "I am so sorry that cheating on me has been such a strain on your conscience, darling, but speaking solely for myself, I would prefer that we did not discuss this further, not at Clarendon, not anywhere. I am willing to go forward and pick up our life as it was. I am ready to do that, I wish to do that, and I feel it is best to put this behind us with the minimum of upset."

His voice was quiet when he answered me. "And I do not. I'm sorry, Sunny, it must be as you wish. If you don't wish to have a long overdue honest discourse at Clarendon this weekend, I cannot force you. I will remain in the city and begin making arrangements for the removal of my personal belongings."

Panicked, I assured him that if it was *that* important to him, I would meet him at Clarendon for a talk and that I hadn't realized how unhappy he was etc.. He murmured his thanks at my understanding and said he was looking forward to seeing me.

After our subdued goodbyes, I lay awake for hours in the darkness of my room, smoking and crying, both of which are very wrong things to do following a face lift, but I could already tell that, new face or not, my husband had little interest in looking at me again. And I should have called him back and told him to go ahead and remove his personal things. That was what my mother would have expected of me; anything else she would have indeed judged as pathetic.

I did not do that. I lay awake, crying and trying desperately to think of the right offers to make him during our upcoming meeting at Clarendon. Money meant nothing to me personally but I knew it meant a great deal to my husband. I merely needed to find his price point.

Chapter 24

I now see that I am a better woman dead than I was while I lived. If I could have been brought out of my coma coffin at any time during the twenty-eight years I was trapped there, I would have risen a kinder woman than I was when I was put there. Time and regret caused improvement in me. Put into a ghastly situation where nothing I wanted happened to me, I became more patient and understanding. Given years of misery, I realized too late that I was but one human being in a vast ongoing flood of people who had needs and dreams and lives I had never considered.

Forced by circumstance to hear day-in and day-out the stories of my nurses and attendants as they spoke of their lives, I was exposed to the realities of others; something I had never been made to do, or desired to think about, while I existed among them.

There is an old saying that best describes my entire time as a living person. 'There are two roads to destruction: one is to receive everything you ever asked for, and the other is to receive nothing that you have asked for.' I became, by circumstance, the rare creature who in one fractured lifetime lived out both of these tragic scenarios, and it changed me.

Dead now, I look back at the woman I was. I float unfettered through the beautiful rooms I lived in and I see myself in my former incarnation. I want to reach through time and shake her / me into awareness, but that cannot be done, and so I suppose, in some odd way, I am haunted by myself, though I have moved past fear and despair finally. All of that was long ago used up in a small airless hospital room where the daily delivery of roses could never quite disguise the smell of my own waste and decay.

Unfortunately for both my husband and me, it was the woman I was then who appeared that Friday evening at Clarendon.

I was a bit late as I had spent several hours in the city, meeting with my trust officer, Morris, and my lawyer, Sims. I had decided to disregard my mother's advice and to marshal my resources to keep my husband.

I knew that regardless of their private thoughts on the matter, both Morris and Sims would do only as I asked and never dream of proffering advice. I was always more comfortable with those whom I employed than people in positions equal to mine. My husband was trying to become my equal, and rather than feel compassion for him, I felt attacked and thwarted, and I did not like it one bit.

I arrived just in time to be seated for dinner with my husband and daughter. I was delighted to see both of them, and little Cosima at least returned that delight. The evening began on a sour note, as my husband had taken the liberty of giving our chef carte blanche on the dinner menu. I despised rich French foods and my husband was aware of this. I did not see any reason to be amenable, and instructed our butler to return my plate and bring me back a hamburger.

My husband did not bother to conceal his disdain, and our daughter quickly became aware of the atmosphere of tension and excused herself to bed quite early. After accepting her kisses, we rose without words and adjourned to the privacy of our library.

The library at Clarendon was, and remains, one of my favorite rooms in the world. With a great profusion of mahogany paneling and a masterpiece of a fireplace that rises two stories, it holds a deep comforting richness. It seems warmer than the other rooms, as the floor in there is one of intricate parquet wood and not the marble which covered the rest of the floors.

Once we were comfortably ensconced in our favorite chairs, drinks in hand, I wanted to forestall, or, if possible, forgo completely, the conversation we were there to have. It was such a beautiful room and I fancied in my mind that we made a perfect picture in that lovely setting.

I only wanted us to go on as we had been before. There seemed to me no need to say anything. After all, we were at home and together, and that was enough.

I looked up at my favorite painting, a Gainsborough, that hung over the fireplace, and sighed in contentment. My husband followed the trajectory of my glance and laughed bitterly. Setting down his drink he turned to face me. "I know exactly what you are thinking, Sunny."

I shivered inwardly. He was going to force this confrontation through after all, and I can still say with honesty that I felt a certain amount of pity for him going in. After all, I held all the money, thus all the cards. I smiled politely and said, "Oh yes? Then please tell me, darling, what am I thinking?"

"You are thinking what a lovely room this is and how well that painting becomes it, and you are wondering why in the world a man privileged enough to live in such surroundings cannot be content. You were also hoping that I had settled down from my current aberrations and would suggest we have a backgammon game instead of this conversation. I apologize for disappointing you. You do so hate it when anyone disappoints you, don't you, Sunny? Would you like to know what I see when I look up at that painting?"

I nodded. "If you wish."

"What I see is a masterpiece that belongs in a museum where it can be viewed and appreciated by all. What I see is another thing that you have collected merely because you wanted to have it, without considering that it might be better served elsewhere. That's what I see."

"I see, well, darling, you see so much, don't you? Tell me, when you look at that *thing*, as you call it, do you also see or consider its value? And pardon me for my crudeness, darling, but this time I am not speaking of the painting's value as an object of beauty but its value in dollars and cents. You must remember the day we purchased it from Sotheby's. I paid nearly four million dollars for it, do you recall? It's worth many times that now, I understand. Isn't that really what you see, darling, all those millions of dollars hanging on a wall in one room in one of my homes, just hanging there so close but as useless to you as the treasure of a sunken Spanish galleon?"

If he was startled by my counterattack, he gave no sign of it. Despite his believing he was a broken shell of his former self, my husband had retained a great deal of his personal power and old negotiating skills. It was one of the reasons I still loved him.

He smiled slightly. "I see that you have been a busy girl, Sunny. Who did you speak to before coming up this weekend - Morris or Sim?"

"Both of them, actually. I was hoping to avoid pressing some home truths upon you but I wished to be prepared if it became necessary, and now it has. Maybe it would be better if I laid out my cards, so to speak, and then you can tell me, if you still wish to, what your current plans are."

He nodded. "Go on."

"Alright. I want to remain married to you. I have loved our life together. For Cosima's sake and for mine as well, I am willing to forget, if not immediately forgive, your unfortunate alliance with Miss Isles. In time, if your behavior returns to its former state, I will indeed forgive you. Meantime, we can resume our marriage. You must understand, however, that if you should decide to terminate our relationship, you will be doing so without any financial help from me. When we married, and several times over the years, I have offered to set up a trust for you to give you some independence. That you consistently refused those offers spoke well to your character and affection for me. Those offers are no longer on the table as you have hurt me a great deal. If you choose to stay, in time who knows how things may change. I am not clairvoyant and therefore cannot tell you how I may feel in a year or so, but -"

"It's unfortunate that you lack clairvoyance, Sunny, but I suppose you have so many other things going for you that one can hardly mourn this one inexplicable shortcoming. Who needs clairvoyance anyway when you can tell the future by owning it, can't you? After all, you seem to own everything else, don't you?" He made a sweeping gesture around the room, including himself in it.

"I do seem to own everything, as you say, yes. So please, let's cut to the chase. I have stated what it is I want, and now you can tell me the same, and one way or another we can begin to move past this. I'm tired and wish to sleep."

He arched an eyebrow. "I'm not surprised that you are tired, Sunny. I'm exhausted myself. I could have never imagined twelve years ago how incredibly exhausting it would be to do nothing with one's life. I had hoped to talk to you about things that mattered to me, and gain some understanding from you, but I should have known not to bother. I've tried for years and you continually ignore me, just as you ignore the world around us and anything else that doesn't interest you." He rose in agitation and began pacing as he spoke. "I have met someone who loves me, Sunny, who sees me as a man, a person, not just as some fucking lackey, some adjunct. I have taken a position with a man half my age, Mark Millard, in the hopes of reclaiming some of the ground I have lost in my long, slow slide into apathetic nothingness. You think I'm so welded to this life? Well I am not, Sunny, I am not. I do think, though, that yes, you should grant me a reasonable sum of money for time served. Wouldn't you do the same for anyone of your loyal servants, and I have been a fine servant, haven't I, Sunny? Oh God, if you have ever cared for me as a separate person, someone who is not you, but a living breathing human being who is choking from lack of air, then let me go with some dignity." He sat down near me and took my hand, looking at me searchingly. "Please, for both our sakes."

I stood and backed away from him. "No, no, no. I don't want you to be like this. I don't want you to talk like this. You haven't even said if you think I look pretty yet!"

He made a small sound that may have been a strangled sob. "I'm sorry, Sunny, I'm sorry if this is upsetting to you, but I have feelings and needs too and -"

I put my hands over my ears and began childishly wailing. "No, no, no, I won't listen to you anymore and I won't give you any money if you leave me, and then your whore won't want you either. See if she wants some stupid old man who has to live in a ... a ... a basement somewhere. She just wants your money, as you wanted mine, and she can't have it."

He came over to where I was standing and I could see he was finally really angry. He yanked my hands away from my ears and he shouted, "By God, she is no whore. Why, she has accomplished more in a week than you have in a lifetime, and I will -"

Neither of us ever got to hear what he would have said. Whether it was, 'I will leave you whether I have a penny or not', or whether it was 'I will kill you', I can only speculate, because, blinded by tears and rage, I broke away from him and fumbled with the French doors to the outside terrace.

I tore them open and ran outside to escape his detestable words. It was raining and I was in heels. I caught my heel in a crack on the flagstones and went plunging down the wide steps to the terrace below. I smashed into the stone and felt a terrible burning pain in my hip.

An ambulance was called; the first of four times an ambulance would come to Clarendon over the next eighteen months.

After that night I walked with a pronounced limp for the remaining months that I was able to walk at all.

Chapter 25

He stayed, and I made assumptions because he stayed. I assumed he remained because, after all, he bore me some affection. I wasn't quite enough of a fool to imagine that the lifestyle our marriage provided him wasn't the primary reason he was still there. I was, however, fool enough to believe that he had resigned himself to his rather enviable lifestyle and had ended his affair as per my demands.

He did keep his silly little job and made much of it, spending far too many hours cloistered in his study on the phone having long discussions about other people's money. I did not like this change in our routine but I was clever enough to know that I needed to make some sort of allowances, and I thought I was being rather supportive letting him alone for several hours during the week.

Inevitably he wanted more, and left with little notice for a week-long trip to dreadful Los Angeles, and I could see the writing on the wall. Christmas was approaching, and when he returned, I let him know in no uncertain terms that I expected the two weeks of the holiday at Clarendon to be one of *uninterrupted* family time. He was adjusting his tie in the mirror when I spoke to him of this, and so I was addressing his back, though I could see the tightening of his jaw in the mirror.

He said, "When you say uninterrupted family time, I imagine that means you wish to decline all of the invitations we have accumulated to Christmas events in Newport."

I made a little moue of distress, but it was wasted on him as he was not looking at my reflection in the mirror behind him. "Darling, you know, since I shattered my hip, that prolonged standing or walking is painful to me, and -"

He cut me off abruptly. "Yes, of course your injury must certainly act against your natural social inclinations. I quite understand."

"That isn't fair, and why are you acting this way? I thought -"

He turned to face me. "Oh leave off, Sunny. If you don't wish to go, we won't go. Nothing changes. You know, a curious thing happened to me at the club today."

"Oh, what?"

"George Milford came by and patted me on the shoulder, and in a rather embarrassed way asked me if I would care to discuss your situation with him. He said he'd been through something similar."

"Something similar? I don't understand. Betsy has never broken her hip. Maybe he was talking about his mother, she -"

He sat down beside me on the bed. "No, Sunny, he wasn't talking about hip injuries. He wanted me to know that he had been through the difficulties of dealing with an alcoholic family member, his sister I believe it was. He recommended a nice little facility up in Westchester. Said I should contact them for you."

I sputtered in rage. "An alcoholic? I am certainly not an alcoholic. My God, where would he ...? Oh, I see, he got that from you, didn't he, darling? It's you that has been spreading that story about. It explains so much. Mother called yesterday and said that she had been waylaid, is how I believe she put it, by Gloria Rutherford after their luncheon. It seems Gloria's son has been recently sent to Menninger's, and she wanted to commiserate, one mother of an alcoholic failure to another. Mother was furious but of course didn't let it show. Tell me, why would you start this awful rumor? Surely there can be no benefit to you in it, and it makes me look dreadful. I want you to stop it immediately, and to the people you have already told, seek them out and say you were mistaken. You will look foolish, I realize, but you brought this on yourself, after all. Good Lord, what were you thinking?"

He stood, unperturbed, and walked towards the door. Turning, he smiled slightly at me. "No, I'm not going to do that, Sunny. You see, you must realize that while you have a vast limitless indifference to what people think about you, it is not a feeling I share. For over a decade I have been perceived as the silly lapdog of a spoiled woman. Now I am perceived as the rather tragic caretaker of my alcoholic wife. It creates a certain sympathy among the people whose opinions I do care for. They all thought you were somewhat mad or phobic. A problem with the drink is much more palatable somehow."

I sat up and thumped my fists onto my lap. "I will not have this!"

He laughed outright. "Then accept an invitation, Sunny, venture out into the world, flags flying. Prove me a liar."

"But ... but you know I don't have a drinking problem."

He shrugged. "I suppose, but I don't know that you aren't somewhat mad. I wonder at times."

I lay back, exhausted by this exchange. "You know what, darling, you're right. I don't care what they think, and personally I have never met such a boring, insular group in my life. It's rather pathetic that you care so much what other people think of you. It seems rather, oh I don't know, *desperate*, actually. Do you ever feel that?"

He shrugged again. "Yes, well not everyone has your grand and glorious indifference to other people and the world. It happens that I do care what people think and that I do enjoy company. Were I to share the sad truth of the matter with them -"

"What sad truth is that, as you perceive it?"

"The sad truth is that you think other people are beneath notice. If I told them that, I would be shunned by association, and that I will not do. You see, Sunny, you have your world and it's enough for you. It is not enough for me, nor do your own children seem to share your desire that they abdicate life in the existing world and orbit around you like lesser planets. No, I'm afraid that your world is not that tempting. But don't let it bother you, darling, you're the queen of your bedroom and couch, and your kingdom is forever safe from usurpers. Now, I really must be going. I'll see you later this evening."

He blew me a kiss and swept out the door. It might be asked why I would endure his insults and his public lies about me. From this side of the veil, even I have a hard time justifying that. At the time I told myself that I truly did not care what others said and thought of me, as long as I could be left alone, alone but with my family when I wanted them. I also felt that, in spreading these silly rumors, my husband was getting some of his own back at me for the events at Clarendon when I had made him soundly face his future, or lack thereof, without me.

I felt that in time he would calm down and all would be well.

He did seem daily to gain in stature and confidence in those weeks going up to Christmas. I know now that it was because he had finally steeled himself to kill me, and because for the first time in years he could see a future that interested him.

I merely thought he was acting like a small boy and preening at his little job, a job, I might add, which paid less than a tenth of what I spent annually on plantings for my gardens in Newport.

The Christmas holidays passed without incident, and then on the evening of December twenty-sixth he shot a syringe filled with insulin into my holiday eggnog and I became immediately lightheaded and had to have both he and my son carry me to bed.

The events of the intervening hours I remained in ignorance of for some time as I had slipped into a coma, and when I awoke, three days had passed and I was in a small hospital room at Columbia Presbyterian in the city.

Chapter 26

I had never liked hospitals, and when I awoke in one, I focused on all the wrong things. I was so stunned to find myself back in a hospital for the second time in a few months that, instead of requesting a full investigation of my condition, I argued with the nurses and my poor doctor about the rules against smoking and complained of the food, insisting that Maria or my husband send out for my meals.

My husband, I noted, looked terrible but I imagined it was out of concern for me when now, obviously, I know he must have been both terrified of exposure and horrified at how badly his attempt to kill me had gone awry.

My doctor ordered a round of blood tests that came back with shockingly low levels of blood sugar, and he informed me portentously that I had a condition called Hypoglycemia.

I became uninterested in his diagnosis when he told me that I would need to give up sweets or risk becoming diabetic. I told him to go away.

Less easy to dispose of was the fool of a psychiatrist who was sent in to speak with me. He was the result of my husband's rumor mongering about my supposed alcoholism and refused to leave my room, despite my repeated orders that he should do so. Finally, in desperation, I agreed to answer his silly questions. No, I told him, I had seldom been happy or felt fulfilled since leaving childhood. No, I was certainly not suicidal, though I didn't much care if I continued to live, and finally I told him that I hoped my future would be more rewarding than my past had been.

Almost immediately afterward I was appalled that I had said such things to a stranger, that I had said such things at all. I wasn't miserable, was I? I finally reasoned out to myself that the distress and shock of awakening in the hospital with no memory of how I had gotten there had temporarily unhinged me emotionally, and that the words I had spoken to him were merely the party line my husband gave everyone, and that I had only said them because, if I had told him the truth about my deep contentment with every facet of my life, he would have never gone away. Everyone knows, I thought to myself, that psychiatrists expect people to be miserable, and if people say anything else, they are told they are delusional. Now I understand that in a situation of uncharacteristic vulnerability, I had indeed spoken truthfully.

My mother came to visit and she was in quite a state. It seems that she had spoken to my maid, Maria, who had told her that my husband had known I was unconscious for hours before he had allowed Maria to call a doctor. I neither believed nor disbelieved her. I felt it was possible that my husband had grown so resentful and irritated by his presumed injustices at my hands that he might not have looked at me closely, but the idea of attempted, or as I now call it, *failed* murder never crossed my mind.

I had three hundred and fifty days left before I would be returned to this hospital to remain there for the rest of my life. *Three hundred and fifty days.* Looking back, I think, on a very repressed level of my subconscious, I might have known that time was ending for me. I didn't learn that it was my husband who was creating that ending, but in a period of six months I had taken two ambulance rides from my home, one of which I had no memory of. So even my customary languor and self-absorption had been breached.

At any rate, the world that I had heretofore ignored was temporarily upon me. My eldest daughter, my beautiful Ala, was getting married to a very nice young member of the Austrian aristocracy, much as I had done at her age, and I had a wedding to orchestrate, and for once I grasped happily at the opportunity to step outside of myself.

No longer secure in my insular world, I spent the next few months in a state of uncharacteristic busyness, and involved my husband and myself in the necessary balls and teas that precede the union of two great families.

Ala's wedding was to be held in Austria at the grand ducal palace in Vienna, a privilege allowed only to those with the blood of the Hapsburgs, something that both my daughter and her fiancé possessed. All of this necessitated a prolonged European sojourn, and fool that I was, I believed that my husband was as happy during that time as I was. In fact I was enjoying my unaccustomed travels so much that I even agreed that he and I and Cosima could spend a few weeks in his beloved London to allow him to show our daughter her father's old home.

But wait, I'm not telling everything. I have difficulty looking back on this with clarity even now, for it all makes me seem such a terrible fool. My husband was not happy, of course. During our time in Europe, he was continually calling and wiring his mistress and sending her gifts. I had overheard several of his calls. He was not discreet, he was desperate, nearly deranged with his desire to be free of me, although not of my money. You see, he had actually attempted to murder me a second time before we left for Europe.

Two months after I had awakened from my abbreviated coma in a strange hospital room, I awoke covered in my own blood, and drenched in my urine, on the floor of my bedroom at Clarendon. I'm not certain why he always chose Clarendon for these assaults, possibly because in the city there is such a plethora of gifted men of medicine, and in the vastness of the city no-one had heard about my supposed drinking problem. The Newport medical community may have seemed to him unlikely to run nerve-racking tests which would unmask his actions. At any rate, we were at Clarendon for the weekend, our first weekend since my coma. How impatient he must have been for me to die.

I had been a little more careful with my food and drink intake following the debacle at Christmas, and that evening was no exception. I had a plain hamburger and a glass of milk with dinner. Moments after finishing, I became weak and dizzy. I asked my husband to assist me to bed. He did so, and without a word of concern or a suggestion that a doctor be called, he turned off the lights and left the room.

I did not, as before, sink into unconsciousness. I can remember the next few moments well. I needed to use the bathroom, but was afraid that I was too dizzy to walk unaided. I called out weakly for my husband, but if he heard me, he did not come. So I reached for the house phone by the bed to summon Maria, but it was not there.

Despite my sickened state, I can clearly remember the phone, which had always been on my bedside table, was not there that night. My bladder was giving me urgent signals by then, so I shakily rose from the bed. The darkened room spun in circles and I felt myself falling.

I tried to grab for the bed, but missed, and my weakened hip spasmed owing to the shaking of my legs, and instead of falling forward, I collapsed backwards, slamming my head against the marble floor. My last conscious feeling was of my bladder releasing, and then all went black.

I know now that my husband, if he had been the one to find me, would have left me laying there until I bled to death from my head wound. I wish he had been the one to find me, God how I wish that.

Instead, an innocent little girl came in to kiss her mother good night. Turning on the lights, Cosima found me on the floor and began screaming for her father. 'Foiled again!' as they say in the old melodramas.

I was removed by ambulance for the third time in a year. That time I think maybe I had my intuitions, but I would not let myself recognize them consciously. Quietly, I planned some changes that I hoped would lessen such incidents. It was all too late, of course.

No-one tries to kill someone not once but twice unless they hate them deeply. His course was set, and in his own mind at least, there could be no deviation. I think he honestly saw it as either him or me, and in the end we will all try to save ourselves first.

And yet that summer I was given one last chance to save us both, and just as he botched giving me a quick, clean death, I botched giving either of us a clean, dignified escape.

Chapter 27

We returned for my last living summer to Clarendon in July.

July in Newport, Rhode Island, must be the loveliest place in the world. Newport's almost navy blue sky, and the summer aqua of the ocean, provided a flawless backdrop for my beautiful white house and emerald lawns, dotted with the rose bushes and rhododendrons I had cunningly placed for color every few feet.

I was still in my atypical mood of trying to associate more with people. I had actually enjoyed myself in Europe, and my son's coming of age was approaching. I planned my first, and as it happened, last great party at Clarendon that summer.

The invitations exhorted all the guests to wear white, and the party took place at twilight, that most enchanting of hours. I had hired tableaux players to dress in costumes from the Twenties and to play assorted games of croquet at strategic viewing spots. The players, dressed in white flannels and filmy gowns, seemed both eerie and otherworldly in that special setting.

I was, as always, somewhat removed from those around me, but that night as I wandered through my gardens, smiling. I did not feel, as I customarily did, as though I were alone inside a painted world looking out. I felt as though all of us, all two hundred white clad guests wandering through the gardens, had joined me for a moment inside my painted world and were happy in there. Or maybe we had all traveled through some sort of warp and entered the pages of Mr. Fitzgerald's wonderful story, 'The Great Gatsby'. I had created a faux land of perfection, and if the evening held the soft misty focus of unreality, it was one that everyone seemed to glory in.

I looked across the pretty scene with pleasure, hoping to catch my husband's eye. I thought maybe he would feel the pull of it all as well; maybe feel proud and enchanted at what I had created, and look at me, at least for a moment, with his old pride and desire. He did glance across the lawn at me, but instead of happiness, all I could see in his eyes was a bottomless resentment.

I was completely taken aback. Hadn't this been what he had dreamed of when we married? Wasn't this the very sort of night he had spent over a decade trying to draw me into?

The evening lost its soft white focus for me and turned sepia, and the pleasant muted voices suddenly became the usual shrill biting tones I had always avoided. Unnoticed and unmissed by anyone, I drifted away, a ghost at my own gathering, and took myself to bed. If he came in that night, I have no recollection of it.

Foolishly, like an unwanted pet, I refused to slink away to try to find a more welcoming human companion. In the waning days of summer, I tried everything to please him.

I purchased, for the first time, tickets to the Newport Music Festival. He escorted me; of course he did. He had been asking that we attend every summer for fourteen years. But his arm under my hand was as hard as iron, and his face held the set expression of a man determined to get through an unwanted situation as stoically as possible.

Oh, I see so clearly now that he had left me long before. Good God, by that time he had already tried to kill me twice, though in my own defense, that much I did not know. What I did know was that he could hardly bear to be near me. Instead of sitting him down and asking what he felt he needed in terms of money to begin anew, I sat him down and asked him if I gave him a certain amount of independent funding, would he feel happier again?

He was like a hound on a scent when I asked, unable to conceal his eagerness. He came straight to the point. "How much?"

I will admit I was disappointed. I still hoped even at that late date he would refuse my offer and say all of the reassuring things I was longing to hear. I did not show my hurt to him. I said, in what I hoped was a careless voice, "Oh, I was thinking a million or so, would that suit?"

Without pausing he threw back. "Two million would, as you put it, suit much better."

I nodded. "Fine. I'll contact Morris and he can begin to put the wheels in motion."

Quick as a dart he said, "No, don't trouble yourself, darling. I'll write to Morris straightaway and tell him to release the funds. He'll call you, naturally, but since you are the one who brought it up, I can't imagine that you will discourage his going forward with this dispersal."

I looked away from him and merely shook my head.

He moved over, and for the first time in months, voluntarily took my hand. "I do appreciate this, Sunny, I ... well, I thank you. It's for the best, you'll see."

I smiled slightly and excused myself. I felt many things, including disgust at both of us - him for his ill-concealed greed and self-loathing, me for my pathetic gratitude at his use of the word 'darling'.

I hesitated at the door, knowing I shouldn't say it, but doing so anyway. "Tell me, darling. If two million buys me a pat on the hand, what's your rate for a one-time fuck?"

If he was shocked or angered he gave no sign. He laughed slightly. "I don't know, Sunny. No-one has ever asked me that before. I'll tell you what, let's get these two million dollars out of the way, and we can always revisit the situation."

I cannot bear how much I debased myself with him, for him - and for what and why?

I have some theories, for what it's worth. I feared growing older; I feared being left alone, a state I had not yet learned to think of as desirable, though soon I would feel differently; I loved him still and wanted him still, or thought I did, which amounts to the same thing; I had never been able to imagine or plan for the future, so the thought of being left made me feel utterly hopeless; I was jealous of her and could not bear to think of him with another woman; I was unhappy, and since he was the one who had made me unhappy, it didn't seem fair that he should get to enjoy life if I couldn't.

I do know how small and petty that sounds. I suppose it is, or rather I was, but I had never had to share and I'm not certain that jealousy and a desire to strike back are emotions native only to the tribe I was born to.

The most ironic reason, and I think my husband would find it in him to laugh about this, was that I was more terrified than ever before of being alone, as for the first time in my life my good health seemed to have deserted me. After all, when one wakes up not once but twice from a coma-like state, you do begin to fear its recurrence.

All of these things felt true to me then, and so behind his back I contacted Morris. I told him to go ahead and give my husband the two million dollars but to put down obstacles. I told him to act as though it was all his own idea, and to involve Sims if necessary. Like a well-paid lackey, Morris obliged me without questions or advice, both of which I was sorely in need of.

He wrote my husband a series of letters explaining that a one-time disbursement of two million dollars would attract a considerable amount of taxation which would have to be funded additionally from the trust, and that, as my trust officer, he was forced to refuse his request. My husband raged and argued, and it didn't matter a bit, the will of money must always be respected. In the end, Morris set up a two million dollar trust for the Metropolitan Museum. My husband would receive, during his lifetime, the interest from this trust...a little over one hundred thousand dollars a year. The terms of the trust, and the amount, were irrevocable, as was my husband's decision to murder me because he knew there were finer alternatives available to him. In my will he would have received fifteen million outright, as well as the Manhattan apartment, Clarendon and all the contents of both houses - such wealth and power against which no silly bank manager's annual salary of a mere six figures would suffice. He must have foreseen a grand and glorious life with such wealth at his fingertips and, as a bonus, the everlasting freedom from a dreadful, neurotic wife who continually ruined his pleasure in his surroundings.

I imagine he felt he had earned it. I imagine that he even felt I deserved a death sentence. After all, he would have reasoned, Sunny didn't much enjoy life, and he did, just not with her. It was really for the best for everyone.

I like to think that if he had foreseen exactly what he was about to sentence me to, he would have drawn back. I like to think that.

There was so little time left. September came and we returned to the city where Cosima attended school. I had never sent any of my children away to boarding school, or to summer camps. I always wanted them with me. Time is fleeting in all things, but with children its feet are winged.

I suppose I should be grateful that he gave me enough time to see my big pair grow up, but I am not.

Chapter 28

Every year we spent Christmas in Newport, at Clarendon Court. But that final year our plans had changed. My mother was ill and had asked that we celebrate our holiday in the city with her. Later I learned that she had made this request so that I would not travel to Newport again, as she, unlike me, felt that she knew exactly what the genesis of my illnesses was.

I was sorry to miss my favorite holiday in the house I loved so dearly, but I agreed to her request. It was an extraordinarily pleasant surprise, then, when my husband, who had remained distant and emotionally, if not physically, unavailable, suggested kindly that we go up to Clarendon for a three day pre-Christmas weekend. I was delighted.

My son, Alexander, even agreed to meet us up there. He was at Brown and had his own small apartment, and I missed him terribly, so the idea of having him with us for a few days increased my pleasure in the plan.

When we arrived at Clarendon, I immediately placed a call to the local plant nursery and ordered a large tree to be delivered. My husband made an unpleasant remark about the silly extravagance of having a tree for a brief weekend.

I was anxious to please him and also to show my gratitude for this bonus family time, so I refrained from pointing out that it was my money and I could do with it as I wished.

Instead, I smiled pleasantly at him and told him that, yes, it did seem extravagant, but Christmas trees were so lovely, and besides, after we left, the servants who remained at Clarendon year round would doubtless enjoy it.

After being nasty about it, he acted as though he could care less, and wandered restlessly around the living room, picking up and replacing objects to examine them, as though he had not already lived with them for over a dozen years. He seemed very nervy to me and I asked him what the matter was, but he only stared at me blankly.

I tried to make a joke of it, asking him if he was looking over our things and mentally pricing them for an auction at Christie's, but he became visibly annoyed at me again and said that I was being ridiculous and dramatic and, worst of all, tedious, and that if I was going to behave this way, he at least had work to do and would see me later for an early dinner.

I was puzzled how could I be both dramatic and tedious.

I didn't follow him but spent a really lovely afternoon with Alexander and Cosima, decorating the tree and telling them for the hundredth time the stories of each treasured old ornament. Both Cosima and Alexander echoed my views about how much we missed Ala, and I had to restrain Cosima from calling her that very minute. I reminded her of the time difference in Austria and said we would all call her in the morning.

How I wish I had made that last call. While I was able to hear my beloved elder daughter's voice many times over the years when she would visit me in my coma coffin, she was never able to hear me tell her all of the many things about her that I was proud of, and that is just one more great loss and regret to me.

I didn't know, of course, no one knew except my husband, and when he rejoined us for an early dinner, I noticed that he looked pale. But he snapped at me for inquiring after his health and berated me for choosing to have a sundae for dinner instead of the roast that the rest of them were eating.

Cosima mischievously requested the same as I was having for dinner, and I made a face at her and told her that she had to wait until she grew up to be allowed to eat things that were so bad for her.

The children laughed, but not my husband. His face was set in what I thought was a look of boredom at our company and at our planned outing to the movies. I know now that what I saw was a look of stoic determination. He knew the hours ahead would be difficult and was doubtless reminding himself that, like Macbeth, 'If it were done when 'tis done, then it 'twere well it were done quickly.'

I offered to cancel our planned outing to the movies but he turned that around on me, rolling his eyes and saying, "Oh, of course, let's cancel our plans for the evening. Never mind that the children are looking forward to it or that I might have been. Sunny wants to stay in, so let's all stay in."

I was hurt, protesting that wasn't what I had meant at all. The children were clearly uncomfortable as they stared down at their plates. He waved my protestations aside, and standing, strode towards the dining room doors, adding coldly, "If the rest of you are coming, then do come along now. I, for one, plan to see this movie."

Cosima raised her eyebrows comically at me as we all hustled out of the room to follow him. "Goodness, I never realized that Daddy was such a Dolly Parton fan." We all giggled behind our hands.

The movie we were off to see was called 'Nine to Five', and at the time I thought my husband was being ridiculous. After all, this was a man who could sit in an empty room listening to Sibelius by the hour. I understand now that he would have rushed us to a showing of trash barrels emptying if only to speed the evening along. He couldn't do what needed to be done until bedtime.

When we returned from the movie, the children and I went into the living room to sit by the tree and chat. My husband said there was a call he had to make regarding a report that couldn't wait. I shrugged it off. Increasingly he had been using the slightest excuses to avoid me, and I could see that this so-called family weekend was going to be no different.

An hour later, he rejoined us and asked me solicitously if there was anything he could bring me. I was taken aback by his many mood swings but still grateful for his show of husbandly concern. I told him that, yes, if there was any soup left in the kitchens, I would enjoy a cup.

A few moments later he brought it to me and I thanked him. He met my eyes and the look in his was so troubled and sad that I reached up and stroked his face in puzzled concern. It had been so long since I had touched him.

At his reaction, I was sorry I had bothered. He jerked back as though I had struck him, and at my querying expression, he shook his head. "Sorry, darling, I think I might be getting a cold and I don't want to expose you to it."

I pretended to believe him and drank my soup. Within minutes the room began to swirl. That is when I finally understood. It was impossible not to know that I had just been drugged, and if he had drugged me, then ...

It all fell into place.

I rose shakily and my son, concerned, rushed to my side, asking what was wrong. I told him not to worry, I was just feeling a bit weak and had better go to bed. I started to move towards the doorway but my legs buckled and everything swam around me. My son picked me up and carried me to my bed, Cosima and my husband on our heels.

Alexander wanted to call the doctor but I waved him and Cosima out of the room. I fully planned to see them again but at that time I needed to be alone with my husband. Dizzy and sick though I was, I felt I could still make myself clear, at least clear enough for long enough to let him know that I knew.

He moved towards the bed where Alexander had laid me, his face looming above me as though through a dirty window.

I blinked trying to clear my vision. "Help me undress, please," I asked him.

Solicitously he assisted me. I could feel the drug working against my consciousness but I fought it. I was no longer afraid.

When I was in my nightgown and propped against my pillows, I weakly patted the edge of the bed. "Sit down, please."

He did so wordlessly. His pupils were pin points; I believe he had taken a smaller dose of whatever he had drugged me with.

"You have drugged me, haven't you? It's been you all along, hasn't it? There was nothing wrong with me at all. My God, my God, you stupid man, you have been trying to kill me. For what, the money in my will? God you're a fool, they'll never let you have it. My mother will stop you."

He looked at me sadly. "Maybe she will, maybe she won't, but either way, Sunny, you will not be here to observe it. You are going to die tonight."

His words, even in my weakened state, struck me as ridiculous. He sounded like a bad actor and I told him so. I ordered him out of the room, saying that I planned to sleep off his latest concoction and that we would finish discussing this in the morning.

He didn't move. He remained sitting there, staring at me with eyes that finally, far too late, created a frisson of fear in me.

I realized he was completely serious, he honestly meant to kill me. I opened my mouth to scream, and so quickly I never saw it coming, he struck me hard, splitting my lip. Before I could react, he shoved his hand over my mouth and began muttering to himself, "Jesus, Jesus, you fool, you imbecile. There can't be blood." Then to me, "Stop it, stop this struggling."

He pushed me down to the cold floor, keeping his hand over my mouth all the while. He straddled me, and using his legs to restrain me, he reached inside his pocket with his one free hand, producing a syringe. I was screaming in utter panic, but all sound was muffled by his hand.

He leaned down close to my face and whispered, "Goodbye, Sunny, goodbye, darling tormentor."

He lifted up my gown, tightening his knees around me to prevent movement, and reached inside my panties to push the hypodermic between my legs. When he depressed the needle, it went through soft tissue and the instant burning pain made my back arch in agony.

He maintained his position on top of me until there was no longer any need to do so. He blinded me - that was the first thing that happened – and the world went instantly black. I thought I was drifting away into unconsciousness, but I wasn't quite yet. It was simply the first nail in my coma coffin, sudden blindness.

I heard him sobbing and repeating over and over that he was sorry, so sorry, but he had no other choice, so sorry, sorry, sorry. I felt his weight leave my body and he must have stood and grabbed me by my ankles, for my next sensation was one of movement and discomfort as my nightgown rode up to my waist and the cold marble pressed against my back as he dragged me across the floor.

I did not know for a few moments that he had pulled me into my bathroom until I heard the water begin to run in the sink. He must have decided that nobody would fall onto the floor and end up flat on their backs with their clothes shoved around their waists like that, so I felt him touching me again to roll me over on my stomach. I tried to speak, to beg, to ask him to stop; to at least pull my nightgown down. The floor was so cold against my stomach.

But I couldn't make my mouth move. My tongue felt swollen and huge. I heard the crick of his knees as he knelt down beside me and I felt his panting breaths against my cheek.

He said aloud, "I'm sorry, Sunny. I have to close your eyes. I can't bear you staring at me like this."

I was dazed, terrified and confused. What did he mean close my eyes? My eyes were closed. All I could see was blackness, but then I felt his shaking fingers against my lids as he gently tugged my eyelids down, and I knew that I was blind.

Inside I wailed and screamed with the loss of my sight. Outwardly, at best I made a small moan of protest.

He heard me and sighed. "I know, but it's not for much longer now. Sleep, Sunny, go now."

I heard him stand and I heard his shoes clicking across the marble. Every sound was magnified in my black fear.

I listened curiously as he opened the windows and when the icy night air blasted across my prone body, I understood. My bladder released in terror and he made a small disgusted sound, followed by a strangled laugh.

"Sorry, darling, I wish I could clean you up a bit, but you've just erased the last possible bit of evidence and so I'll have to leave you like this."

Those were his last words to me.

I did not lose consciousness all that quickly after all. I felt the pain in my mouth and the rapidly increasing coldness of the room. My body began to spasm and everything started to hurt, and I felt it all. It seemed to last forever until finally the blackness in front of my eyes was matched inside my head, and for a long time there was nothing at all.

Chapter 29

It's been a year since I finally died. I can't speak for the rest of the dead, but I can say that, for me, so far it's been wonderful.

I didn't wait a minute after I was released from my coma coffin by my long overdue death to begin my return home to Clarendon. Over the thousand or so years that I seemed to have spent trapped in my coma coffin, there were times when I was able to rise temporarily from my body but never when I wanted to, not when my children came, nor when they eventually brought their own children.

It was always an involuntary thing, that sudden pull and I was out for a few minutes. When I was out, I was able to see again, and oh how marvelous that was - at first. But it's like the old saying, 'What mine eyes beheld.'

What my spirit eyes beheld was a scene of such horror that I would immediately recoil from the ugliness of it all and squeeze my eyes shut again. My body on that bed was an abomination; there is no better word to describe what science had made of me.

I had been a slender, pretty blond woman all of my life. I stayed that way right up until the night my husband tried to kill me. But how quickly, and how hideously, I deteriorated. The thing on the bed, the thing that was, me was a twisted, deformed shell.

I perceived thin limbs, hands that protruded in claws, and feet that were in the strangest, most unnatural positions. My hair was gray and nearly gone. My face ... my face was that of an idiot, but one who was suffering, an idiot with a twisted mouth and an expression of agony. Well, that much was true. I was in agony during those years.

The infrequent escapes from my body were usually brought on when the touch of too many strange hands doing too many ugly, intimate things to my poor body would shock me into awareness and send my spirit spiraling up towards the ceiling. The novelty of this wore off quickly because, try as I might, I could never get any further away from my shell than a few feet.

I could not leave that God-forsaken, cursed room of living death. I used to try. I would attempt to pry my spirit self through the window, or try to float out the open door into the hallway, but every attempt at escape ended the same way. I would be slammed back into the decaying darkness of my body coffin, and ten years might pass before I was able to rise up again for another futile view of freedom and a peek at how much worse my living corpse appeared.

It's over now and I won't look back. I said I can't speak for how others who are dead find death, but I did see many dead on that blessed day when I was finally released. I caught glimpses of them as I floated free at last through the hospital corridors.

I heard their pleas to me to stop, to join them, to go where they were going, to be with them in the light. I did not pause once in my flight past them. I breezed through the corridors and out the lobby doors, and for the first time in twenty-eight years, I was outside again.

For the first time in all of memory, I was happy. It's ironic, I know, but maybe there will always be people who are better at living only after they are dead. I know I am one of them.

I found that I could fly, and I rose high over the great city of Manhattan and laughed aloud at its beauty. I do not chastise myself for what I did not grasp or do during my walking life. Whatever my failings had been, I was punished a thousand times, a million times, seven hundred million times over. I simply enjoyed the view from on high.

Slowly I followed the enchanting New England coastline to Newport, and watched the ocean off to my side. Funny though, when I tried to join the breezes and drift out over the waves, I found that I was tossed back to land.

This ghost business is all rather new to me and it is possible that crossing water is one of the things we cannot do. Well, no matter. There is nowhere I wish to go and no-one I wish to see.

My husband, who is now I suppose my ex-husband, since he divorced me a year into my coma, would say that by that statement I haven't changed at all. He would be wrong. I am utterly free, in a way I never wanted to be before the last night of my waking life. I reside between the rooms of my beautiful house and the shore, along the water's edge, with a light spirit. Oh, that is not correct, is it? I reside as a light spirit.

My house, which I still think of as mine, was sold long ago to another family with a great deal of money. Mercifully, they made few changes and they spend very little time here. I think they will spend less time now that I have returned. I don't mean to be a haunting presence, but I can tell that they know I am here, and while I am sorry that it disturbs them, I will not be leaving again.

I am perfectly aware that there is a place beyond here. You don't have to be dead to know that. Anyone who has ever stood on a shore after a storm and watched the black clouds break to allow in golden light, knows that there are other places, maybe better places, but here is my place, and here I will remain.

I do not know if I am turning my back on heaven or somewhere in-between. Heaven, I suppose, as I never did hurt anyone while I lived, and I don't plan to do so now that I am dead. I lost my rage a long time ago, and wanted only to be somewhere familiar and beautiful again, and here I am. Besides, heaven is full of strangers, and I was never comfortable in new surroundings.

The Fourth Death

Colette

The Ghost of Castle Drive

Chapter 30

Of course I didn't see it coming. One minute I was going on with my life, and then I was fighting for it, and then it was over.

I never saw myself as special when I was alive. I think maybe if I'd been given time I might have become a little special; at least I was trying. I never stopped trying, not after I had to drop out of college because I was pregnant, not during the rough hurried years of early marriage and motherhood which happened to me simultaneously. No matter how little time or money, or how few my chances were, I kept trying.

I was taking an extension class the night my husband killed me. I was pregnant again for the third time in five years and, like always, we were living somewhere I didn't much want to be because he was trying something new.

The night he killed me I was a very ordinary woman who was struggling to become someone that things didn't just happen to, and my husband ... well he was his ordinary self too. The thing of it is, though, my husband had never been ordinary and nothing ever just happened to him. He was a rainmaker, and what he wanted, he achieved. When he was around, people could barely restrain themselves from clapping. I was supposed to clap too, and I had, I almost always had, except for that one night - one rainy night when I was tired and pregnant again and maybe feeling a little sorry for myself and for the whole camp-follower lifestyle I was living. I didn't clap and I didn't pay enough attention to him. I didn't try to make it up to him, even though I understood the rules. Despite how he saw himself, and how I knew by then he wanted to be seen and to be living, I treated him like an ordinary husband and father. I asked him why, just for once, he couldn't have washed the dishes for me.

We had a silly little argument; at least I thought it was silly. Instead of just answering me or shrugging it off, he started a recitation of all that was on him: the responsibilities, the constant need to shine, the expectations, and how he didn't need to hear complaints from me, of all people, because who should know better than me what he sacrificed.

It was the kind of argument every married couple has had hundreds of times over the course of a marriage, but those kinds of arguments weren't the norm in our marriage. I had spent our years together listening to his stories and applauding his accomplishments, and if I clapped hard enough and acted very excited, then he might deign to ask me about my day, or even better, play with the girls for half an hour or so.

I knew all of that. I knew it that night.

I knew he saw himself as the big hero for having let me go to class and for having stayed in for three whole hours with the girls. I understood my script too. I was supposed to rush in and thank him at least three times for letting me go off gallivanting to the university's extension class and then encourage him to tell me either his latest story of heroism from the emergency room or the story of someone else's incompetence and how he had to go in and clean it all up.

This was our routine, but it was late, and I was wet from the rain, and pregnant and tired, and I slipped up. Instead of going into the kitchen and just pouring us both the aperitifs he liked to drink before bedtime, I went into the kitchen and saw the sink full of dirty dishes and asked him why he couldn't have washed them for me.

That's a normal enough question, or I imagine it's normal enough in other people's marriages. It was atypical for us, though, and the stunned look he gave me made me feel like I had asked or said something much more explosive than my innocuous comment.

We had some undetonated landmines in our marriage, he and I. Governments were doing that back then, back when I was alive. They buried bombs in the ground. I think they said it was to protect our battle lines, but they didn't seem to work like that, the buried bombs, because it seemed like every night on the news I was watching Walter Cronkite tell some sad story about an innocent civilian who had stepped on one and gotten blown to kingdom come.

That's a pretty good description of what happened to me, an innocent civilian who unknowingly detonated a buried land mine and got blown apart. There were children who stepped on the mines too - they are called casualties of war. My children sleeping in their beds that night became casualties of war.

Seeing the look on his face, I backed down. I always thought that some place out ahead of me in a Colette I wanted to be, but wasn't yet, I might in truth set off some real landmines. I might, for instance, bring up the other women and the lies - my God there were so many lies - but it wasn't going to be that night.

I was too young and my babies, including the one in my stomach, were too young, and I hadn't had enough life and time yet to become the future Colette who could begin conversations like that. It was a pretty big breakthrough for me to even bring up the dishes but, seeing his face, I backed down. You couldn't criticize him and I knew that. I started backpedaling. I tried to make a little joke about saying it, telling him that I was turning into an old nagging, pregnant shrew.

He didn't laugh but he did take the little glass of liqueur I poured for him. I tried to shore him back up, asking about his new on-call job at the hospital, but he was too displeased with me to engage and I was very tired. I decided we were both exhausted and that maybe it wouldn't hurt anything if, just once, I just went bed and left him unappeased. I told myself I would be extra-attentive in the morning and I would remember never to ask him to wash the dishes again and it would probably be fine.

He let me kiss him on the head and told me that, no, he was going to stay up and read for a while. He said it was the first chance he had had all night to be alone. It was a direct hit at me, a reminder that I had made him stay with the children.

There was this entire subtext to his remark as well; in that at least we weren't so different than other married couples. In every marriage something as simple as 'Good morning' can mean 'Are we okay?', 'Are you still in this with me?', 'Do you still love me, like me, want me, want us?'.

In my case, that night, since he was punishing me, his remark meant *I am trapped in this small cramped apartment with you and two children I never wanted. I am trapped in this ill-fitting life that I don't belong in, and it's all your fault, and instead of trying to make it easier on me, you nag me about doing women's work.*

I was pretty versed in marital speak, and in my husband's not so subliminal signals, by then, so I got it in one. Maybe if I had turned back to the living room instead of towards bed, we all would have gone on living - maybe not happily ever after but at least gone on. I didn't feel like sitting down with him, though, and stroking his ego back up with a gratitude I didn't feel anymore.

I guess, if I thought about it at all then, I thought that we would get up and face another day, and if the days were starting to drag for him, then it wasn't any different for me. That phrase 'chain of days' can be pretty apt.

What I understood, though, and saw too late, that he didn't, was that this was simply the life that people went through when they were young and had small kids and not much money. I understood that it would change over time and get easier.

Our parents, and their parents before them, had gone through it and I figured we would too. I also understood that us getting through it with the minimum of trauma and residual resentment rested mostly on me. It was up to me to keep the waters as smooth as possible for him so he didn't give into his desire to make a run for it. If I'd had to declare the state of our union that night, I wouldn't have said his level of disappointment or boredom or frustration was any higher than usual. Nor was my level of stoically concealed sadness any more apparent.

It was just one more night for an ill-suited couple who had been forced by circumstances into a marriage that probably should never have happened, but had anyway. In that, we were pretty typical, I imagine, of millions of other people at that time and place in our country. I thought we would get by, or if not, that it would take a few years longer - at least until the kids were a little older - before it ended.

How could I have known that for him it had become truly unbearable? He didn't tell me; well he couldn't have. That would have been an admission of failure, and at least in his own eyes, he could never fail.

So there we were: the tired pregnant woman who, if not happy, still thought she might become that way; and the tired desperate man who had begun to feel like he couldn't breathe anymore, and I had, without knowing it, put a spark to the tender of his growing anger.

It was inevitable that his anger faced outward at the girls and me; nothing was ever his fault. So, if you can, try to look through his eyes that last night. There he was, a young brilliant surgeon, a winner by any standard, trapped in a small on-post apartment that dissatisfied him, never mind that it was by his choice alone that he had landed us there.

Chapter 31

I'm a ghost by choice but I don't know if that happens in every case. Seconds after he shattered most of my bones and carried me back to our bedroom for me to finish bleeding, I saw the light that people talk about. I even saw my oldest one standing inside it, smiling, waiting, not broken anymore. If I could have left, I would have. I didn't want to stay in this terrible little apartment, a place where even before he killed us we had never been happy.

I stayed here, and have continued staying here, because I am a mother and my tiny one would not come to me when I called her. There is a long and terrible story leading up to our entrapment here, but I need to look further backward to put it in context.

I didn't live very long, but half that short time was spent with my husband. We met when we were twelve and eventually I fell as madly in love with him as a thirteen year old girl can be with a thirteen year old boy.

Life came at me pretty fast in terms of pregnancy, marriage and babies, and trying to keep it all together in increasingly stressful situations, and I had to grow up or we all would have been in a lot of trouble and, as for him, well, he just didn't.

It goes like that sometimes, I think. I learned about it in one of the psychology classes I took. In some people, a series of traumatic events will either create sudden maturity under pressure or they might become frozen at the age they were when things began to become too much for them.

I don't know what happened to my husband that locked him in time and kept him stuck there as a boy. Sometimes I think it was nothing traumatic at all, it was just that he was such a wonderful boy and my husband, despite his emotional immaturity, could still be so smart, so maybe he purposely chose to remain a boy forever because he was good at it. I don't know. I remember that when I used to read the story of Peter Pan, first to Kimmy and then to her and Kristy, I always kind of thought I was reading them the story of their father, or how their father wished he were.

Excerpts from old phone calls and letters float around me like the dust motes in this old apartment. When we were thirteen he wrote me, 'Colette, it's official,

I am going to make varsity this year. Just watch me!' When we were eighteen and not yet dating again, during my freshman year at Skidmore and his first week at Princeton, he wrote, 'Colette, I have decided for certain now, I am going to pursue medicine and become a doctor.'

I made the mistake of sharing his letter with my mother. I meant it to be a funny thing, something she and I could maybe laugh about, how kind of sweet but funny it was that he hadn't changed much, that he was still the same adamant impulsive young guy he had been a few years before. She missed the underlying context and instead began using all her might to push me back into his arms.

I didn't want to return there. Young as we had been when we started, I had shied away from him, sensing something that might cause me hurt down the road. Against all popular opinion from my family and my girlfriends, I told him goodbye. He was so hurt and I hated being the one to do it. I told him that he'd be glad one day, that I was too simple and small town for him, that he was meant for a bigger life than a girl like me could give him. I told him that he thought it was love but it was more about winning and that I knew what he felt for me was a very temporary thing with him, which of course it was, but by the time he realized I was right, the only way out he could see was the knife, the club, the ice pick.

When I shared his letter with my mother, I was just beginning college and loving it, and I loved something else too: a sweet, quiet boy named Dean who wanted to be a teacher.

My mother gave me a rough summer that year. She told me she hadn't raised me for the life of a poor teacher's wife. She said a lot of hurtful things that only make me sad for her when I think about them. I know she must have been tortured by them later on. I did love Dean but I had loved the man I married first, so I gave into my mother and agreed to see him again, to see if I had been wrong in breaking it off a few years earlier, to see if he had grown up a little, become a little easier about things.

He hadn't, but all my old feelings for him revived with a vengeance anyway, and then I was pregnant and it was too late for regrets on my part or the realization on his that I had been right after all about his feelings being a temporary thing, because we had to get married which is a very permanent sort of thing.

Overall I was a quiet sort of person and what I had felt with Dean was a quiet sort of love. With my husband it was different. He had always been overwhelming and dazzling. Being near him made sunspots appear in front of my eyes and I felt dizzy and excited and proud that he wanted me. I didn't understand fully why he wanted me, or ... well no, that's not true ... I guess I did understand and it worried me.

He wanted me back because he had always, without fail, gotten everything he had wanted, and when we were sixteen I had ended our relationship. I had good reasons for doing it and it all would've been fine if only it had been him that had said goodbye, not me. It must have eaten at him, the need to change our ending, and so he began to write to me when he went to Princeton and I went to Skidmore. It's such a waste of all of our lives that he could not move past the one girl who forgot for a moment to be filled with approbation.

If it had only been him who walked away, he would have quickly forgotten me and moved on towards the kind of girls he belonged with; women who had his kind of star quality. All he could have ever wanted from someone as ordinary as me was the chance to reverse that one rejection.

What else could he have ever seen in me? I was pretty in a plain un-showy way while he was beautiful, magnificent. I was smart enough but I didn't have his quicksilver brilliance, the kind that allowed him to grasp every subject, and challenge and master it in a day.

I was adoring, certainly, but everyone treated him that way. He was a golden boy, and at my best I was silver, and all I could offer back in return for his glory was his reflection. Maybe at first that felt good enough to him.

Phone calls after we got married ...

'Colette, I'm going to be a surgeon, I just decided this morning.'

'Colette, can you believe this? I've been asked to scrub in on an appendectomy, the only one in the class who got asked.'

'Colette, I want to take the internship at Columbia Presbyterian. It just feels right, so that's where we're going.'

'Colette, I've been drafted. You'll have to move in with my mom for a while.'

'Colette, I've joined the Green Berets. It's the most elite group even in the special forces.'

'Colette, I won't be able to see you or the girls for a while, but I made my first jump today. It was tremendous. My superiors say I've got what it takes.'

'Colette, this is fantastic, I've been asked to join the boxing team as team doc and I'll get to accompany them to Russia.'

... letters and calls from a little boy who could become so easily excited, and more easily bored, with each new experience.

His initial triumph at wooing me back to his side lasted maybe six months. My parents gave us a very pretty wedding in New York and there was no contest that day - he was the star of the show - and then there were all the people in his family (and this is kind of embarrassing), and in mine too, who treated him like a hero for marrying his pregnant girlfriend.

My own mother told him that she hoped that the baby and I wouldn't be too much pressure on him with med school coming up. I felt small and foolish and very, very grateful to him for marrying me. I know he liked that, the way everyone looked at him with shining eyes for being so noble. Mine were the shiniest eyes of all.

I vowed privately that I would always make sure that he didn't regret picking me, that he would always come first, and that one day down the road he would see that the baby and I added more than we took.

Marriage was a novelty for him at first. It was the beginning of his junior year at Princeton and this time he came back with me, but other than that I worked really hard to make sure he didn't miss out on the Ivy League experience, that his life in college wouldn't be ruined. I was his private cheerleader, typist and geisha, and I clapped the loudest of all when he joined a top fraternity and eating club.

He liked people around all the time so I made our tiny apartment the friendliest place on campus, just the way his mother had made their house back in Patchogue the fun place to go. I never let myself think about Skidmore or Dean, or anything at all except him. And at first I know he really was glad he had married me. Thanks to my efforts, his life at Princeton was even better than before because now he had sex on request, and a mother there to take care of him and shout for joy when he got an A on a paper or was toasted at his eating club by the football team. I understood him so well and I did work very hard, but the reason we had gotten married was that inevitability a baby was coming along. Kimberly arrived, becoming my much-loved little girl and his much-feared foray into a less than golden adulthood. I knew within a week that my careful, adoring balancing act was going to become a tough high wire job.

I had had a difficult labor with Kimmy and ended up needing an emergency Caesarean. I spent a week in the hospital with her, and the day I was released I was still pretty shaky and weak, and a little overwhelmed, knowing I was responsible for this new tiny life. My mom had come to help and I felt that, with her there and maybe a few days of rest, I could manage this immense new thing, becoming a mother while still being a wife to him first.

When he picked me up, he could barely look at me or the baby. I asked him if he was alright and he just nodded. He said he had a surprise for us. I was nervous and so exhausted but I played along, pretending to be dying of curiosity and excitement. Finally his shoulders loosened up and he was grinning with obvious relief, thinking maybe after all things weren't going to have to change too much. I saw the dozens of cars at the curb and inwardly groaned, but outwardly I was smiling with pleasure when he walked Kimmy and me inside our small place to hear thirty of his fraternity brothers and their girlfriends yell 'Surprise' and raise up their Princeton beer steins.

Two-and-a-half years later, Kristy came along - another girl.

And then I was eight months pregnant with our third child.

In the small apartment that fatal night, he brooded because thanks to his unsatisfactory union he had been made to spend an evening babysitting – *babysitting*, and not even for sons, no, just for two unwanted little girls. His seemingly continuously pregnant wife hadn't even managed to give him a son with her repeated unplanned pregnancies.

Then as a topper to a boring, miserable night, his wife, instead of showing the proper appreciation for the sacrifice of his limited free time - of his life, if you pause to think of it - instead of showing him gratitude for everything he did, asked him why the dishes weren't done.

As he watched me striding up the hallway, clumsy and pregnant, I imagine his fists were clenched with all that rage he believed he hid so well. I can't know this for sure but I think he must have spent the next few hours pacing, trying to read, trying to calm himself down, to convince himself that he could get through this life with us, if only for a while longer.

But, for whatever reason, he couldn't totally manage it, and on that night he remained angry and frustrated, knowing he had to be up and at his unsatisfying army job in the morning, a job which was yet another indignity. He had expected to be in Vietnam becoming a hero, not ordering sanitation reports in North

Carolina.

I think all of his disappointments must have fused together.

He would have walked slowly down the hallway to our bedroom, probably almost staggering from the weight of a life he hadn't asked for, and when he got to his bed and he saw one of the unwanted little girls lying in his spot, his anger flared again.

As if her intrusion wasn't bad enough, he found that she had urinated all over his side of the bed. Sometimes it's the very smallest of domestic moments that caves in our carefully held up house of cards.

Within fifteen minutes, the girls and I were all quite dead and he was left standing in the carnage he'd created.

I never did get the chance to find out what I might have become, because what he made me become instead was a dead thing - a ghost, if you prefer.

He, on the other hand, started to live out his real life, the life for which he thought he was destined. I'm still here and I think now it is because I need to filter it all down - our lives, our marriage and how it all started - so that I can understand us today and maybe finally be able to visualize what our ending, if any, is supposed to be.

Chapter 32

He finished Princeton in only three years.

I didn't ask him to do that. It was purely his choice. I was beginning to see that once he conquered something, it was over for him. All conquests were only as good as the competition, and then it was time to move on and shine at something else. He couldn't ever pause and enjoy what he had once he passed his own high bar, and he passed them all. He owned every situation and won every contest he ever set for himself, and I alone understood the terrible emptiness of those wins.

Afterwards, no matter what it was, the excitement and the applause of winning would die down, and since he couldn't live without constant approbation - or had convinced himself he couldn't, which is in the end the same thing - he had to find another world to conquer, another school, another high bar in sports, another woman.

There is an old saying, 'It's lonely at the top'. I said that to him once half-jokingly.

He missed the humor in my remark and answered seriously, "Maybe, but the top is the only place I'm interested in being, Col."

He had his pick of medical schools and he chose Northwestern in Chicago. The summer between Princeton and Northwestern was a bad one for me and it tested every resolve I had about keeping my promises to always be grateful to him for not leaving me and Kimmy behind. We went home to Patchogue and I understood that he wouldn't want to stay with my parents. He was never totally comfortable with my mom. Despite what I saw as her pretty blatant adoration of him, he thought she was critical of him. I tried to tell him that she was less critical of him than of anyone else alive, including her own husband and kids, but the damage had been done during a Christmas visit to Princeton.

It was such a little thing. She had asked him if he would mind watching Kimmy while she and I went grocery shopping. He laughed off her request as a joke and said he had a basketball game. I shot her a look, beseeching her to leave it alone, but my mom was almost as strong willed and set on getting her own way as my husband, so she persisted. She reminded him that he was a husband and father now, that things had changed, and that he needed to share in our new responsibilities.

It was horrible being caught between the grinding wheels of their two determined personalities. I felt ground up into dust. All that came of it was that my mom and I inevitably ended up taking Kimmy, and then I had to listen to my mother demeaning my husband all afternoon. I didn't argue with her but I did beg her never to criticize him to his face again. I told her he couldn't stand any form of criticism. She looked puzzled and asked me why. I could have thrown it right back at her but I just said it was his quirk, and please, for my sake, never do it again.

My husband proceeded to punish me first with sullen silence and then by absenting himself for the rest of her visit. Sometime later, when I suggested that maybe Kimmy and I could stay with my mom and dad during the summer, since he would be gone during the week anyway as he had a summer construction job lined up in Montauk, he sneered and said, "Sure, if you don't mind not seeing me even on the weekends. I'm not comfortable with your mom, Col, and if you don't think I deserve some peace and quiet on the days I can come home, go ahead. I'll pick you and Kimmy up in September on the way to Chicago."

We moved in with his parents for the summer. They had a small house and the biggest bedroom in it was theirs, but since we had the baby, my husband suggested that they move into his and his brother's old room and give us theirs, which they did.

He started his weekday construction job on Montauk, and since it was such a long commute, he camped out during the week in the office on a cot. He came back to his parents' for two weekends and then announced that for extra money he had taken a weekend cab driving job on Fire Island and he didn't know if he'd be able to make it back to Patchogue except for 'fly bys'.

I didn't blame him for wanting to avoid the house; it was a tense and crowded situation. My husband's father, Mac, was a gruff, sometimes loveable, always opinionated, man. He started off each morning by reciting how badly his back hurt him sleeping on his son's old twin mattress, so I begged him and my mother-in-law, Dorothy, to let Kimmy and me move into my husband's old room, but Dorothy, who I always liked but was also a little afraid of said, "No, no, Colette, you and Kim are staying right where you're at. You know he wanted you two in there, and if he gets even one day off, I want him to be comfortable."

My in-laws had three children - two boys and a girl, Judy. Judy was a nice girl, pretty. She worked hard in school and did everything her parents asked, and was nearly invisible to them because my husband's family were son worshippers.

The oldest boy, Jay, had been a quarterback in high school and was voted most popular and most likely to succeed. Back then it drove my husband - his little brother - up the wall. I can't count the number of times that he would tell me how badly it hurt when he would be playing J.V. games and score a touchdown, only to look up in the stands and see his parents weren't there. They were at Jay's games instead. Ironically, Jay wasn't a competitive guy. He was an athlete because it was fun for him; he was popular because he was easy-going and laid back, and everyone liked him.

But as the years passed and high school ended, he drifted aimlessly into a bunch of dead-end jobs, and of course my husband became the school's quarterback and the most popular boy, and then there was Princeton and med school - all of the honors.

I think in the beginning Jay was honestly happy for him, but that wasn't what my husband wanted. He wanted Jay to feel like he was the one looking up at a row of empty seats where no one was watching him. Later on, when Jay got into drugs and trouble, my husband played the part of the helpful brother to the rescue, but I knew he was really happy to see Jeff fail.

That summer Jay was in and out. Judy was still living at home and going to high school, and Kimmy and I took over Mac and Dorothy's bedroom. Every morning without fail, Mac talked about his back killing him and my husband never came home at all. When he would call from Montauk or Fire Island, he tried to sound self-sacrificing and stressed, but I knew him better than anyone and I could tell he was having a blast. I wasn't. In fact my strongest memory of that summer was trying to be invisible and to keep Kimmy quiet so as not to bother anyone, but I didn't say any of that to him. He couldn't stand criticism or hassles.

Sometimes I would get so frightened at night knowing that Kimmy and I weren't novel or fun anymore, I wondered if he would even stop by the house to pick us up on the way to Northwestern or if he would just head straight there and pretend none of it had ever happened - me, the marriage, the baby - so when I talked to him I was extra-cheerful and would ask him all kinds of questions about his job, and I made a point of telling him to try and take some time for himself and have fun too - don't just work all the time. I guess it paid off because he did come back for us and loaded us up into the car my parents had bought for me that summer.

The drive from New York to Chicago is almost a thousand miles, and we made it in one horrendous, non-stop twenty-hour drive. My husband said we had to save every penny from his summer jobs if we were going to make it through the winter and that we couldn't afford motels. My dad had given me two hundred dollars for emergency money and I showed it to him, asking if we couldn't use just maybe fifteen or twenty for a room somewhere in the middle of Indiana.

He yelled at me that he was really trying to get all of us through this, but honest to God, if he had to listen to me whine for another five hundred miles, he would explode. He took the money and gripped the wheel with white knuckles. Of course his yelling had scared Kimmy, who started to cry, and then, because she was hot and tired and cramped in her little seat mashed in amongst all our boxes, she wouldn't stop crying and his face got redder and redder.

He told me to make her stop, but I couldn't, and then I started to cry too, and we drove another two hundred miles without him saying a word, with me sobbing silently and my baby screaming in the back seat until she cried herself out.

When it finally got quiet in the car, he suddenly jerked the wheel over to the left, shooting us into the breakdown lane of the highway. That woke the baby up and she started to cry again in this funny hoarse voice because she had been at it so long. He lowered his head against the wheel and I saw that he was crying too. I didn't reach out to comfort either him or Kimmy because I didn't have anything left. I was doing my best not to start screaming myself. I thought if I did I might not be able to stop, and that he would open the door and leave both of us there on the side of that hot highway.

Through the dusty windshield I stared out with the only dry eyes in the car and saw the silhouette of that great Midwestern city ahead of us in the distance.

Chapter 33

If I had to guess, I would say that my husband would describe our first year in Chicago as a rough one, but for me it wasn't that way at all. For me it felt like I was finally a real wife and a real mother.

Of course, after the summer with my in-laws, any place that I wasn't in the way would have seemed like heaven to me. So, after the initial hassles that come with moving into a new place with a young baby, I was able to catch my breath and look around, and I started to get happy. My parents, my brother and I had lived for a few years right in Greenwich Village in New York and it had been a pretty great experience for me, so I was wide open to getting to know Chicago, which is kind of the New York of the Midwest.

My husband had gotten some leads ahead of time from the housing assistance office at Northwestern and they had lined us up with a tiny one bedroom almost across the street from the medical school. It was small, sure, but it was my first real apartment. I hadn't felt that way at Princeton - there I had just been kind of camping out, trailing my husband around - but that first little place in Chicago was all mine.

We turned a corner of our living room into Kimmy's bedroom – well, anyway, we put her playpen there and I called it her bedroom. I made her a bright red comforter and sewed up curtains for the living room and for the kitchen window out of the same fabric, so everything matched and it looked really cheerful and nice.

In our bedroom I saved up until I could buy a nice navy-colored bedspread, because I knew he liked that kind of neat masculine-looking stuff, and for our first Christmas there I had all his certificates from Princeton framed and hanging right across from the couch so he could see them when he had time to come home and watch TV.

It was a year of beginnings for both of us. He was a first year med student and that's hard for everyone - huge amounts of studying, trying to prove yourself and, in his case, trying to shine more than everyone else. It wasn't happening overnight for him as it usually did, though. Northwestern is a really top medical school and all of the med students were either from the Ivy's like him, or were geniuses who had made the cut from less famous schools than Harvard and Princeton. So, for the first time in a long time, maybe since the days of being Jay's little brother, he had to run just to keep his place.

I hated seeing him hurting and worried like that, but I'll admit it, I loved how he was turning to me for reassurance. I felt like he was glad I was there to type his papers and iron his shirts, and to wait up for him from a night class so he could tell me that he had gotten the highest marks in a dissection or whatever they were doing.

And I was finding out that I had a little tiny bit of star quality of my own. Being alone with Kimmy most of the time in the apartment, and outside when we explored Chicago, I found out that not only did I love being a mother, I was good at it.

I hadn't really had a chance to develop being Kimmy's mom at Princeton or during the summer in Patchogue. I mean I was crazy in love with her from the beginning but it seemed like the first months of her life I spent mostly trying to just keep her quiet. In Chicago that changed. We were alone together and we really got to know each other, and I found out that I had a knack for making my baby happy.

I don't want to make it sound like I was special or better than other mothers, though I did notice that my baby seemed brighter and happier than the other babies I saw when Kimmy and I went to the playground, or took our walks to the grocery store or the laundromat together.

My dad had bought the car mainly for Kimmy and me, but my husband didn't like to be seen walking in front of some of the other med students, a lot of whom were from very wealthy families, so he took it. I didn't mind. Kimmy and I made an adventure out of everything. I talked to her all the time, all day long, and I could tell she was a super smart baby early on. Her big brown eyes could look so serious when I was telling her about how hard her daddy was working to become a doctor, or when I would discuss with her whether or not I should make meatloaf for dinner or spring for pork chops.

She was so cute. Sometimes I could tell that she was really following me to the point where her little forehead would wrinkle up in concentration, and then I'd have to grab her up and kiss her tummy to make her laugh. She had the sweetest little laugh - like bells - and she laughed all the time. I knew how to make her happy and it was the richest experience of my life.

She loved her daddy too. When he was home, her eyes would follow him around everywhere he went and just gleam. I think she was a little star struck by him. Of course he didn't have a lot of time for doing baby stuff - his school workload was incredible and he had picked up a couple of nights driving a cab - but he did try. His idea of a game with her was to spin her around in circles till they both got dizzy, but she hated that game and would start to cry every time till he would almost toss her back to me.

Later, when we had Kristy, that became Kristy's favorite thing in the world, being spun by her daddy, but Kimmy was always a quieter, gentler little girl. My husband said she was too timid but I didn't see it as timidity; she was simply a lot like me and it took her a while to warm up to new experiences.

But Kimmy adored him. I remember a few rare times when he would pick her up and let her fall asleep on top of him while he was studying on the couch. She looked blissed out, in that quiet way of hers, at being close to him. A couple times he'd conk out too, and I could stand there and just look at them both, my tired golden boy working so hard to stay golden and my little girl.

I think I never knew what real happiness was until Chicago.

We lost our wonderful apartment during his sophomore year in medical school and had to move several miles away to a kind of bad neighborhood, so it was a blessing that he had the car, otherwise he would have spent hours riding the bus back and forth to classes. It was a little harder on me and Kimmy, though, because the only grocery store was nearly twenty blocks away and Chicago has freezing winters, and that name - 'the windy city' - well it's not just a tag.

But I'd bundle her up like a little papoose and as we'd do our errands, I'd make up stories about Kimmy, the Eskimo baby, and she'd just grin and chatter back to me the whole way in her own language, which I called Eskimo. I started taking in typing from other med students that my husband knew, and I built up a pretty good little cottage industry. When I finished with them, Kimmy and I would ride the buses up to the medical school and deliver them for an extra five dollars. She loved the bus rides, and since they only cost me fifty cents, I made quite a profit on our delivery system.

That funny old neighborhood brought me my first real friend since high school too. Rosa was this great Italian lady who lived downstairs from us. She was married to a nice guy named Sal who worked for the city's power company and she had four rowdy little boys that Kimmy was scared to death of, but I thought were adorable.

It was Rosa who suggested that I do what I was always talking about and take a couple classes at the city college to try and eventually finish my degree in English. She said she'd watch Kimmy for two dollars a night if I wanted to do it, and oh did I want to do it!

I talked it over with my husband and he wasn't enthused, but he didn't say no. He reminded me that we really needed the money I was bringing in from my typing, and that he would kind of like me at home for some dinner and company when he was around, but if this was something I felt I needed because I was unhappy or whatever, to go ahead and do it.

I rushed in to smooth him down, explaining that I was totally happy and that I would never neglect him or Kimmy or the typing jobs, and that if I couldn't line up classes for the same nights he had his two night classes, I would forget about it.

He seemed appeased and said okay, but it's funny, it was Rosa and not him who showed up a couple days later with all this student information from Northwestern about free classes for family members of enrolled medical students. When I asked him, he said he hadn't known they offered that, but of course I wonder now.

Anyway as great good luck would have it, I was able to enroll in a Wednesday night junior level English class that got out at the same time as his lab did, so we were able to drive home together. It was my first time back into the college atmosphere. I loved it and it was a special thing to me. How wonderful I felt walking outside afterward into the icy night air, my arms filled with books and my head filled with ideas beyond dinner for the first time in two years. A couple times, instead of waiting at the car for me, he'd have walked over to stand outside my classroom and we'd have coffee together on campus. I'd ask him all about his lab work and his eyes would shine at me, just like Kimmy's did when I made her laugh. I'm sure my own eyes must have looked just as star struck as hers did when I looked back at him, and I know I made him happy then, made him glad he was with me.

So sometimes it's very hard to understand all the things that came later.

Chapter 34

When you are very young, and I was very young when we lived in Chicago, one good day can make you feel like everything is fine. And I had more than one good day, I had two sweet years behind me, when I made the decision that it would probably be okay to let myself get pregnant again.

Now, with Kimmy it was definitely an accident and I know I'm to blame for it. He didn't like condoms and he got a friend of his, a doctor in Patchogue, to write me a prescription for birth control pills, but I wasn't very good about remembering to take them, and so Kimmy came along.

Over the next few years we hadn't talked about having more kids except in a kind of vague way. My husband had so much on him with med school, and I knew he had a long road ahead of him, but after Chicago I felt like he would be keeping me and Kim with him on the road. I loved being a mother and I didn't want her to be an only child, and anyway, sometimes we did talk about the future, and when we did it went like this: he would finish med school and get a top internship, after which he thought probably Yale would ask him to join their surgical staff and to teach at their med school. We would buy a farm in Connecticut and have a big house filled with sons for him, and horses and dogs for all of us. He didn't bring this up much, usually only in the very rare times when he had gotten enough sleep and we had made love, and he didn't have to rush off to study or work one of his part-time jobs.

I understand now that the job at Yale and the farm in Connecticut were only one of the possible lives he envisioned for himself, and only on the days when Kim and I seemed more of a blessing than a burden to him.

I think on other days he looked around and listened to his fellow med students talking about being Park Avenue surgeons and partying in Manhattan, or becoming team doctors for some pro team, and that he probably saw those lives just as clearly. But of course he couldn't tell me about them since I was the very thing standing in the way.

He was always a boy, as I said, and, like a boy who dreamed in his room of being an astronaut but told his parents dutifully that he wanted to be a lawyer, he kept his private dreams to himself. I was the parent that wouldn't have understood.

In my own defense, at the time I wasn't even twenty-three yet and I was in love with my husband and with being a mother, and if I chose to disregard the vagueness in his voice when he talked about the farm in Connecticut, I didn't do so to trap him. I believed what I wanted to believe because that is what young women do when they are in love and feel they are loved in return, or, I don't know, maybe I did know that Yale and Connecticut weren't truly his dream, but I hoped that if I clung to them hard enough, they would come true anyway.

Whenever he would talk about it, I would just listen with shining eyes, maybe adding that I knew for sure that he would be the youngest chief of staff Yale had ever had, and things like that. I didn't tell him about my own little hopes of how, after I finished my English degree, I would like to attend Yale myself towards a graduate degree and maybe one day become a professor.

It would have bored him and he might have seen me as being in competition with him for household achievements, and he would have hated that. So I stayed quiet except for my remarks about his future achievements and, in return, he rewarded me by talking about our imaginary future farm.

During the summer before his junior year of med school, he landed a great job working at the Chicago Tribune's medical clinic and we found an amazing old duplex in one of the city's historic neighborhoods that we could afford to rent. I went ahead and let myself think that our future, not just his future, would be golden too, and without telling him, I stopped taking my birth control pills.

I got pregnant almost immediately because I remember having to catch him right before his September classes started up and ask him if he had a minute to talk. He looked at me impatiently. He had been made the Sigma Nu medical officer and the fraternity had a game that night, which was totally typical of our lives back then. He was always gone, or coming home to shower and be gone again. There was school, work, sports, and maybe other things that I didn't like to think about, but I couldn't question him about his time. It was an unwritten rule and I never broke it.

That beautiful Indian summer night, though, I caught him between the shower and the door, and asked him if we could sit outside on the porch swing and talk for a minute.

He looked at me annoyed. "Come on, Col, I'm late already." He glanced around for something to distract me and noticed for the first time since he'd walked in the door thirty minutes before that Kimmy was not in the house. I had taken her by bus over to Rosa's after lunch and, without explaining, asked my friend if she would mind keeping her until before dinner.

Rosa had given me a long troubled look and I started moving backwards out of her door, holding Kimmy's hand. I hated being a burden to anyone and I was already apologizing when she stopped me and leaned down and picked up Kimmy. "No, no Colette, I don't mind having this bambina here. She's a delight, and every time I have her, I think maybe her good manners will rub off on my boys. No luck yet but you never know." She smiled and patted me on my arm. "I'm sorry, I must have looked at you funny. It's just that there is something different about you today." She waited for me to fill in for her, but I only smiled and shrugged, telling her I had set my hair in a new way and that I was imposing on her because it had been so long since I had had anytime alone with my husband, and I was hoping to …

I let my voice trail off when I answered, hoping that Rosa would assume I wanted to seduce him unexpectedly.

Rosa was very open, uncomfortably so I had always thought, about her own love life, so I figured she would assume the worst of me and start to laugh, but she didn't. Her face was unaccountably dark as she stood on the landing holding Kimmy.

"Rosa?"

"Colette, you're pregnant, aren't you? That's why you want me to watch Kimmy. You're pregnant and you are about to tell him so."

I was floored. I had only had my suspicions confirmed the day before at the health clinic and, if anything, I was thinner than usual that summer. I looked at her shocked and she met my gaze squarely with her warm dark eyes which appeared sad and sunken in the dim hallway gloom.

She shrugged. "I see by your face that I am right. Don't ask me how I knew. All of us Italian women have the second sight to one degree or another. My grandmother …" Seeing the look on my face she tried to smile and lighten up the air around us which had suddenly gone thick and still. She held up her hand in reassurance. "Don't, Col, don't look frightened of me. The sight can come in very handy. For instance, I knew the pipe under the sink was going to burst last week and I told Sal that -"

I interrupted her. "But Rosa, why did you look so funny? You've been staring at me since I got here like you thought something terrible was going to happen to me. Do you see something bad about my baby, or, oh God, Kimmy?"

She shook her head quickly. "No, not at all, I'm just ridiculous. It's nothing. Most of the time what I see, or what I think I see, never comes true at all."

"What did you think you saw, Rosa?"

She shook her head firmly. "Nothing, I saw nothing. Go on home, Colette, and tell that handsome hunk of yours the good news. Tell him he's going to have a son and all of you will be as happy as the cows in the field."

I felt a sudden spurt of joy. "Is that what you saw, Rosa, a son? Oh, I know he'd love to have a son."

She tried to smile back but I could see it was a forced attempt. She half turned away from me heading back into her apartment. "Oh yes, a son. Maybe not this one, but one day soon. Like I said, Colette, I don't know what I saw. Go on now. Kimmy and I need to start lunch for my boys before they eat the furniture."

And then my friend who had never let me leave without trying to press cookies or homemade wine on me, or hours of conversation, gently shut the door in my face. On the bus headed back home, I tried to tell myself it was just old country nonsense but maybe she was right about the son part. I didn't know what she meant about 'someday'. I toyed with, and then discarded, telling the story to my husband. He didn't think much of Rosa anyway and somehow I didn't think it would add to my announcement.

So later that day when he was trying to slip past me and he asked me where Kimmy was, I just told him that Rosa had asked if she could have her for a couple hours. I offered him iced tea, lemonade or a beer, all three of which I had stocked for our talk, but he refused them and said in an annoyed voice, "No, I don't want anything to drink. I have ten minutes tops for this, Colette, so spit out whatever you have to tell me that's so damned important, okay?"

My wonderful announcement, which I had pictured taking place in the porch swing with me nestled against his shoulder while we watched the sunset together, instead happened in the hallway outside the bathroom door where I had managed to block his exit.

After I told him, he didn't say anything for a long time. He just stared over my head at the doorway to outside with a lost expression in his blue eyes.

Chapter 35

After my big announcement and his small reception of it, the long tense quiet months began. I had wanted another baby, maybe to add to our family, maybe just to increase my own sense of security in our little family by shoring us up with one more member that was on my side - the side of family, and love, and farms in Connecticut.

But what I had created along with this baby were all of his old feelings of fear and entrapment, and I think the first seeds of desperation.

My pregnancy with Kristy was the beginning of his 'me or them' mentality, a feeling which time did not lessen but made larger until he felt that something had to break open or he would suffocate and die. What broke open, as it happened, was my skull, but that came later. I had a few years left to try and fix things, and I think I nearly made it, until a few strokes of bad luck pulled the rug out from under me again, and then of course it was too late because sometimes you can't un-ring the bell.

With my second pregnancy I still had our pretty little place in Chicago and my girl, my friend and my classes, but I had lost him. And, because there was no happiness or security for Kimmy and me and the new baby without him, I was psychologically, if not physically, back in his parents' old bedroom, trying to keep us invisible so that we wouldn't bother him to the point that he would just leave.

At the time, back then, I thought that would be the worst, the very worst thing that could befall us - for him to leave. I understand differently now, but hindsight is so useless.

Other things that fall and winter made me feel as I had during that long uncomfortable first summer of Kimmy's life. I had known then that when he had stayed out on Montauk, or over on Fire Island, he wasn't always alone at night. I knew it, but of course I never confronted him. After all, what would that have gained me? He might have lied, which would have made me feel even smaller, or worse, he might have shrugged and said 'So what?', and how could I have answered him then?

During the winter that I was pregnant with Kristy, when he cheated, he wanted me to know about it. He was very angry at me. Sometimes the look in his eyes made me afraid that he was going to hit me. Hitting me was something that was not completely impossible, I knew.

Back when we were just two young kids in love and dating, he had struck me a few times - nothing major, just a slap or a shove, or if I had really enraged him, he might grab me and hold my arms tightly enough that I'd have to wear long sleeves for days afterward. He had a terrible temper when we were kids. It had eventually caused me to pull away from him, which had in turn made him chase me, win me and then wonder why he had bothered. But in the years since we had gotten back together, he had never raised a hand against me, or against Kimmy either, but that winter I could tell he wanted to.

Since he had managed to steel himself against doing so, he had to strike out in other ways. He was a child, always a child, and children will not, cannot, suffer silently. If they are upset, and you ignore them, they follow you around the house until you are forced to acknowledge their unhappiness.

And so that winter, when he went to the other girls, he changed his pattern of concealment and gave them all our home phone number.

He was almost never at home and I know a lot of it was legitimate. Med school is so hard, and during that winter he kept his summer job at the Tribune's medical clinic. It made things extra hard on him. But he told me sullenly that my little typing work wasn't going to help much in paying for a new baby and so he would have to manage both school and the job somehow. I cringed with guilt, and because of my guilt, on the nights the phone would ring, and there would be hang up after hang up, I never said a word.

In every way, that third winter in Chicago seemed colder and harder than any in our history. It truly was a cold winter. Lake Michigan nearly froze over, and between the winds and the snow, it didn't warm up to much above ten below all winter long.

Kimmy was uncharacteristically irritable and hard to please, and when we did have to venture outside to the grocery store or the laundromat, she would wail in her stroller all the way there and back from the cold, saying 'No Eskimo' when I would try and make up our old stories.

When my husband was home, he didn't touch me and he didn't look at me, and when I was in disgrace, Kimmy was also. So she suffered from his distance, and my guilt was doubled by her lack of interaction with the daddy she adored.

Finally, in spite of my fear and sadness, spring eventually did come, and in May, like the first best flowers of the year, Kristy was born. It was a rough labor, no question about it, and after ten futile hours of trying to deliver my girl, they wheeled me in for my second C-section and brought her out.

She was bigger and blonder and louder than her sister had been from the moment she was born. I only had a tiny glimpse of her in my husband's arms before the drugs took me under again, but I could tell right away that this little girl was going to be a fighter like her daddy, and I hoped a winner like him too.

The next morning I woke up and the edges of my hospital room were cloudy. I could see my husband but only through what looked to me like white cumulus strands. I would find out later that is how we ghosts always see things, but that morning I was still alive - barely. He leaned down over me and his face seemed huge and engorged to me. I tried to raise my hand, and found I couldn't.

I could feel my heart fluttering like a wild trapped bird inside my chest, and then I was slipping, oh so gently, out of my body, and suddenly I was no longer on the bed but watching my husband's back bent over me from my spot in the corner of the ceiling.

It looked as though he was studying me for a long time, but maybe it was only seconds. Time is very different on the other side. I watched, detached and uncaring, as he stood up straight and ran his hands through his hair. His face appeared to me to be twisted with indecision but maybe it was simple fear. I have no way of knowing.

He sat down hard in the chair beside my bed, pulled my limp hand into his, and began. I listened, curious but not alarmed, from my perch in the corner.

"Col, honey, I think you might be bleeding inside. I think you are going into shock. You might die, Col. Col, I don't know what to do, I don't want you to die, you know that, right? I would never want you to die but, oh Col ..." He lowered his head over my lifeless hand and began to sob. I had never seen him cry before. "Col, I don't want you to die, I just want you to go away. I ... the new baby's a girl, did you know that? Col, I feel like I'm dying too. I didn't want to feel this way, I don't want ..." His shoulders shook harder. I was beginning to grow alarmed, my worry for my girls overcoming my strangely removed state.

He didn't get up, though I was willing him to with all my might. *Go, hurry, get help, please.*

"The thing is, Col, sometimes I feel like I'm the one who's in shock and bleeding to death inside, and I don't want to hate you, or Kimmy, or the new baby; I don't want to blame you for how I feel, but who else can I blame? I mean, think about it, Col, I -"

I watched in growing fear as my body on the bed below began to convulse. An alarm went off and a nurse ran in. I bowed my invisible head and whispered a prayer of thanks. When the alarm had begun to beep, my husband had quickly stood up, and when the nurse rushed into my room, he turned and shouted at her, "Jesus Christ, call a code, stat, you idiots! My wife is unconscious! I walk in here and I find my wife like this. My God, we're losing her. Tell her doctors to check her goddamned blood pressure. I think she's got an arterial hemorrhage."

Within seconds he was shoved out of the way, paddles shocked me back into my poor body, and I was sent back to surgery to repair what did indeed turn out to be an arterial bleed.

My husband was widely praised by my doctor and the nurses, and by my mother and by me, for his brilliant diagnosis which had doubtless saved my life. I did not remember any of my near death experience with finality until after I was dead, and by then, of course, it was too late.

Chapter 36

My husband's senior year of medical school was a time of recovery in our marriage. I had knocked myself out to make it up to him for getting pregnant, and I think he felt a little more warmly towards me since I had nearly died. And even though Kristy was another girl, she was his girl.

Brave and tough almost from the get go, she cried louder and laughed louder than her sister ever had. She was, for want of a better description, a showy baby. She was beautiful too. I wasn't beautiful, and neither was my Kimmy - except to me - not that she wasn't completely adorable and super-bright and loving. She was; she was all those things. But Kristy looked like a tiny version of him right from the beginning - perfect small features and big blue eyes. She didn't go through the red faced wrinkled stage. Like her daddy, she was a showstopper from her first day to her last.

He couldn't resist her and she was so obviously his for the asking. When he'd walk through the door, her little head would come up and she would start waving her arms and feet, like the joy of seeing him was so great that her tiny body wasn't big enough to contain it. He always responded well to adoration and it didn't hurt that everyone who saw her said the same thing.

"Look at this little one. She looks just like her daddy. She's going to be a heartbreaker when she grows up."

Of course, she didn't grow up, but yes indeed, my Kristy is a heartbreaker like her daddy.

He had a lot of exciting new distractions and wins that year. Fourth year med students get to wear the white lab coats and examine patients, and he was gorgeous in his lab coat, there's no other word for it. He looked like Robert Redford playing doctor, and I told him so. He loved that. By this time he had started to pull ahead of the pack of other med students. At Northwestern they are all the very top, and he was on top of the top, coming in ahead of the ninetieth percentile.

He was asked by a reigning surgeon if he wanted to scrub in on an appendectomy, and I waited up for him until three a.m. so he could tell me all about it when he got home. He really liked that I had waited up, I could tell, and he made love to me, and afterward he held me in his arms while we watched the dawn come up outside. And, to reward me, or so I thought, he talked for a while about his plans.

He seldom confided his plans to me. It wasn't because he had a secretive nature - far from it. In fact, I think I would have preferred if he had been a little more secretive. He didn't confide them because he didn't make them. Part of that was because he stayed such a boy, and the other, I think, was because he always had so many more choices than other people did.

I don't hold that against him - it has to be hard to decide what's best when everybody wants you - but that morning he did tell me, with this rare little tentative strain in his voice, that he thought he could probably get any internship he applied for. He said he wasn't sure and didn't have any real feel for the place that would ultimately be best for him. I was pretty excited that he had confided that much in me. It wasn't his way and I didn't feel hurt or anything that he hadn't mentioned the girls or me in his decision making process. That just wasn't how he did things.

In fact, I was so flattered, that it was me who brought up him taking the trip along with some of his friends to go check out different residencies. He had mentioned it kind of in a passing a few days before and I hadn't really responded, but that morning I felt so flattered that he seemed to be kind of leaning on me for advice that I encouraged him to go.

I guess in retrospect, which I have so much of now, he had probably planned it that way; given me a little attention and manipulated me right into telling him to go off and have a good time. It doesn't matter. Even if I had known then, I would have told him to go because I did understand how hard it was for him sometimes to have to come home to us night after night when there was a whole world out there that wanted him too. I was grateful to him for not leaving. If that makes me sound pathetic, then I'm confused. Is it wrong to see another person's side, to empathize with them? I always tried to understand where people were coming from, so how could I have done less with the man-boy I was married to and whom I loved so much?

I figured I had time on my side and that any temporary unhappiness I might suffer would be erased or forgotten as we both got older and grew up a little. I had already lived through something pretty terrible and I had held on, and after a while everything had become okay again. I held closely to the story of my personal resurrection when got down and afraid in my marriage. My husband wasn't the first man I had loved who had wanted to leave me.

When I was eleven years old, and my brother Bob was fourteen, he and my mom had driven home one dark winter's day from one of his games and pulled into the garage. Hanging from the rafters in front of them was my handsome father. Unlike my poor brother, I was spared the actual sight of his body, but oh, I saw it a thousand times over in my head.

I knew it had to have been me, that I had failed him somehow, and so he had gone away forever. I knew it couldn't have been my mother. She was beautiful and they had always seemed so happy, and my brother was exactly the son any father would want, smart and nice, and he played baseball just like my father had wanted him to.

So it had to be me.

After my father's suicide, our formerly good lives fell apart. I watched anxious and helpless as day by day my mother began to fade away in front of my eyes until eventually I was sure I was going to lose her too.

I couldn't fix anything. All I felt I could do was to be as good as possible, to try not to get in the way and to try to hang on and hope things would get better. And it worked. It worked better than even my most fervent prayers, because a few weeks before my thirteenth birthday, my mother brought home Freddy and said they were going to be married. Funny-looking, sweet, wonderful Freddy, who from the very first became not a stepfather to me but another father. That's how I always thought of him, as my second father.

The lesson I learned from my father's death, and my response to it, was that if you held strong and tried your hardest, and stayed good to people that you loved, in the end everything would be all right again.

And it was that sad little girl, who used to keep a bright smile pasted on her face, who waved off my husband the day after his *summa cum laude* graduation from Northwestern.

It's funny, my girls' different reactions that day.

All Kimmy cared about was trying to make me smile for real. She brought me graham crackers and her doll, and finally her most prized possession in the world, her snuggle pillow, to try and cheer me up. Kristin meantime roared with outraged betrayal all day, not understanding one bit why her beloved shining star of a daddy had left in a car. She knew it wasn't a school day. She was a bright little girl and could easily tell the difference between when one of us was leaving her because we had to for work or school and when she was being left behind because we wanted to do some grown up thing without her.

I tried to comfort her while Kimmy tried to comfort me but it was a waste of time. All three of us were too sad to be cheered up. When, in despair, I suggested that we all go to bed, even though it wasn't dark out yet, two sad little blond heads only nodded, though normally neither of them would have accepted such an outrage. He was the center of our lives, and knowing he was going to be gone for six weeks was the same for us as if we had been told the sun wouldn't rise for over a month.

He had a wonderful time - I could tell from his infrequent calls that a wonderful time was being had. In fact, so good was his time that he was more comfortable talking to the girls when he did call home.

It's very hard to have a conversation with a three year old little girl and a baby, but still easier I suppose than trying to have one with your anxious wife, especially if you are calling from a strange bed with a strange woman laying beside you in that bed.

When he did finally come home in late July, he looked suntanned, handsome and pleased with himself. He announced that the trip had been a really good thing as far as being able to make an informed evaluation about the prime residency. He said he had decided on, and hoped to be accepted at, Columbia Presbyterian in New York.

His announcement didn't come as much of a surprise to me since I had seen the acceptance letter from them that had arrived about two days after he had left on his trip.

Chapter 37

Bergenfield, New Jersey. How can I describe our family's year there?

It's important to me that I remember this correctly because I think now that so much of what went wrong happened because of my husband's residency year. If we had been an annoyance and sometime burden to him during med school, then it was during his intern year at Columbia Presbyterian that we became a stranglehold. I know there are other couples who get married during med school, and maybe even have babies, but I am going to guess that for them it seldom works out well either. And if there were couples like us, I never got to meet them. I think it would have helped us both - less isolation for me and less feeling of being embattled for him.

That year started tense, degenerated to fraught, and ended up with both of us in our separate corners licking our psychological wounds like embattled cats. Of course he wasn't the type to take disappointment well, or really to take it all, and there were consequences.

I did try, I did, but there were so many things stacked against me being able to make him glad that he had the girls and me that year. New York is the most expensive place to be. No matter how badly you try to live cheaply in New York, you will fail.

Columbia Presbyterian is in the city, and if he hadn't had us, he could have lived as an intern at either the Columbia or the Cornell dorm. He would have been able to walk in five minutes to the hospital by crossing Central Park. In the so few hours of freedom available to interns, he could have returned to his room and slid into clean sheets in a quiet dark room. And, of course, there would have been the cafeteria and the downtown art scene, and most of all the camaraderie of living and working alongside the only other people in the world under the one-of-a-kind thrilling and horrifying pressure of being an intern at one of the country's great hospitals. Instead, because it was all we could find or afford, there was a tiny one bedroom apartment twenty miles away in Bergenfield, New Jersey. A forty mile round trip from New York City to Bergenfield is not quick, so when he got off a thirty-six hour call and had ten or twelve hours to try and recover, instead of crossing the glorious park to his dorm room for silence and sleep, he would have to get into the car and make an arduous drive to Bergenfield.

He would come dragging in. I tried to keep the girls quiet and to have something he liked ready-made to eat, but there were always problems. I would make breakfast when he had wanted dinner, or vice-versa. The girls would keep quiet for fifteen minutes but Kimmy might get excited and come running to the kitchen to show me something she had drawn, and the sound of her voice would wake him up. Kristy was a year old at the beginning of our year there, and she was exploring and trying to talk, and she would wake him up.

I would put the TV on so low that my little ones would have to huddle inches from the screen to hear, ruining their eyes - anything to keep them quiet - and inevitably they would see something they liked and start to giggle, and they would wake him up. So, instead of ten hours sleep, he would get an interrupted seven, and he blamed me.

Then it was time to return to the hospital but he would have to leave an hour ahead of time because of traffic, and he blamed me. His anger about the drive was about the only time I did defend myself. I pointed out that we were two minute walk from the train station and that not only would the trains get him back and forth in half an hour without worrying about traffic on the expressway, but that he could catnap during the trips. He looked at me like I had suggested he walk naked down the street. "Isn't it bad enough," he asked me, "that I am stuck making this goddamned commute back and forth to this godforsaken shit hole in the first place, without you expecting me to sit pressed up against a thousand sweating freaks from God knows where? Jesus, Colette, what more do you want from me?"

I held my tongue and apologized. I didn't say that he would only be commuting with other regular people who were going back and forth to the city for work, just like him. I understood that argument wouldn't have gone over well. They weren't like him at all, he would have answered - they weren't doctors. He would have asked me if I knew of any doctors who had to ride the trains with sewage employees and Indian waiters.

I didn't mention how much I could have used the car with two little ones and the grocery and laundry errands to make. It was my mother who made that mistake when she and Freddy came up for Christmas.

They stayed in a hotel, naturally, but on Christmas Eve he was actually off for fourteen hours through a miracle of scheduling, and we were all together at the apartment. I had tried my best but I could see from both my mother's and husband's expressions that I had failed in their eyes.

Kimmy's little bed and Kristy's crib were in the living room - there was no other place for them - but I had tried to turn Kimmy's bed into kind of a combination bed and extra couch. I had made a bright red cover for the couch and a matching one for her bed, and that night I had put out some little homemade Santa pillows. I thought with the red bows on the trees it looked sort of festive. To my elegant mother it just looked tacky, and to my fastidious husband it looked crowded. Only Freddy complimented me on the room.

We put the girls to bed in our room after dinner so the four of us could talk and catch up. Freddy had brought a bottle of champagne and my husband went into the kitchen to get it. On the way back he tripped over a carton of soda and the milk bottles I had out to remind me to take them back for the nickel returns. He went flying and so did the champagne bottle.

He was furious at me, and in front of my mother and Freddy, he yelled at me about what a mess the place was and why hadn't I returned the bottles yet? I was trying so hard not to cry, and before I could explain about what a long walk it was and how hard it was to drag out the girls, my mother uncharacteristically decided to defend me.

She said every wrong thing imaginable. She reminded my husband that she and my dad had bought the car for me and the girls, and that, instead of complaining about bottles in his living room, he should be grateful that he had a wife who was so thrifty and could even manage on a twenty-five dollar a week budget with two little girls.

She said he was probably wasting that much every month in gas by driving when there was a train. And didn't he think it was very selfish to use the car for only himself while leaving her daughter and grandchildren to have to walk everywhere in what was so obviously a bad neighborhood?

I had once reminded her never to criticize him but I understood she was trying to defend me, trying to address him adult-to-adult, but she didn't get it, that despite all his wins and strengths, he was never an adult.

Like the boy he was, he reacted in rage.

His face was bright red and I could even see his lips were trembling. Still wet with spilled champagne and without saying a word to any of us, he grabbed his coat and the car keys, and stalked out of the apartment.

I was too upset to try and comfort my mother who was confused and devastated by how things had gone so badly so quickly, and poor Freddy just sat there looking at two crying women and the empty champagne bottle on the floor. I think he was a little scared by all those female tears and he was so easy-going and bent towards making people happy that he didn't know how to try and fix the broken evening. After a bit he stood up and said jovially that, what the heck, he was in New Jersey and he bet that if he tried he could find one open liquor store there on Christmas Eve.

Neither my mother nor I answered but he went on talking.

"Sure that's what I'll do, I'll get us another bottle of champagne, no two bottles, that's what I'll do, and when he comes home in an hour or so, why we'll have a fine little celebration." He looked at our tearful faces, his own big kind face wrinkled in worry. "Oh come on now, girls, this was a little storm in a teapot. Why, I'll bet right now he's sitting outside in the snow on a curb feeling a little bit silly. You two watch, he'll be back before I am."

Freddy hurried outside, clearly relieved at the prospect of driving around New Jersey at eleven o' clock on Christmas Eve rather than staying inside with my mom and me.

My husband was not home when Freddy returned an hour later. He called at six a.m. from the hospital, telling me tersely that he had decided to show up three hours early for his call assignment. He didn't mention the night before or ask about the girls or my parents. I didn't tell him either but I did ask him where he had spent the night, and he said shortly that he had just been out walking all night.

I was so upset, but I didn't want to make things any worse, if that was possible, so I cleared my throat, and trying for a bright voice, I asked him if he had seen anything neat during his all-night walk.

Humorlessly he answered me, "Interesting? Maybe. I walked by a recruiting office, Colette. You know they are getting pretty desperate for doctors."

I tried to laugh a little. "You found a recruiter open in the middle of the night on Christmas Eve?"

"Yes, I did, Colette. The war doesn't stop, you know."

I didn't address the obvious stupidity or pomposity of his remark. I knew him well enough to know that if he was challenged he would always have to prove himself, and if he had only been trying to frighten me by mentioning Vietnam, I didn't want to escalate him any further.

I agreed with him that of course the war didn't ever stop and that I was so grateful that he was in New York and not in Vietnam. I told him that was the only thing I wanted at Christmas. It pacified him enough that before he hung up he told me he loved me and to kiss the girls for him. He didn't mention my parents.

I found out later that of course there were no Army recruitment stations open all night long on Christmas Eve or any other time of the year. He had gone to a nurse's room at the dormitory attached to the hospital. I could get over that - I was used to that - but after Christmas the mention of his near miss with volunteering to go to Vietnam never quite went away, and I knew that the girls and I were on trial in a very real way.

Chapter 38

Nobody can live on sheer nerves all the time and no one stays on stage twenty-four hours a day once they grow up. When we were young kids in love, he used to stage these situations in his head of the perfect evening we would have, which back then, since he was a fourteen year old boy, usually meant making out like crazy whenever we saw each other.

He wouldn't tell me what he was planning for the night. I would stupidly go into the situation whatever it was - a sledding party, a group movie, hanging out with our friends - thinking that was what we would be doing, but he would have built up this night of grand passion in his head, well grand passion within the limits of two suburban virgins who lived in Long Island in the Sixties.

And more times than I can count, the evening would end with him storming off, and me in tears, because I had stupidly thought that he had come to the event to be with me and have fun, and since I didn't know, and didn't always want to spend my whole night wrestling with him on a couch or a snow bank, he would become enraged.

Then, like clockwork, he would call my best friend, June, at whose house I was spending the night, and tell her that he liked her better and that he was totally done with me. I would panic and do what he wanted, and this silliness went on for the first three years of my girlhood until I had an epiphany that while I might have loved him, I was also beginning to fear him, and even to pity him a little. I broke it off, and to my shocked mother and girlfriends, I explained that, yes, he was a winner in every way, but I wasn't looking for a life of competition, and that while I hoped down the road he might find someone he could love, that person wasn't me. Who knew, maybe he'd grow out of it, but right then the only person he loved was himself.

Obviously I hadn't forgotten any of that when I returned to him years later, but once I had re-committed myself to loving him, and then marriage and having his babies, I had put it firmly out of my mind.

That last grim winter and spring in Bergenfield, some of our worst moments from the past came back to me. He didn't have my best friend to complain about me to, but he did have the option of running to other women and having grown up sex with them.

I don't think his overall approach changed much, though. I can't know of course, and I never asked, but I can guess that after he had spent himself, he probably launched into their sympathetic ears a diatribe of my failings. I didn't blame them then, and I don't blame them now, if they joined him in agreeing what a shame it was that a man like him, so young, so handsome, such an obvious winner, was stuck with such an unsupportive, nagging, demanding failure of a wife.

While I have never been able myself to criticize people I don't know, I do understand how easy it is to see only your own point of view, and he presented as a victim so well. In college I had read and loved 'The Lord of the Flies'. My husband hadn't liked it very much, and he never could see, as I did, that he wasn't like the powerful savage leader of the dominant troop of boys, but instead like one of the frightened followers.

My husband was only aggressive with his equals behind their backs, and only tried to dominate those that he knew ahead of time could never fight back. So the girls and I became a target in the place of every surgeon that didn't pick him first at rounds, and every older nurse who didn't jump when he said move, and we suffered under his reign of cowardly terrorism.

I didn't fight back. At first I just tried to smooth things over, and when I couldn't, I withdrew more and more into silence.

Kimberly was a peace-loving little girl, like me, and she sensed, though did not understand, his displeasure that year in Bergenfield. She developed a slight stutter and began wetting the bed.

Kristy, on the other hand, was irritated by the atmosphere she lived in, and being only a baby, expressed her displeasure by biting and long inconsolable screaming sessions if she didn't get her way immediately.

A vicious cycle of anticipated boredom and displeasure on his part created in us behaviors guaranteed to make him even more disgusted that he was still a part, however marginally, of such a disappointing little family.

What I remember most of that winter was how cold I was all the time. I walked around our tiny overheated little apartment swathed in a heavy old sweater like the little old ladies I would see at the grocery stores. At the end of March, when my Freddy called and asked if I could come up on the train with the girls for a few days over Easter, I jumped at the chance. He sent me the tickets, and without explaining why to either him or my mother, I stayed home for two weeks.

Those two weeks were wonderful for the girls, and good for me as well, but I didn't lose sight of what was awaiting me back home; or maybe to be clear, I should say that I tried to puzzle out what was awaiting me.

I didn't burden my parents with the state of my union, and since I was never exactly boisterous, I don't think they noticed if I was quieter than usual. My brother and his wife came to visit, and it was only once alone with Pep, my sister-in-law, that I broke down and cried. I didn't tell her about how unkind he was to us, or how frightened of the future I was, but I did tell her that I thought he was cheating.

She seemed so horrified by that revelation, which to me was the least of my worries, that I didn't feel I could go further. I didn't want the people I loved to judge the man I loved - still loved.

He didn't call for the first week, and when he finally did call, there was a strange excitement in his voice.

I knew what he was going to say before I even heard the words. "I've been drafted."

I didn't bother to point out what an amazing coincidence it was that the draft notice only arrived after my departure, or that it was surprising that he, a married man with children, had been drafted at all. I only cried.

It was a terrible feeling hearing his happiness at the prospect of going off to Vietnam. I knew then with a terrible clarity how badly I had failed to love him, to keep him happy. If he preferred to risk his young life in that terrible war rather than be with us, what did that say about the life I had created with him? I felt that if he were badly wounded or killed in that far country, that it would have been just as if I had done it myself. Remembering this, how I felt then, what I believed, it makes me feel terribly foolish and short-sighted.

In my defense, I didn't know what he would do to be free, and until the last stroke of the knife finally took my life, I don't think I completely understood that there was more at work in our marriage than mere dissatisfaction.

He hated us.

I took the girls back to Bergenfield, and thanks to my mom and Freddy, all three of us had beautiful new dresses to wear to the reception given for the completion of his internship. His orders were to report for basic training in Fort

Sam Houston within fifteen days. Given everything, I was shocked when we got home that night and he reached inside his jacket, handing me two tickets to Aruba.

We had never been on a vacation - there had never been the money or the time. I wanted to but couldn't ask where he had gotten the money for this. At first I couldn't say anything. I sat quietly on the couch and looked at the tickets.

He took my hand. "It's great, isn't it, Col? Don't even ask how I got them, just be happy we have a chance to do this."

I looked up at him. "I am happy, I just -"

He cut me off, his face already darkening - a child whose present wasn't being received properly. "You just what? If you're worried about the kids, for Christ's sake, I already talked to your mom and mine. They're both going to chip in and take care of them. So what is it now? You're too busy to go? Maybe you don't think I need a little break, a little tiny fucking rest after this year, and before I head off to basic training and then fucking Vietnam where you have to realize, Colette, I might just get the shit shot out of me and come back in a coffin. Fuck it, I just wanted to have a little special time with my wife and now I guess I'm the asshole."

Then because my poor boy could always convince himself that if he said a thing, then it was true, he buried his face in his hands and began to sob.

I saw a chance to do and say the things he needed, and I rushed in with soft kisses and reassurances of my love and of my pride and my gratitude, and I apologized for not having jumped up and down immediately. I said that I had been stunned, disbelieving, that the idea of time alone with him, let alone time on a Caribbean island, had temporarily overwhelmed me.

I asked if I would need money for a new bathing suit or would I be inside the hotel room the whole time?

After a half hour or so of adoring comments and kisses and stroking, and calling him Doctor Amazing, he perked up and even felt generous enough towards me that he said he was sorry he wouldn't have time to help me pack up the apartment before we left but he needed to finish up some stuff with the sports team he had been overseeing.

I laughed and told him that, with the prospect of five days in the Caribbean with him, I would be super-charged and that he shouldn't even think about it.

I did it too. In four days I had every single possession that we owned either boxed up or sold to our neighbors. We had decided that I would stay with my mom and dad while he was in basic and, unsaid - but there - while he was in Vietnam. My parents did not like clutter and so filling their garage with all of our second hand furniture was not on.

My husband was in a terrific mood that week, and when he was around, he would hug me and remind me that after this time in the army was behind us, he would start his residency at Yale, and we would have our farm, and I could shop for French antiques if I wanted to.

He only ever brought up the farm when he was pleased with me, and though I guess on some level I knew it was just a pacification technique at most with him, I would respond joyfully because I hoped so much that maybe in reality it would become his dream one day too.

Chapter 39

I think our time in Aruba was as good as it could possibly be, considering the weight of the past year that we were both carrying, as well as the prospect of the coming separation - a separation that I knew might be permanent.

In some ways that I didn't let myself think about, I was starting to plan life without him. Before we had boarded the plane at JFK, I had managed to ship those of our meager belongings to my parents and deliver in person the only things of value that he and I had yet produced in our marriage - my girls.

Everything had happened so quickly since his draft announcement, and the closing up of our life in Bergenfield, and then the trip, that I hadn't had a chance to sit down and take stock, to plan the future he had suddenly thrust on me. For me that is what those five days in Aruba became; a chance to look forward without him. I had not asked for that. If I had been asked, I would have said it was the last thing in the world I wanted, but it was here and I was finding it dismayingly easy to adjust to his newest plans.

Maybe Aruba isn't the prettiest island in the world, but it is the only island I ever got to see, so to me it will always remain a vision of perfection. I'll admit that I was a little disappointed at first at the way he had gone ahead and arbitrarily picked our first, and as it happened only, vacation spot. Since I had been a girl, I had loved everything French and had learned to both read and write in that beautiful old language, and when I let myself dream of traveling one day, it was always to France itself, or at least to a French-speaking country - Quebec, the French West Indies maybe - but waking up in our motel that first morning in Aruba, it caught my heart and imagination immediately.

I felt so out of context, but in the best possible way. Our motel was located close to the island's big public beach, Eagle Beach, and from the windows that morning I looked out stunned at the loveliness, the sheer blueness of the ocean. This is what I meant about being out of context because that magic turquoise water that nearly shouted out, 'Come swim in me. Become lost in my seductive warmth and beauty', was the same old Atlantic Ocean I had grown up near for most of my life.

Gray and forbidding and murky at home, here it was at its southern end, transformed into a place of clear blue enchantment. It made me realize that if something as vast and impenetrable as an ocean could exist at all times as both a somewhat fearful thing and also a place most welcoming, then I in my own small life should be able to mutate a little too; grasp some of the bright blueness of the world and not always hide in gray shadows. Unable to stop myself, I edged quietly out the door of our room and ran down to the water's edge. I was still in my nightgown, and I remember being a little shocked at myself, but I couldn't resist that marble colored water and the white sand.

I waded to the edge and then, without thinking about it, I plunged in head first and let the silky warmth encircle me. Coming up gasping and laughing, I floated on my back and stared at the perfectly matching sky above me. It occurred to me that there was an entire world of beauty and wonder that I could enjoy, could teach my girls to enjoy. Disloyally, I also thought that morning that it seemed the sun could after all shine brightly on me if he wasn't standing over me blocking out all the rays for himself.

Of course, during the days and the nights we did what he wanted. He would give his enthusiastic shouts of "Col, watch this dive", or, "Col, I think I want to try parasailing. You stand over there and shoot some photos", shouts so reminiscent of my baby Kristy reminding me sternly, "Watch me, Mommy. Look at what I can do, Mommy". This time he didn't have all my attention but he didn't seem to notice that my smile was a little fixed or that my eyes might have gazed over his shoulder at the horizon beyond him. During the nights, when he reached for me, I was merely compliant, no longer eager. My sighs were not those of pleasure anymore. Too many other women had worked to please him, and with my new distance, I realized tiredly that many more would continue to. No, I was there in body with him but my mind was beginning to sit up and take notice of a world in which he wasn't front and center.

On our last night in Aruba, over dinner, when he droned on yet again about having managed to make the top ten percentile during his internship year and how he wondered if maybe he should consider trying for Special Forces when he entered basic training, I listened and nodded and smiled, and looked beyond him and beyond us to the ocean. He was always very attentive to any lack of attentiveness, and broke off in mid-sentence to ask me what I was thinking about that was so much more interesting 'than my boring stories about how I should try to stay alive in Vietnam'.

I didn't do my usual damage control. I only smiled and said, "Your stories aren't boring, sweetheart. I just have a lot on my mind, you know, about where the girls and I will be spending the next few years and what we'll do while you're gone. I've been thinking that since we'll have to live with Mom and Dad, I might enroll at the city college, or maybe even NYU, and finish up this darn English degree. Who knows, by the time you get back, I may have my Masters done and be heading for the P.H.D., and we'll have two doctors in the family. It's a long -" I broke off at the appalled look on his face. "What's wrong, darling? You know I've always -"

"No, no, Colette, I can't say I have always known that you were planning such a big career. Wow! Wow, this is pretty amazing. I mean I'm so glad that I got fucking drafted into the United States Army so that you would have this chance to really go out there and grow as a person." Ignoring my hurt expression he continued on, his voice rising up enough that we were catching the attention of other diners. "See, I didn't really envision it going this way, Col. I thought, stupid asshole that I am, that this was going to be a pretty hard time for you worrying about me over there, and here I've been trying to think of ways to cheer up my girl; but you're going to be fine, aren't you, professor?"

I sipped my wine and thought about, and then, discarded all that I could say to him.

He drained his glass and looked at me with tears of self-pity shining in his eyes. "The girls?"

"What about the girls? They'll be with me and with my parents."

He sneered. "Oh, your parents, well sure. So let me get this straight. I work my fucking ass off, nearly kill myself for the last five years, then when all I can think about is taking my little family to Yale and starting life on our farm, maybe even having a son one day ..." his voice broke, "... instead I get orders to go to Vietnam to get my ass blown off, and yeah, maybe this makes me a pathetic jerk for wishing that my girl, my wife, would be waiting at home with my kids, and I don't know, maybe missing me just a little bit, but what a chump, huh? You'll be so busy conquering the halls of academia that you probably won't even notice I'm gone. And my girls, well what the hell, they'll be all the time with your parents who will probably never mention me to them, and they won't have time to take them to see my mom, who unlike you, Colette, is pretty upset about maybe me being killed and all."

I stared at him for a long time; I was at a loss for words - not because of him, but because of me. How had I gotten here?

I wondered if this was going to be it. Would I spend all of my life trying to appease this overgrown child and never once gain even an inch of ground I could call my own? The image of my father's body as it must have appeared to my brother flashed into my mind. Family - you had to stay and live the life you committed to for your children, for the promises that you had made.

I forced a smile and stroked the back of his hand. "I'm sorry, darling. Can you ever forgive your silly girl? I'm so lost at the thought of you being gone, being in danger, that I came up with these ideas. They're just castles in the air. You know that if anything happens to you, I'll die, and if you want me home with the girls waiting and knitting socks like the girls in the old war movies, then that's just what I'll be doing. Silly love, of course I'll see your mother all the time. I know she's upset, but sweetheart, not as upset as I am. No-one on earth loves you as much as I do, you know that. Please, sweetheart, can we forget this?"

He studied my face suspiciously for signs of deceit. Apparently I was a better actress than I knew, because his own features cleared. He threw some money down on the table. "Come on, Col, let's walk on the beach. It's a great night."

I rose willingly and gave him my hand. Once we had walked beyond the stretch of sand where the lights and music came from, he pulled me against him and I tried to relax my tight muscles as he lowered me to the sand.

He said, "It's just like in the movie from 'Here to Eternity', isn't it, Col? And you'll be waiting for me, and when I come back we'll both have everything we ever wanted."

I let him make love to me on the sand. Afterward I told him all the things I knew he had wanted to hear: that these five days had been the best ones of my life; that his eyes were the same blue as the ocean here; and that the memory of this time would sustain me while he was gone.

In reality, though, all I could think of was that my husband was like the other Atlantic - the one I'd grown up beside - gray and stormy, except on rare perfect summer days. I was always afraid of my own native water. I didn't like swimming out where I couldn't see the bottom. I always felt like something frightening and unknowable was right there just beneath the surface, waiting to pull me down.

Chapter 40

Our first date was to the movie with the song by the same name, 'A Summer Place'. Afterward, throughout the years, whenever I heard the song, whether I was with him or apart, I would stop for a minute and hum the tune.

> *There's a summer place,*
> *where it may rain or storm,*
> *yet I'm safe and warm.*
> *For within that summer place*
> *your arms reach out to me.*

In the half world I exist in now, a place I have now lived far longer than my life amongst the living, irony abounds. '*Your arms reach out to me.*'

I am thinking of that song now as I revisit memories of our last summer; the one with just the girls and me.

He had headed off in a shower of admiration to Fort Sam Houston and basic training, and what I at the time assumed was the beginning of a year's long separation. I did miss him, I did - I think I did - but it was so good to be home again. My mom remained, as always, a little bit critical of me and my care of the girls - were they dressed right, had I remembered enough sun screen, snacks, and diapers? I didn't mind really, because with the girls themselves, she allowed herself to just be with them as their grandma, and they were crazy about her. If my mother meant old-fashioned stories and dress-up plays and tea parties, then Grandpa Freddy meant endless games of hide-and-seek and tag and wrestling; Kristy, naturally more than Kimmy, enjoyed the latter.

At first they were a little shy around him. They were not used to adoring male attention that lasted more than the requisite three minutes. Soon, though, they were lying in wait behind the front door for him to come home from work. They had never done that with their own daddy; he didn't encourage spontaneity and interruptions from them.

That last summer was the first time in years that I didn't have to parent alone and worry about pleasing someone all the time, and I took full advantage. I had a chance to look up all my old friends, and by then some of them were married with kids of their own. There were play dates for the girls and talk dates for me, and by July, all three of us were as fat and tan and happy as kittens in cream.

In July I left the girls with Mom for the day, and clutching my transcripts in my sweaty little hands, I made the train and bus trip into the city and enrolled in NYU's seniors' English program for the Fall semester.

Then he called from Texas.

It wasn't me he called. First it was his mother, but the girls and I were over visiting her for lunch that day. I heard her say his name and watched her face light up with the special softness and pride she held in reserve for this, her youngest, finest and most loved child, the son of all hopes. I didn't mind that he had called her and not me - we had a bi-monthly call schedule set up to save money - and if he wanted to call his mother spontaneously, then I was glad for her.

I listened with half an ear until I heard her exclaim, "The Green Berets? But why, sweetheart, why paratroopers? That is so dangerous." I could have told her why but she was pushing the receiver towards me, saying to him, "No wait, honey, tell Colette. She and the girls are here."

Reluctantly I took it, saying brightly, "So, doctor, what's this about the Green Berets?"

His voice was scratchy on the connection but all his old boyish excitement was there, an echo of other earlier decisions. "Did she tell you, Col? I did it, I joined the Green Berets; I'm going to jump out of planes."

I laughed a little. "Okay, doctor, now why don't you tell me why in the world you want to jump out of planes?"

His words rushed out. He was too excited to reason. He sounded just like Kristy. "Because it's the best there is, Col. It's the most elite of the Special Forces, and this guy that talked... You should have heard him. Oh, and Col, you just wait till you see the uniforms. They are the best. You know what else, I'm going to get to go to Fort Benning next for the training. It's really an honor, Col."

Despite his mother's eyes on me hoping that I would try and talk him out of this latest adventure, all I said was, "That's great, sweetheart. It's nice to hear you so excited." Unsaid was that even in the massive harm's way situation that existed at that time in Vietnam, it seemed a body jumping out of a plane presented an enticing target by land and air. It wouldn't have changed a thing if I had said that, except to anger him, to ruin his moment and to add emotional distance to our physical distance.

At home that evening after I put the girls to bed, I shared his news with my parents. They seemed bemused. My mother, I think, was worried about me becoming a young widow with two small children, and saddened about the very real possibility that her dreams for me as the wife of a Yale surgeon might never come true. But she was not critical of my husband, merely quiet. Freddy, on the other hand, was a former war hero himself and he became sentimental speaking of his memories, and he appeared touched and proud by my husband's bravery. I had my own thoughts as to why he had picked Special Forces but I was not in the custom of sharing feelings regarding my husband or our marriage, so I merely listened to my parents and murmured agreement or reassurance where it was appropriate.

Ten days later he called from Fort Benning to give me the latest news. His voice on the phone was much more subdued this time. "Hey, Col. Well, this call is going to put you over the moon."

I asked him if he was calling to tell me that they were going to promote him from Captain to General.

He liked that and his voice loosened a little. "No, not yet, but hey, I knocked it out of the park on my jumps. You should have seen the face of my C.O. and the other guys. Jesus, they made a mess of like their first ten jumps but I had mine down flat on the first one."

I congratulated him with what I hoped was the proper degree of enthusiasm and awe, and I waited. I knew there was more to come and that at least from his viewpoint it wasn't all good news.

He cleared his throat. "So, yeah, the jumps were great and I got really good marks straight across the board. I was pretty sure that maybe I'd make group surgeon for one of the platoons, but well, and this is a real honor too ..." His voice trailed off.

I spoke encouragingly. "But what, sweetheart?"

"Well, you know, Col, the JFK Center at Fort Bragg, that's the elite for the entire airborne, and the Green Berets are the elite of the elite, so anyway it looks like instead of Vietnam, it's going to be Fort Bragg, at least for a while. I'll be a group surgeon there under one of the real heroes, guy named Colonel Kingston. So what do you think, Col?"

I hesitated. I was of course happy that he wasn't going to Vietnam. I knew, though, that was what he secretly wanted - maybe not Vietnam so much as just get away - so I answered carefully. "It is an honor, sweetheart. Even I've heard of the JFK Center at Fort Bragg, and hey, Captain, you know for me, every day that you're safe on U.S. soil is a good day. So are they going to give my soldier boy any leave to see his girl between assignments? I can meet you at the train just like in the movies, or maybe I could come down there for a couple days if -"

"No, you don't understand, Col. I'm going to be in Fort Bragg permanently for my time. You and the girls will be coming there as soon as I have quarters assigned. You can be with me full-time for the duration, you know, unless I get sent over, and even if that happens, you and the girls can stay there; free housing on the army, huh? Can't do you better than that, right?"

I don't remember what I said to him. I don't know how I got off the phone. I think I checked on the girls and they were with my mother or something. All I can remember is walking on shaking legs to my old girlhood bedroom and falling onto the bed. I let myself cry all afternoon for all the years I hadn't given into tears.

We would all be together again, we four, together in a distant place where I knew no one and there was no ivy-covered college waiting for me in the Fall and no charming Montessori school for Kimmy. I had reserved a place for her at the same wonderful little French-run school I had attended twenty years before. My mom was an interior designer, and she had been planning to construct and decorate a doll house with the girls. Instead, we were headed to a place where the girls and I would be cut off from the assured affection of my parents, and reliant once again on only his, and that affection I knew was far from assured.

I pulled myself together because there was no other option, and after I washed my face, I went out and brightly told my mother the news. Her face fell at the prospect of separation again but she reminded me how lucky I was to be able to be reunited with my husband, and that it was a miracle - those were her exact words - *a miracle* of luck that he was not being sent off to Vietnam to fight, and perhaps die, there.

That evening Freddy was, as he always was, loving, kind-hearted and able to find joy in any situation. He told me that he had a surprise for me. He said he had gotten together with my Aunt Helen and jointly they were going to buy me a car. I was too surprised to speak. My husband had sold the first car they had bought me when he enlisted – oh, pardon me, when he was drafted. He had said that the girls and I wouldn't need it living in New York with my parents. For all I know, that was how he paid for our trip to Aruba.

I told Freddy I could never accept another car, that it was far too generous, but he waved down my protests. He said he had checked out Fort Bragg, and that while it was our nation's largest base, it was also ten miles to the nearest town of Fayetteville, and I needed a car for school, groceries and the girls. I murmured that I wouldn't be going to school, and he hugged me and laughed and showed me information he had already gathered about the college extension courses right on the base. He said that he was planning to buy a new suit for my graduation, so I had better not disappoint him. I began to cry again and, knowingly or not, he chose to misread my tears as those of happiness. He said that his other surprise was that he was going to take off from work for a week and move me and the girls down personally in the new car. Did I think the girls would like that, he asked hopefully.

There was nothing left for me to do but hug him fiercely and thank him, telling him that, yes, the girls would like it almost as much as I would.

In the second week of August, my husband called to say that he had secured married officers' housing for us in the Corregidor Courts area of Fort Bragg, near his office. He said we would be living in a large airy apartment, with a bedroom for everyone, on a street called Castle Drive.

Chapter 41

Freddy and I arrived with the girls at 544 Castle Drive in Fort Bragg at the beginning of September, 1969. Except for Freddy, the white Impala that pulled up at the curb was a carload of incipient corpses. My daughters and I had twenty-two weeks to live, one hundred and fifty-four days, which comes to three thousand and eighty hours

One of the few mercies of our lives was that we did not know this on that bright September afternoon. One of the few mercies of death is that you do not measure time in hours.

I am trying valiantly to tell the story of those last few weeks unclouded by how they ended, and I may well fail at this. If I say that from the minute I walked through the door of my last home, I felt a constraint, would that be true, or are the events now too shrouded in four decades of blood-stained memories?

I can only try.

I think my first feeling upon seeing the apartment was a faint alarm, because it was completely empty. My husband had told me that the army had lent us temporary furnishings but when I first walked in, there was nothing but a few friendly dust bunnies.

I'll back up for a moment and describe our reunion. I need to do this because, to my mind, it is the only unclouded happiness that the four of us ever shared at Castle Drive and it ended the moment we walked inside.

That sounds ominous, even to me, but again I can think only with the hindsight of death and we dead are constantly looking back at our lives and remembering events in ways that seem portentous.

Once in Chicago I visited the art museum. There was a painting there where at first all I could see were some people standing near a copse of trees, but as I studied it longer, it deepened. It became something puzzling and unknowable, and so it is with certain events in our lives; the more we study them the more unfamiliar the landscape can become.

We arrived late in the afternoon, during that time of day when heat has settled on the land and holds it tightly in a suffocating grip. My husband was waiting outside Castle Drive when we pulled up. He had commandeered a military Jeep, and as Freddy cruised to the curb, I had a minute to look at him unnoticed.

Sitting there in the open Jeep, one leg casually up on the dashboard in his greens, he looked as young and carefree and unfettered as the boy from Long Island I had met half a lifetime before. I watched as he caught sight of us in his rearview mirror, and immediately his shoulders tensed. I could not see his expression, and by the time we had pulled in behind him, he had arranged his face into a mask of happiness.

He knelt and held out his arms for the girls, and his eyes met mine above their heads. I saw a small flash of happiness and a larger one of confused fear.

I always understood him so well and I knew he was trying to puzzle out how to do this again, how to take up the mantle of husband and fatherhood that had always created a sense of frightened resentment in him. And yet he and I were friends, so in his eyes I also saw that he wanted me to reassure him, to make sense of it for him. Maybe he hoped I could explain how he had ended up back here in front of a row of family housing when he had been so close, so very close, to escape.

I didn't have answers for him or for myself, either. I could only try to shift back into my old role of adoring helpmate. As it happened, I never quite managed it again during our remaining time. I was tired and confused as well.

By then I had long known that our marriage should have never taken place, that he had been unfaithful too many times to count, and that there had been no letter from the Government requesting the pleasure of his company. The weight of his lies and disenchantment with us had become too heavy for me to carry lightly any longer.

And so, standing outside on a hot Fall day in foreign humid air in the middle of a place I had never wanted to be, the best I could manage for him was a small smile and a shrug as if to say, 'Here we are, let's hope for the best, again'.

Once inside the apartment, any fragile attempts I might have made at cheerleading this latest adventure disappeared when I saw the empty rooms in front of me. We had *nothing*. At his orders we had sold every stick of furniture, including our plates and linens.

We were there, and I was hot and tired and filled with apprehension, and expected to do what, twirl around in delighted surprise at how much space we had, make it seem like an adventure to my little girls, becoming Eskimos again? I suppose that is exactly what he expected of me, but that afternoon I didn't try.

I turned to Freddy and not my husband for reassurance. That was a mistake, but disenchanted and exhausted, I was not in the mood to be wary and pleasing, two states which are not meant by nature to exist simultaneously in the first place.

Freddy gallantly stepped in and took care of us. He jovially made jokes with my husband about the inefficiency of the army, asked him about his work and how he liked the new car he had brought us, and somehow he managed to do what I could not, or would not, do. He raised the spirits of everyone in our empty apartment and hustled us all off to a hotel with a swimming pool. Before he left in his cab for the airport, he had prepaid the room for the week and handed me a check for three hundred dollars for furniture.

He did all of this in such a manner that it appeared to my husband that Freddy was nearly begging him to let him help out since, as Freddy said, my husband was not only a Green Beret but a doctor, and how could he possibly have time to sort out stupid domestic details?

Freddy had instinctively chosen the perfect approach, and later that night in the hotel room, with our girls asleep in the next bed, my husband reached for me to show that, despite my shortcomings, he still wanted me. I was reluctant to have him touch me. We had been apart for nearly five months and I wasn't comfortable yet in his presence. He seemed to me both bigger and smaller than I remembered. He seemed unfamiliar in the way that this new state and life did. I needed time to acclimate myself.

I didn't bother saying that, I merely said truthfully enough that I had stopped the pill when he had left in May for basic training.

He asked me why and I tried to turn it into a joke, telling him that any other husband would be glad to hear that his wife didn't feel the need to practice birth control in his absence. I reminded him that the birth control pills had always given me terrible headaches and suggested lightly that we put off our reunion lovemaking until I could make an appointment with a new doctor there on the base, or at least until the PX opened in the morning and he could purchase condoms.

When I said that, I was being deliberately provocative because I did not want to make love to him, not that night, and not with my little girls a foot away and liable to wake up at any moment.

Of course I knew that he must have had an ample and handy supply of condoms, but by speaking first of my lack of birth control and my reasons for it, I had hamstrung him.

His anger towards my provocation was fierce and sudden. His rage towards me was always readily available, sometimes held loosely, but I think always he had lightning in his hands.

I didn't die that night and I now know I could have, that we all could have very easily. I didn't die because when I saw the veins begin to cord on his neck, I instantly backed down and put my arms around his neck, pulling him towards me. I cannot remember my exact words, something like 'Oh, what does it matter? We're married. I didn't mean that.'

I did not mean that I was willing to risk another baby, a baby which at that time neither of us would have wanted. If I did indeed speak words to that effect, it was only to tamp down the rage I saw in his eyes. I did not believe that the world or nature would be so randomly unfair to me if just one time I wasn't careful.

How I could have thought that, I do not know. After all, it was one other random night, five years before, when I had wanted to please him that I had allowed unprotected sex and the clear result of that night was laying inches away from me, sleeping beside her baby sister.

Once again I took on the burden of being responsible for his unhappiness, and of being the one who had to fix it. By that time, of course, there was no way to do it. I understand too late that it was the fact of us that created his limitless stress and anger, and as proven by our deaths, we were always one bad minute away from annihilation. One false step or forgetful moment on my part, and chaos would ensue.

None of what happened to me, to us, at his hands was ever fair, so it is surprising to me now, so long afterward, that the sharpest pain I feel is that he was so obviously willing to use the protection he claimed to hate with all those faceless women, and yet not once with me.

And then, having failed to protect me, he would always blame me, look at me as though I had set out traps for him to fall into. He never considered me; he never asked me how I felt about anything. He judged me and he sentenced me, and I never got to be heard at all.

Chapter 42

Whether we made a baby that night or another night, it does not much matter. Before Halloween, during the time I had begun to try and clumsily make costumes for my little ones out of the cheap pajamas I had bought for them at the PX, I knew. I put off my first missed period in September to stress from the move, but by the end of October, I knew. I just didn't know what to do about it.

I had never held strong feelings against abortion. I understood the ways that unplanned love between a man and a woman could result in new life that they were in no way ready for. I had been raised by a liberal mother, a mother who had indeed advocated strongly for me to end my first pregnancy in an abortion. Her reasons had been sound: I was just twenty, he wasn't even that; we both had years of school ahead of us and no money; he said there was a right time and place for starting our family. Ironically it was him, my not-yet-husband, a nineteen year old boy, who had held the day. He had called his cheerful strong-willed mother up on the phone and begged her to come to my parents' house and explain to them why we should have the baby.

At that time, and I suppose for the remaining years of my life, I was the sort of girl-woman who was swayed by the strongest voice in the room. I was so moved, so elated and proud, that it was him who had brought in his warrior mother to argue for early marriage and parenthood. I thought it showed a deeper longing for a life with me than I had believed in up until then. Now, of course, I know that it was only a momentary desire to win that made him come down on the side of our baby that day. Maybe I knew that then as well, but tiny speck though she was, I already loved her deeply, and if she can hear my words in her faraway heaven, I hope she will know that she was a very wanted baby.

Kristy, of course, was a different thing altogether; I sought her out purposely at a time when I felt secure in my marriage and my motherhood. I had been right about the latter anyway, and though I nearly died having her, she, like her sister, was the center of my heart from the day she came.

So when I realized that we had created a new small life, my feelings of fear, even horror, were not because of the baby itself. I knew that I would love my baby with all my heart, and that he or she would make me glad every minute that they were in the world.

I was afraid I might not be in the world with my new child, or my girls, if I went forward with the pregnancy. It was too soon - too soon in every way. Physically I wasn't up to par - and my doctor in New York had advised me to wait for several years after Kristy - and I didn't think my marriage could take a new baby. I was living in the foreign land of an army base thousands of miles from home, trying to figure things out, trying to make it okay for the girls, for me, for him too.

Fort Bragg was so hard on him, I knew that. Poor baby, he had gone so far as to join the army in wartime, for God's sake, to get away from the family he had helped to create. He had expected to be ten thousand miles away in a sweating rat-infested jungle, either proving himself or maybe just trying to gain breathing space in the only way he knew how.

If I could have talked to him about it, I would have told him I understood that parenting, which came so easily and joyfully to me, was only a burden to him. I would have told him that while I knew I could love him forever, I knew that he wasn't sure he could say the same. I could have even laughed with him about how strange all of this was. He had been striving to be in the jungle with other lost boys and I was meant to be at NYU, and we were supposed to meet up a couple of years down the road and see if we would continue on together or separate.

But, instead, we were in a situation of more enforced grown up intimacy than he had ever had to experience before. The army had assigned him a desk job. For the first time in our marriage there was no high-pressured school or internship, no bars to raise and jump over, no challenges, and probably worst of all from his viewpoint, no other places he had to be at during the night hours.

He must have sat there day after day in his stuffy little army office, drowning in frustrated disbelief at how, in attempting to run, he had locked himself into this life, a life of boring duty and the inescapable knowledge that every day at five the other men around him would get up, eagerly or dutifully (because how can I know), to go home for dinner with their own wives and children.

He was so alone, without anyone around that he could ask, 'Is this it? Is this all there is? And if this is all there is, how do you cope with it?'

He could have asked me, I would have helped him, but because he had told that stupid lie about his enlistment, he couldn't bring it up.

Because he could not stand any form of criticism, or ever to be caught lying, I couldn't bring it up.

In cowardice and indecision, I became the liar in our marriage. By October, my every move and gesture with him was false. I made love to him, and I listened to him griping about his low-level boring job, and I smiled at him over dinner, and all the time I was locked far away inside myself, trying to make a decision I didn't know if I had the right to make.

I would look at my girls, and they were beautiful and happy and thriving in our little apartment on a street of identical houses with trees planted in a row with military precision. They didn't know that their father was burning himself to death with internal misery or that their mother was terrified for the future. They looked at us and they loved us and they trusted us, and they feared nothing. He and I, well I think by then in our own separate ways we feared everything. It was inertia and my love for my girls that let the pregnancy continue through October and into November, and then it was Thanksgiving and my mother-in-law was coming for her first visit, and oddly, once again it was she who decided if he and I would have a baby or an operation.

I liked my mother-in-law; at times I even loved her. Perry, as she was called, was a big lady, not in size but she had the magnetism passed on to my husband that made her fill every room she walked into. My husband adored his mother and he had brightened up perceptibly by the second day of her visit. In her he found no ambivalence. If he said he had volunteered for the army, so it was. If he said he was underutilized at his medical job there, it was all true. If he said that he needed to look for moonlighting work at night to augment his paltry salary, she wanted to type up his resume that minute.

Actually, somehow we did seem to be sliding into a worse financial morass than before. How that was I didn't understand because, for the first time ever, he had a regular salary and we were living rent-free. Freddy had bought our car and our living and dining room furniture. My husband and I had together built beds and bookshelves for the girls, but still we were in trouble.

I didn't realize how bad it was until he nearly had a stroke when he found out I had spent fifty dollars at the PX for groceries. He screamed at me in front of his mother and the girls, and stormed out of the apartment saying he was going for a run. In my hurt and embarrassment, I turned to her for comfort and somehow I blurted out that I was sure I was pregnant again and I had no idea what to do.

Capable as always, and radiant in a crisis, she sent the girls outside and steered me to the couch. "Colette, this is wonderful news. A baby is always wonderful news, and you know I can just feel it; this one's going to be a boy, the boy he has always wanted."

I was glad that she was so sure but confused as to why. "Perry, I'm glad you feel that way, but you know, he's not ...well, sometimes I think maybe he'd rather be other places." I laughed a little to remove any sting of criticism as she was as wary of any critique of him as he was. "I don't mean that he isn't wonderful, but don't you see it even a little? He's restless, I think -"

She squeezed my shoulder. Her eyes were warm but intent when she said, "He's not restless, he's driven. You know how hard it was on his father working all of those years doing an engineer's job but without college qualifications. He just doesn't want to let that happen to him, to fall behind like his dad did. Colette, I know my boy. Maybe he is a little silly sometimes, needing so much approval the way he does, striving so hard to be first, but that's just him. His need for success, it's not restlessness, you see, it's ambition. And sure, kid, I bet it's hard sometimes to live with such a driven guy, but it's all for you and the girls that he does it, all so that you can have that big house and farm in Connecticut one day. Everything my boy has done since he left Princeton and went to med school early has been for you and the girls. Now, you tell me that you don't think he'll want a son. Why, Colette, that's so unfair to him. What has he ever done but his best for all of you? Oh don't look at me that way, honey. I know it's probably a little early after Kris, and that you are a little scared - three kids, all the work, a busy husband, you're feeling hassled, right? You know I'll talk to him for you if you want me to, ask him to help out more, but ..." her eyes twinkled, "don't expect miracles, kid. That son of mine is all boy and you know how that goes. I don't think his dad washed a dish or changed a diaper in his whole life. On the other hand, Colette, I never got to look forward to what you have in front of you. Look at the life you're going to have. You're on the cusp of getting everything you want, so try to be a little patient with him, okay? He is trying so hard."

There was nothing I could say to that kind woman, or nothing I *would* say at any rate. I hugged her and thanked her, and I wasn't even surprised later when I overheard her telling him my news. I think I was relieved.

If he was stunned and horrified at the idea of yet another baby, another link in the chain that he felt binding him, he didn't let his mother see it. He rose to the occasion, going out for a bottle of his favorite Cold Duck, and later the three of us sat around the living room toasting to our bright future and to the new baby.

But I didn't believe a word of it. There was darkness at the edge of his eyes, a creeping fear. I wanted to reach over and take his hand, to say something real, or at least to reassure him that I knew, that I was unsure too, that I felt we might try our best and still fail, but that ultimately we would probably live through this.

I didn't do it. I couldn't break out of my prescribed role, and neither could he. The only real happiness and satisfaction in the room was from his poor mother who didn't know one true thing about either of us anymore. Nobody lives in our story.

Chapter 43

As with the previous year in Bergenfield, we settled into another winter of discontent. I was nervous and vaguely guilty. I knew intellectually that I hadn't gotten myself pregnant but I also knew that from the minute his mother had returned home he had been hoping that I would ask him to arrange for an abortion.

One grotesque rainy December night when he came home, he suggested doing it himself. I tried to minimize it. I asked him lightly if he would be saying this if he could know for sure that the new baby was a boy.

He nodded. "Yeah, I would, Col. I don't want more kids." He shrugged and looked away, his eyes darting around the room, trapped, anxious. "I don't think I want the ones we do have. I don't think I want …" His voice trailed off.

I had to help him, I was always willing to help him. "You don't think you want me anymore, is that what you were going to say?"

He nodded. "I'm sorry. I … we're too young, Col. I'm too young for all of this stuff." He waved his hand around our small cluttered living room.

I smiled humorlessly at him. I was tired. "We are too young, I guess, sweetheart, and yet here we are." I gestured down the hall. "There are two little girls sleeping in their bedrooms who belong to us and in here …" I tried to take his hand and lay it against my stomach but he jerked away as though I'd burned him. I nodded, "Okay, well thanks for that, darling, but as I was saying, this might not be … no excuse me, Doctor, Captain, if this is not where you want to be, it doesn't matter because it's where we are. I know all of this rubs against you - me, the girls, the new baby, a desk job you feel is beneath you, maybe a whole life that you feel is beneath you - but what do you think I can do to help you? Don't you know that if you can't take it here, can't take *us*, then I can't stop you from leaving? Go, go and don't look back. I don't know how I'll manage, but I will." I broke then and began to cry. I slapped ineffectually at his shoulder while he stared at me, his expression unreadable. "Damn you. I told you this years and years ago, that all your grand declarations of love were temporary. I told you, and you wouldn't leave me alone, and now … now, with two little girls and another one on the way, you have finally figured out that I was right. Well then, go, goddamn you, go, because I might not be very strong, and I might be terrified of what will happen to all of us without you, but it's better than this. I can't take another year of you looking at all of us like you wish a magic genie would make us disappear. I can't take the guilt - and its guilt for existing that you make me feel. Don't you know how sick that is? So go. It's almost Christmas, go see your C.O. and ask for leave. Go home to your mother and all your old friends, and try to start figuring out how to shine in this one. It won't be easy, I know. The pregnant wife, the two little girls, it's hard to make it seem heroic, but I have faith that you can turn it to your advantage somehow. Don't worry, I'll never say a word. I'll be too busy trying to survive. So go on, get up. What are you waiting for?"

He hated even the perception of rejection. I think the sane practical part of him, the one that allowed him to breeze through Princeton and Northwestern, was probably thrilled with my telling him to go, but he lived, poor darling, with a duality of nature, and it would always cause him in the end to do the worst thing for himself. If I had stayed silent, or if I had begged him not to leave me, maybe he could have gone, but the idea that I might survive without him was too much for him to bear, so he decided to stay.

It was almost a year to the day since he had run out of our apartment in Bergenfield and impulsively decided to go to Vietnam. If I had only remained silent he might have done something equally desperate to get away from us, but I had told him he could leave and it triggered his endless insecurities, so in a complete *volte face*, he took my stiff body into his arms. "Col, come on, how could you even say stuff like that to me? You know you're my girl. I was just blowing off steam but I guess around here a guy has to be happy and excited twenty-four hours a day or you tell him to get out, huh?"

Once again he had twisted my words around. I could have pointed that out to him. I could have insisted he leave. I could have done anything but fold against him in relief, which is what I did.

I still loved him, and despite my brave words, I had no idea how to care for the girls and the new baby without him. My assets were small, actually nonexistent. I had two and a half children and a car, and a three-quarters finished English degree. I didn't feel well in the new pregnancy and sometimes I thought I might die in delivery. Sometimes I thought it would be best for him and me if I did die in delivery but I worried about my girls, so I resolved yet again that night to try harder to make him happy; to think less about his lies and how we had gotten to where we were, and to think more about the future.

In bed that night he made love to me enthusiastically and I responded, but afterward, pregnancy or no, I resolved to begin classes at the community college on base in the new year because nothing had changed. His renewed passion for me and his marriage that night would, I knew, fade quickly.

Chapter 44

My mom and Freddy showed up for Christmas two days later and I felt like I could exhale for the first time in weeks. My husband loved company - even my parents were better than being alone with me - so he perked up, and though I knew he was only pretending enthusiasm for the girls and the idea of the new baby for my parents' sake, it still improved the atmosphere.

Freddy and Mom had brought stacks of presents for all of us, and we had the tree up and the eggnog flowing at night, and I don't know, for a few days there I wondered if maybe we weren't just like every other struggling young couple who had hit a rough patch but would ultimately be fine. And then Christmas morning came and he gave the girls a live pony and I realized for the first time that he might be more than impulsive and childish; that he might in fact be insane.

We had the neighbors in for cocktails the night before and everyone had stayed up a little too late for the morning barrage that the girls had started at six a.m. looking for Santa Claus. They were so cute that I didn't mind the sleep deprivation, though my poor parents looked a little worse for wear. My husband, who didn't need much sleep ever as far as I could tell, was unusually involved with helping the girls open their presents that morning, and when I went into the kitchen to start waffles for everybody, he and Freddy followed me in. They were both grinning from ear to ear when they told me we were going to have to wait on breakfast because there was a surprise first.

I was puzzled but willing. I thought I knew what the 'surprise' was. My husband had been talking about buying a stereo for a couple of weeks and I had been trying to talk him out of it because it was nearly two hundred dollars and we were so broke at that time that I had decided to forego a private doctor in favor of an army doctor for the baby.

But it was Christmas morning and I decided to put a good face on the purchase. I made funny faces at the girls, asking them what did they think it could be, as he herded us into the car. He said that the surprise was still in the store window and there hadn't been time to deliver it yet but he wanted to show it to us. I was a little puzzled by how happy Freddy seemed since I knew he was getting tired of funding our marriage, but I made up my mind that if he could act excited about the stereo, then I could too.

My husband turned away from Fort Bragg's main street and pulled off into a small agricultural area that was kept for supply drops. We got out of the car, and he led us over to a small fenced area and pointed to a little shaggy pony that was standing there. I looked at him startled but he was already lifting an excited Kristy and a reluctant Kimberly onto the pony's back. He didn't meet my eyes. My mother squealed in admiration and Freddy put his arm around me.

"Look at that, sweetheart. He got the girls a pony for Christmas. He's really something, isn't he?" I know Freddy misunderstood my expression because he laughed. "Don't you see, Colette, it's for your farm, the first thing for your farm in Connecticut, that's what this means."

I couldn't speak, and both he and my mother mistook my tears for delight.

I was frightened for the first time in all our years together. I couldn't cope. Less than a week earlier he had offered to abort our child; he had told me he didn't think he wanted any of us, and then he bought a pony. I knew him too well to believe that he had undergone some epiphany. I knew the pony was a message to me but one I could not understand.

I somehow survived that endless Christmas Day and that night in bed, when he reached for me, swelled up with wine and self-satisfaction from all the approval and adoration, I didn't refuse him, I only hesitated, but it angered him.

"What? Jesus, what now Colette? What haven't I done right now?"

I placed my hand against his face. "Don't ... don't be mad, sweetheart. We'll do whatever you want. I'm just confused, that's all."

He rolled away from me onto his back and loudly blew out air between his lips. "You're *confused*. What exactly are you confused about? I bought the girls a fucking pony. Isn't that your big dream, Colette, ten kids, a bunch of dogs and horses, the *farm*?" His voice on the last word came out in a near growl.

I shuddered, thought about it, and discarded my questions, deciding that maybe it was better not to ask, not to know after all.

I rolled closer to him but he resisted me saying, "I can't do anything right, can I, Colette? One time, one lousy fucking time, I try to tell you that I'm feeling a little overwhelmed here and you are never going to let me forget it, are you? I do everything for you, give up everything, give into everything, buy a fucking pony for the girls because that's your dream for me - fucking Farmer John, country doc, with fifty kids and a goat in every room - and even then it's not good enough."

I laughed a little. I wanted him to calm down. I was sorry I had tried to question him.

"Farmer John, huh? Well that's one way of looking at Yale, and as for the fifty kids and a goat in every room, I think I'm willing to negotiate that, doctor. Sweetheart, listen, I love the pony, the girls love the pony, I just think that maybe we need to slow down, to wait and see. This might not be where you want to be and I -"

He leaned over me suddenly and I felt his hands clamp down on my shoulders like iron. I tried not to flinch.

"It doesn't matter, does it, Colette, where I want to be, what I might want? Isn't that what you told me, that it doesn't matter because this is where I am and no matter what, there is no way out of here, isn't that what you said?"

"No, that is not what I said. I tried to tell you that -"

"Shut up, Col. Whatever you said, I know what I heard. It's you and me and the girls and this baby, and the next one after that, and one day I'll be so fucking old and tired that I don't care anymore, and I guess that's what I was trying to say with the pony, okay? I was saying you win, you got me. I'm here, isn't that what you wanted?"

I was afraid to either agree or to disagree. His eyes were bright red with rage and tears. I was afraid of what might happen next. I told him I loved him. I told him he was too good for me. I'm not certain of everything I said, but I kept talking until his hands loosened and his eyes cleared and his breathing slowed.

After a while he tried to make love to me but he couldn't, and when he said that it was the baby, that the baby between us made him feel funny, I accepted the blame for that as well. After he slept, I crept out of bed and moved over to the chair in the corner of our room. I sat there for the rest of the night, watching his hands as they knotted and unknotted convulsively in his dreams.

Chapter 45

There was very little time left, and I think if I had been watching the last weeks of my life at that time, as I do now, with the curious distance that death brings, I would have known. Looking back at that small endangered family, you can almost cue the spooky music, the kind that is meant to make people sitting in darkened movie theaters bite down on their knuckles in anticipation of the horror to come.

Long dead now, I can safely view the young man's growing desperation to depart from the scene. I can watch as he spends the last weeks before he slaughters his pregnant wife and two little girls, trying to find a different way out. I can view my old self, my living self, as I tried to prepare for an onslaught I could feel but not articulate.

Look as the young man begs his commanding officers to send him to Vietnam. *Watch* as he vainly pleads his case and, finally losing hope from that direction, *watch* as he joins the Army boxing team after hearing that the team might involve travel.

> *"You ask if there will come a time when I'll grow tired of you. Never my love."*

See the young woman that I was rush around despite the sickness of her third pregnancy. *See* how she frantically signs up for the classes that will earn her the teaching degree she is convinced she will soon need.

> *"How can you think love will end when I've asked you to spend your whole life with me?"*

Look at the little girls as they adjust to the new busy young mother. *See* my Kimberly as she embarks on her first days of mid-winter kindergarten, such a brave girl on skinny legs, proudly clutching her new Cinderella lunch box, throwing me a shaky hopeful smile as she walks into her first classroom - a sweet, hopeful little girl who had learned at home to conjugate her first French verb but was much more daunted at having to navigate the trickier waters of her first interactions with children her own age.

There is my brave Kristy, striding forward on her fat little legs to her preschool. She never looked back once. Her words to me on her first morning there were, "See you soon, Ma." And it was his grin she flashed as she went inside. Kristy, like her daddy, never once doubted that if she wanted to succeed at something, she would. She had his beauty and his determination, but she was also a warm open-hearted little girl who seemed to greet the world around her as a place that she never doubted would be delighted to have her.

She was right. My tough, funny little one had made friends with every neighbor on Castle Drive before we had been there a week and had quickly established a routine of visiting people at will. Kimmy used to stand wistfully by my side and watch Kristy's small blond head bob down the walkway, wanting to break out of her shell of shyness, but never quite able to.

I knew that my new routine of school had possibly forced Kimmy into more social interaction than she was ready for, but she was so bright and eager to please, and so inherently loveable, that I felt she would carve out her own little niche at school if only given the time to adjust to her new surroundings. I know she was a little frightened of kindergarten, and I think too that she knew I was running on nerves and determination in those last weeks, and that her father, always a loved but somewhat fearsome mystery to her, was running on something as well. I recognized it as his building up high octane rage, but smart and sensitive though she was, I like to think she never saw what I did and merely put down the growing look in his eyes to his usual restlessness.

I was a little worried about her because she had started coming into our bedroom again on an almost nightly basis. She was wetting the bed again too, as she had during the previous dark winter in Bergenfield. Usually I could get her back, and the bed changed, before my husband came in, because during those last weeks his night-time habits had changed. He wasn't making love to me; he was barely looking at me. It seemed to me that he had become more nervous and restless than ever before. When I asked him if anything in particular was keeping him from the bed, he grinned and shook his head.

"No, Col. Why? Do you need it really bad right now or something?"

Embarrassed I looked away. "That wasn't what I meant. I'm just worried about you. You're staying up so late reading every night and you have work in the morning, and there is your new moonlighting job, you're not eating very much, and I wondered if -"

"Well don't, don't wonder. I'm not sick, and if I'm grabbing a few hours of quiet time to read a fucking book instead of trying to hang onto my six inches of the bed - that is if it isn't soaked with piss - do I need your permission, Mommy?"

I walked into the kitchen, wanting to let it go, wanting to get away from him.

He followed me. "Oh, what, for Christ sake, what did I do now to offend you, Colette? If you must know, I am having a little trouble sleeping. My boxing team coach suggested I drop a few pounds, so I'm taking a few Eskatrols for appetite suppressant and they make me restless, okay?" I nodded, afraid to speak and say the wrong thing. In those last fraught weeks it seemed to me that nearly everything I said was wrong.

He strode around our small kitchen. Seemingly nervous, he picked up and discarded items on the counter. He opened and closed the refrigerator a couple times.

He stopped in front of me and spoke to the air above my head. "I want a decent fucking TV set. I'm so sick of that goddamned black and white piece of crap. I should be able to have a decent TV set to watch, shouldn't I, Col? Maybe you don't want me to have one. You probably think I don't work hard enough."

I shook my head, mute and frightened.

He laughed and rubbed his head. I could see his fingers were shaking. "No, no colored TV for me, right? We need to save up money for the baby, don't we? You want a private doctor, don't you? Army docs aren't good enough for you, right?"

"I never said that, honey. I'll go to one if you want me to. I'm just worried because Dr. Calin who delivered Kristy said -"

"Oh well ... Dr. Calin. Geez, Col, I forgot that any other doctor besides me is always going to be your go-to guy, right?"

"No, that isn't what I said and that isn't what I meant. Sweetheart, could you stop pacing for a minute, you're making me a nervous wreck?"

"Sure, sure, Col. You want me to stop walking around my own kitchen? I'll sit." He slammed into a chair and stared at me challengingly. "See, I'm sitting." He couldn't maintain it for a minute, though, and jumped up, jerking open the refrigerator door again. "Is there anything decent to eat in this house? I'm starving."

"Well, I don't know. You could have a Popsicle." I laughed a little. "They aren't fattening and you said -"

He slammed the door. "Oh, that's perfect. My swollen mess of a wife is telling me I'm fat."

I sat down heavily in his vacated chair. "Wow, thanks, Captain. I guess you are saying I'm fat now? I've only gained six pounds, and that's pretty good for over four months. I -" The expression on his face checked me; I continued in a softer tone. "Hey, no problem. I know you're under a lot of pressure, and if you are dieting, that makes it worse. I'm lucky I'm getting a pass on it right now, you know, having an excuse to be fat. If you are hungry, though, honey, I can make you some scrambled eggs. Dinner tonight is going to be kind of rushed. You know I've got class tonight and -"

"Oh fuck. Again?"

My own brittle control began to slip. "Yes, again. It's Monday. I have class on Monday. We've been over this. You told me it was fine. It's one night a week, you're not on call, and you don't have practice with the team." I stood up and shrugged, trying to head past him. "If you don't want to stay home with the girls tonight, fine, don't. I'll call next door for a sitter. If you don't want scrambled eggs, go to the officer's club. Do whatever you want, because so help me, right now I have about had it with you. No matter what I say, you complain, and moan, and tell me every single thing the girls and I do is wrong. So go have fun. I need to pick up the girls and stop by the PX. Are you taking the car. or can I?"

He clamped his hand around my upper arm, halting my progress towards the living room and points beyond. "Jesus Christ, Col, all I said was 'Is it Monday again?'. I am so sorry that I'm not more enthusiastic about being stuck in this shithole little apartment all night playing what - dress up - with your daughters? And we can't afford a babysitter every time you want to traipse off to class. What are you planning to do with this degree, if you ever finish it anyway?"

I didn't answer him. I just stared at his hand on my upper arm.

He loosened his grip, throwing both hands up. "Oh, sorry, was I bruising you?" He laughed. "Let's not start a big hassle, okay? You're in a lousy mood, I can tell. Don't worry about dinner for me or the girls. I'll take them out to see the pony, and then we'll go get burgers or something. And, yeah, you should go pick them up now. Better start walking because I am going to need the car for a couple of hours. I'll meet you back here at five or so tonight."

He walked out of the apartment. I could hear him whistling by the time he got to the curb. My husband seemed to be running on nerves and conflict; I was running on nerves alone.

I left to walk the mile to the kindergarten and preschool to get the girls. I knew they wouldn't mind walking home, especially Kristy who made an adventure out of everything. I also knew it would take us an hour to get back because of their pace, and that there wouldn't be time to give them a snack and a nap before their daddy arrived to take them to the pony, and that subsequently they would be cranky - and I worried about them being cranky around him in those days.

I shouldn't have been worried; my husband had worked out a way to manage the evening ahead beautifully. He was home and waiting for us when we walked up. He had the front door open for two guys who were struggling to shift an enormous box through the narrow doorway.

When the girls and I walked around to the back to enter through the utility door, he was standing in the living room with an expansive grin on his face. He reached down and pulled Kristy up into his arms and gestured Kimmy to his side. "Look at this, ladies, look what daddy bought for a surprise. It's an early Valentine's present. Do you like it?"

My little ones didn't know what it was, but if he was excited, they were more than willing to be too. I didn't say anything. I watched quietly as the men unpacked the boxes and set up the speakers for the enormous new color TV and stereo.

When I ran out to class an hour later, he waved at me from the floor where he was laying, one little blond head tucked under each arm.

"Have a good class, honey. The girls and I will be right here breaking in our new toy. Drive safely."

Chapter 46

Our last holiday together was Valentine's Day. I awoke early to make two batches of semi heart-shaped cupcakes for Kim and Kristy's respective classes. My husband came into the kitchen and made a joke about how the cupcakes looked more like broken hearts, and that he thought I had used too much red dye. He said they looked like they were covered in blood, I think I might have even laughed when he said that.

The rest of the day was uneventful. I cleaned house and threw up a few times from the fumes as my last pregnancy was not a smooth one.

I had had my first prenatal visit two days before with a gruff Army doctor who told me that I seemed in fine fighting form to him and he reminded me to take vitamins and walks. I had asked him about the veins in my legs which were beginning to bulge and were becoming somewhat excruciating. He chided me against vanity and recommended support hose. We did not discuss my fears about placenta previa or the need for a third C-section. I was afraid to bring them up as I didn't think I would be able to keep a straight face if he heartily advised me to be a good soldier and shared with me the parallels between pregnancy and basic training. Of course, as it turned out, my fears and my aches and pains would prove groundless.

That last Valentine's, I didn't feel well but I didn't feel sick enough either to ruin the girls' pleasure in the day, so I volunteered in both of their classrooms, and was appropriately enthusiastic about the homemade cards they made for their daddy.

I didn't mind that neither of them had made me a Valentine. They always knew they were my favorite Valentines and, little as they were, they knew he needed to receive constant wooing from them.

He came home on time that night, sporting a large box of candy from the PX. He playfully slapped my fingers when I reached for a piece. I hadn't even wanted the candy, I had only been trying to join in his fun with the girls. They were jumping for the candy and he kept raising it a few more inches over their heads. When I made a grab for a piece, he comically wiggled his eyebrows at the girls.

"Oh, should we let Mommy have a piece? Do you girls like your new fat mommy? Should we let her have one?"

The girls, eager to please him, shouted 'No!', and I knew how stupid, even childish, it was to be hurt, but all the same I felt tears start. Not wanting to ruin their fun, I went off to the kitchen to check on dinner.

I had splurged on a whole chicken which I was planning to garnish with small red potatoes carved into hearts. I thought the girls would get a kick out of it and I hoped my husband would at least think they were funny.

He must have thought I was so pathetic with my heart-shaped potatoes. He followed me into the kitchen and stood watching as I pulled out my chicken to check on it and his lips twisted when he saw them.

Abruptly he left the room and came back holding one of his uniform jackets. "Hey, Col, I really need this jacket back by Monday. We're having a formation and this is the one that fits me best. Can you make sure to get it to the cleaners in time for it to be ready Monday morning?"

Puzzled by his seeming urgency, I took the coat from him and looked at it. It seemed spotless. Maybe it needed a going over with the iron but it looked fine to me.

I smiled at him. "It's Friday night, sweetheart. The cleaners won't even be open again until Monday. I'll press it for you, though, okay?"

He seemed to weigh out his answer before speaking. "Well, that should be okay, I guess, but do you mind getting to it tonight before bed. I need to see if it looks okay. Otherwise I'll plan on wearing something else."

Sometimes his vanity tickled me and it did that night. I kissed him and promised that I would have it in inspection-perfect shape before Johnny Carson.

Later, after I put the girls to bed, I explained to them yet again that there was no Valentine's fairy, so not to bother looking under their pillows. Invisible fairies had preoccupied them since November when Kimmy had lost her first tooth and found a quarter under her pillow.

I went into the utility room and set up the ironing board. I then banged my shin hard on one of the leftover boards we had used for making the supports for the girls' beds a few months earlier. Cursing, I tried to jam it back beside the washing machine but it fell forward again. Worried that one of the girls would be hit by it, I took it into our bedroom and shoved it under the bed. Ruefully I reflected how grateful I was for bed skirts as the space underneath our bed had become yet another closet, an all-purpose holding area. When I went back in to finish ironing my husband's jacket, I noticed that his left pocket was bulging so, unthinking, I reached inside to clear it for the iron.

I pulled out a handful of envelopes. I stood very still, looking down at them. I remember being devastated, not because my husband had received *billets doux*, as the French say, from various assorted women, but because he had made such a pointed effort to share them with me.

I walked into the living room and threw the jacket at him, and when he turned surprised, I tossed the handful of cards in his face. Wordless, I walked back to our bedroom and began removing my clothes.

I was always a pretty modest girl, and even after two babies and six years of marriage, I was never very comfortable with nudity, but that night I felt strangely removed from my own skin. And for no better reason I can think of than some hidden masochistic streak in myself, I walked naked to stand in front of the dresser and stare dispassionately at my reflection.

I was only twenty-six but three pregnancies had taken their toll on me. My breasts, though not sagging yet, were scored by ugly white stretch marks, as were my thighs and belly. I traced them absently. I purposely avoided looking at my legs. I had always hated my legs; they were too skinny and short. I had longed for long shapely legs all my life. That night I only wished that the legs I did have were not marred by blue varicose veins.

I watched in the mirror as he came into the bedroom and moved towards me. Instinctively I put up my hands to cover my breasts. I was embarrassed to have him look at me in the light, ashamed to think that he must be comparing me, and doing so unfavorably, to the others.

He must have sensed a little of this because he kindly turned back to the door and switched off the overhead light.

I stood, still breathing shallowly, as he came up behind me and replaced my hands with his own. I was lonely in the way only a woman who still loves the wrong man can be lonely. I was repulsed by the feel of his fingers on my skin, and yet the places he touched me made me burn for him.

I squeezed my eyes shut, unable to face myself. I felt him kiss the side of my neck.

"Shh, it's okay, Col. You're my wife. The rest of it doesn't mean anything, you know that."

I didn't know that - not then, not now.

I wanted him - the one who had hurt me and the only one who could comfort me for that hurt. I wanted the temporary reassurance his body, if not his words, could give me.

I turned to face him, laying my head against his chest. "I love you. I still love you," I said comfortingly.

"I know. I know you do. It's okay, Col. Come to bed. There's no-one else here tonight, it's just us. You're my Valentine tonight, Col."

Can the dead blush in shame?

They can indeed, for this memory over all of them makes me remember the sharp bite of humiliation and compromise, the lies that the living tell themselves in order to continue to live.

He was gone most of that last weekend. I kept busy taking the girls to see the pony and feed him. He was a cute little guy and he had warmed up to me quickly.

On Saturday afternoon, my mother called. It was nothing unusual, a weekly routine, but on a sudden impulse I asked her if the girls and I could come home for a visit. She was taken aback. An elegant, organized lady, my mother did not encourage spontaneity. She said that of course they would love to have us but to wait until the springtime. She and Freddy were putting in a pool for all of us. She said that the backyard was a frozen mud-covered morass and that the great gaping hole in the earth would provide a dangerous temptation to the girls, especially Kristy.

We both laughed at that and I told her of course, I was just being silly, we would wait until spring.

Monday was the same as always, giving no hint of the horrors to come. Breakfast was rushed and chaotic. My husband, I noted sourly, was dressed in casual greens, apparently having forgotten his planned formation.

I took the girls to school, went home, did some laundry, and threw together a meatloaf for dinner. I spent two hours working on a paper for that night's class which was one of my favorites - child psychology - and then I went to pick up the girls.

It began to sprinkle on the way home, and not wanting to let us get drenched, I forced Kristy to let me carry her the last few blocks, causing both she and my lower back to protest loudly.

My husband came home on time wearing a look of martyrdom and we sat down for our last meal together. He was brooding over the evening ahead and Kimmy, always sensitive to his moods, tried to cheer him up by reminding him that, 'Our best show, 'Laugh In', is on tonight, Daddy'.

He ignored her, and poor little girl, so desperate to keep him happy, she tried again.

"It is so good on the new TV, Daddy."

She couldn't know, my little one, that the new TV had already ceased to please him.

Kristy, impervious as always to our shifting sentiments, announced that she was going to visit the neighbors. 'Go see my buddies' was how she put it.

I shook my head a little at my husband, indicating the heavy rain falling outside the windows. He ignored me but Kimmy caught it, saying, "Don't worry, Mommy, I'll make sure she has her coat on."

I smiled a little at my husband to see if he thought that was an unusually sweet and mature thing for a five year old to say, but his eyes were staring blankly ahead of him. He didn't see us. I don't know what he did see.

For my part, I felt no foreboding when I kissed my pumpkins goodnight on my way out. Kimmy put her arms around my neck and told me to get good grades in school, and Kristy, who was struggling under Kim's hands as she tried to zip up her coat, merely told me, "See ya, buddy." Her little mind was intent on her upcoming visit and petting the neighbor's beloved doggie.

I never saw her alive again.

I left for class, picked up my friend Sheila on the way, sat through class attentively, dropped off Sheila, and made a last stop for a half gallon of milk.

I pulled up in front of Castle Drive and inexplicably sat outside in the car for a few moments. Did I sense the coming apocalypse? It would be easy to say yes, but I think I was just taking a moment before entering the house and resuming my role as his wife.

I watched the cold rain fall against the glass and stared at our lit windows, seeing him moving back and forth in front of the glass. He seemed to be pacing. I sighed, anticipating an upcoming scene of some sort, yet another night of blame and appeasement as he aired his dissatisfaction with life in general. I might have wondered how many more of those I had left in me, but if so, I don't believe I wondered deeply. The living do not have the luxury afforded to the dead of limitless time for reflection.

I turned off the ignition and started up the walkway, entering with a very cheerful 'Hello!'.

Chapter 47

He looked funny. He was sweating.

I should have been alarmed.

I might have been if I hadn't known about the diet pills. He had lost a lot of weight in the preceding weeks and he had been more irritable and restless than usual. I knew he was hiding something the minute I walked in, but my husband being restless and excitable wasn't new to me.

I steeled myself for another round of envelopes or some revelation he had come to regarding our marriage. When I think of what I feared then, I realize how little I ever knew him. Being murdered by someone is an even more intimate act than making love. It is as revealing of character as giving birth, and at the end of the act you know yourself and the person who shared the experience with you like you will never know another person. Birth and death are the opposite sides of the same coin, just as love and hate are.

They are the inevitable sides of our existence.

He wanted to talk to me; he needed my attention, I could tell. I reached up and kissed him and told him I would be right out, that I was wet from the rain and dying to get into my pajamas.

He was relentless and he followed me down the hall to our bedroom. He put his hands up against my shoulder when I stopped at the door of Kimmy's room to look in on her. He blocked my way at the entrance to Kristy's room, telling me nervously that he had a terrible time getting her to sleep and to please not wake her. I glanced around his shoulder and made out the top of her blond mop, and though I wanted to kiss her, I let him steer me down the hall to the bedroom.

He remained in the doorway chatting nervously as I changed. He said it had been a stressful night, he said he was exhausted, he said he had something he needed to tell me and he hoped I would think it was good news.

I told him that I was tired too. I suggested we call it a night and he could give me his news in bed.

His face flushed. "No, I'm not ready for bed. I want us to have a drink. I want you to hear my news. I want to watch TV."

He was acting childish, even by his standards, so I sighed and told him to give me five minutes and I'd meet him in the living room for an aperitif.

After I had changed into my pajamas, I turned to the closet to hang up my coat for drying, and I noticed that one of the set of new luggage we had received from my parents at Christmas had been pulled from the back of the closet and was blocking the door.

I sighed, wondering if the suitcase was part of his news.

I padded down the hallway to join him in the living room because I had no choice. When I walked in, he glanced at me and asked me if I would go and get us both an aperitif. Obediently, I went into the kitchen and was immediately annoyed to see that he had left the dinner dishes sitting on the table and counter. My husband made it a point of pride to never help out with any domestic chore and, God knows, I had stopped expecting it, but that night on my way to class I had made a special point of asking him to please put the dishes in water to soak. Lately, the sight and smell of cold crusted food had been sending me running for the bathroom.

I remember standing there in the dim light from the stove, thinking 'Not even this, this one thing?'. I poured two small glasses of Cointreau and joined him on the couch.

Smiling tentatively at him I said, "Okay, Doctor, I'm ready for your big news but I have to ask, couldn't you have put the dishes in the sink for me? You know I -"

His face reddened and his neck corded. Instinctively I shifted back.

"Oh yeah, I know you do everything and I do nothing, and I'm a bad father and a worse husband, and poor Colette, poor jobless Colette, with her two kids already in school and just home from a night out with her friends, doesn't want to have to wash a dish. Gee, I'm sorry, Col, but can't you just go get another fucking manicure tomorrow?"

I laughed nervously. "A manicure? Okaaay, well if I go and get one tomorrow it will be the first time since our wedding day. But if you insist." I put my hand on his arm and I felt how tight his muscles were. "Don't worry about it. I'm sorry I said anything. Tell me your news, okay?"

He pursed his lips and stared at the TV as he spoke. "Okay, but you're in such a rotten mood now you'll probably bitch it up for me. I don't think I want to tell you now."

I counted to ten. I looked at the ceiling for patience. I waited for my usual seemingly endless tide of understanding where he was concerned to rush through me, and it didn't come.

I took a long drink from my liqueur glass, and said in a much harder voice than I usually used with him. "Fine, don't tell me. I imagine I'll figure it out soon enough. I almost tripped over the suitcase you pulled out of the closet. Tell you what, I'm exhausted and I'm cold, and I think I'll go to bed. You're right about me not being in a great mood right now. Whether I'd bitch it up for you, as you so charmingly put it, is pretty doubtful. You usually go wherever you want and do whatever you want anyway. Tell me whenever you firm up your plans. 'Night."

I half rose off the couch before he stopped me. "Oh, sit down, Col, Jesus, everything is an ordeal with you. My news is that Colonel Essing told me today that I have been chosen as the boxing team's group surgeon and I am going to get to go with them to Russia for their tournament." Encouraged by my silence, or maybe only wanting to twist the knife, he repeated it clearly, savoring the word 'Russia'. "*Russia*. Did you hear me, Col, I'm going to get to go to Russia? It's kind of an honor, don't you think?"

"When is this happening?"

Eager now, he rushed to give me the details. "We are leaving early next month and will probably be gone until the end of June. I don't know how we'll stay in touch behind the Iron Curtain, but -"

I drew in a deep breath. "Late June? So you won't be here when the baby's born?"

His face fell. "I knew you'd act like this. Fuck, Colette, if I had to stay home and miss every milestone of my life for you dropping a kid, there would have been no medical school, no residency, no anything, and then where would we be?"

I nodded like I was considering the veracity of his words. "True, where would we be? God forbid you missed any opportunity, because if you had, I might not be in the middle of nowhere, sick with a pregnancy that I didn't plan either, with no money and two little girls, while trying to walk around you on eggshells all the time because you hate it here as much as I do. But you know it's not my fault, and it's not Kim and Kris' fault that your whole 'join the army and run off to Vietnam' plan blew up in your face. Now you say you're going to Russia. That's a good one, going to Russia. So tell me, Captain, what part of California, or Hawaii - or hell, for all I know, New Jersey - is Russia in these days?" I didn't give him time to respond. I got up and started down the hall to bed.

He was on my heels. He caught me at the doorway and pinned me against the wall. His breath was hot and foul against my face.

"New Jersey? You fucking bitch, and what did you mean when you said I 'joined' the Army? I was *drafted*."

I jerked away from him, went into the bedroom and climbed into bed, adding to his outline in the hallway, "No, you volunteered and I must have hit the nail on the head because I noticed you didn't have a ready reply. Who's in New Jersey - your old flame Carol, or -?" I raised my hand for him to stop as I could see he was getting ready for one of his long furious denials which would be turned around on me and the girls, and he always got loud. I didn't want them to be awakened. "Oh, don't bother. Go back out and watch Johnny Carson on that TV we can't pay for. You know what, you've done me the favor of a lifetime on this. First thing in the morning, the girls and I are going to get on a plane and go home. I hate it here and I want my mother, and I want a real doctor, and one day, a long, long time from now, I might even want a real husband too, not a lying little boy who can't even touch a woman if she's pregnant but can paw any stranger he meets. So you go to Russia and I'll go home."

He was very still.

I said venomously, "About the TV, do you plan to send payments from behind the Iron Curtain or Newark or wherever, or should I just call the store to have them come pick it up in the morning?"

I waited for the storm to break over me but nothing happened. I watched him turn from the doorway and head back to the living room.

I laid there in the darkness and listened to the rain pelting the roof. Strangely at peace, I didn't regret what I had said. I promised myself that, for the sake of my two small ones and the one still in my womb, I would work very hard over the next few years not to regret this failed union either.

I was almost asleep when he returned to the bedroom. He snapped on the overhead light and stood over me. He waved his hands close to my face and a few droplets of water hit me.

In a singsong voice he said, "Oh, Colette, I washed the dishes for you. Who's a good husband, who's the best guy, huh?"

I raised myself carefully. I was frightened. "Hum, you are ... I ... well, thank you. I'm really sleepy, honey, so if you're not coming to bed, do you mind turning off the lights?"

He looked at me, his eyes bulging a little. I had no idea what was wrong with him but I was already aware that this was going to be one of those nights where it seemed dawn might never come, and how right I was about that.

He grinned a little. "I'll turn off the lights, see?" And he did, but he didn't leave. He stood in the doorway breathing heavily.

"So that's not good enough, huh, me washing the dishes, me spending all night stuck inside with the girls while you're out having fun? So what is it you want now, Colette?"

I kept my voice low and careful. "Nothing, I don't want anything else. I'm fine, you're great; you're amazing, a great husband and father. I'm just really sleepy now, okay? I'll get up early and we can have a special breakfast together, just you and me. You can tell me all about the trip. I'm sorry I said that about it not being Russia. I'm just disappointed that you're going away. You know how much I miss you when you're gone, but it'll be fine, honey. We'll all be fine, okay?"

He seemed to weigh out what I had said for sincerity, and finding nothing lacking, I saw him nod in the darkened room. "Okay, okay." He exhaled heavily. "Yeah, that sounds good. We'll have breakfast and, yeah, it'll be fine, everything's fine. Okay, I'm gonna read for a while, okay, Col? I'll try not to wake you up when I come to bed."

He leaned down to kiss me and I managed not to shudder when I returned it.

As soon as he left the room, without turning on a light, I very quietly got out of bed and moved over to the closet where the suitcase protruded. As silently as I could, I unzipped it and put in a couple pairs of maternity slacks and some blouses. Then I carefully opened up my top drawer and reached for some underwear and a nightgown. I knew I couldn't put much of my own stuff in there because as soon as he left in the morning I would fill the rest of the suitcase with as much as I could get in of the girls' clothes. I would only be able to carry one suitcase as I knew he would be taking the car. I calculated that it was a mile to the bus stop, which I could make if Kimmy helped me by holding Kristy's hand. From there we would ride to the front Fort Bragg gate, and then catch the commuter bus to the Fayetteville airport. Once there I could call Freddy, and I knew he would call the airlines and guarantee us seats.

I glanced at the clock - two a.m.. Six more hours and, rain or no rain, me and my small hostages to fortune would be on our way.

"Mommy, Mommy, what are you doing?" I jerked around, almost falling backwards over the suitcase. Kimmy was standing in the doorway, staring at me.

I held out my arms for her. "Shh, quiet baby, it's a surprise. I'll tell you in the morning. What are you doing up, pumpkin - bad dream?"

She nodded against my shoulder, too sleepy to question me further. "So bad, Mommy, can I sleep with you?" She looked over my shoulder, and seeing the empty bed said. "Is Daddy working tonight?"

I carried her over and tucked her in. "No, sweetheart, Daddy's home. He's in the living room, reading. Hang on a minute and Mommy will get into bed with you. You can sleep here till Daddy comes to bed, okay?"

She nodded, big brown eyes already closing in sleep. Hastily I zipped up the bag and pushed it back inside the closet, but try as I might, I couldn't close the door over it and I just had to pray that he wouldn't notice it in the morning.

I climbed into bed beside Kimmy and pulled her close to me, trying to breathe in the scent of little girl and make myself relax. I knew I needed a few hours' sleep if possible, but my entire body was as tight as a drum wire and I could feel my heart slamming against my ribcage.

I suppose I must have dozed a bit, though, because his voice startled me when he came into the room. "Oh this is fucking perfect."

Chapter 48

His voice woke up Kimmy. Instinctively she moved towards me, but before I could put my arms around her, she was sliding away. I looked at him in shock. He had our daughter's legs in his hands and he roughly pulled her off the bed.

I know he dropped her roughly to the floor because I heard her cry out in pain and then, "Daddy, Daddy, Daddy," more a cry of betrayed love than of pain.

My reaction was instinctive and disastrous - or maybe not. Maybe nothing could have stayed the carnage, but in forty years I have had to ask myself over and over, if I had remained still, if I had not reached out to defend my frightened child, could we have lived?

I suppose it doesn't matter or I suppose it shouldn't matter, for aren't we, my girls and I, ancient history to all except ourselves? I did try, though, and in the trying failed utterly. We are long dead and forgotten by all but maybe him, the man whose hand I first held in the movies when we were both thirteen, whose hand I reached for on our wedding day, and whose hand I instinctively clutched at the birth of our children, the blood-drenched hands I loved which destroyed us all with such merciless efficacy.

I watched him looming over my little girl with an expression that terrified me. I didn't think - I was moving only to defend my child. Quietly I lowered my hand and reached under the bed, grasping for the wood slat I had shoved under there a few days previously. I pulled it out inch by inch as he bent over Kimmy, screaming at her.

"You pissed the bed again, *my* bed. You're everywhere fucking it all up for me all the time." He imitated her viciously. "Daddy, Daddy, Daddy. I'll give you fucking 'Daddy', you whining, creeping, sneaking little bitch."

I had to move and I did. I yanked out the board, and holding it, moved behind him to swing at his shoulders.

I wasn't quiet enough. He turned, and when he saw me standing there holding the slat and aiming it towards him, his eyes bulged in shock and rage. In a single tug he had it away from me and I will swear until my last day of eternity that he winked at me as he swung it above him and lowered it against my child.

I heard her scream and felt both horror at his action and relief that she was still alive to scream.

I screamed in return. "Run, baby, run ..." I shrieked at her. "Stop, stop, stop! Why are you doing this?"

Kimmy stood and ran, and didn't make it beyond two feet towards the doorway. I was clutching his pajama top. He let out a high animal shriek and swung at her again and the entire world stilled for a moment as I watched my little girl fly forward from the impact.

She made a tiny sound, a little mewl, for only a second before I wailed in animal response.

There was a silence that seemed everlasting.

I looked at her against the doorway, crumpled, her face covered in blood. I could see my child's bone protruding from her tiny face. My baby's bone was sticking through her skin. I reached for my hairbrush - such a paltry defense - but I hoped to kill him with it as my weapon.

I said his name and he turned around slowly to face me. Even he, the monster, seemed stunned by what he had wrought. I pulled back my arm and slammed the brush into his forehead. He bellowed, dropped his club and smashed his fist into my chin.

The pain was sudden, my knees buckled. I reached out and grasped his pajama top, tearing it as I fell. He pulled me back up by the neck and punched me in the chin again. I fell and rose in primal rage. I screamed his name, spitting out the word in blood. I clawed at his top, ripping off his pocket and scratching his chest, and he bent and shoved me backward.

He reached for the wood, and in one fluid follow through smashed it into the side of my skull. It's true what they say, you can indeed see stars.

I must have turned my head from the blow because he laughed and shrieked at me. "Want another, Col? Here comes another and another, you fucking cunt." He slammed the wood into the other side of my face and the black descended upon me. I do not know how long I laid there unconscious but it must have been for some time, because he did things, unspeakable things, while I lay there.

I am certain that he thought I was dead, for the man who had been my husband, the butcher, was not quiet and the noises penetrated my unwilling sleep.

I awoke conscious of only the most terrible pain in my skull. At first the sounds I heard, grunting and thumping, and a high ghastly laughter, seemed all part of some pain-filled nightmare. I couldn't see and my eyes were sticky. Confused, I raised my hand, wiping at the obscuring moisture. In the dim light from outside my room I could see my hand was black with blood.

Instinctively I started to call out for my husband and then I remembered it was no nightmare. Panicked, I looked to the doorway where I had seen my little girl laying broken what had been either a second or an hour before. She was gone, but an enormous bloodstain marked the spot, bringing home forcibly that this was reality.

I listened intently for the sound that had awoken me. I recognized the voice as my husband's. I could hear him laughing or crying from somewhere nearby.

I heard another sound - a tiny squeak - and I knew. Kristy!

I made it to my knees, driven upward by a fear so deep and primal that my physical pain was pushed aside. I hesitated for a moment, such a small moment during which I gazed at the dim outdoor light coming in through the utility room door ten feet from me, a door that opened to the outside and possible safety. I crawled quietly the few feet forward to the utility room and looked up at the handle above me. I put a shaking hand on my abdomen and asked the tiny life inside me for forgiveness, then I reached into the utility drawer and pulled out a knife.

Rising on my shaking legs, I stumbled down the hallway towards my baby's room, leaning against the hallway wall for balance. Frightened in a way I could never be for myself, I inched into Kristy's room.

I almost made it to her bed but I had not been quiet enough. I had not been fast enough.

"Colette, Colette, Colette, you're alive. No matter where I go, you'll always be right ahead of me, waiting, won't you, Colette?"

I turned to face him. I could beg but he did not give me the chance. The wood was in his hand. He held it high and he swung at me. I raised my arms and he shattered them. He swung again and hit me a killing blow to the head, but still I did not lose all consciousness. No, I was aware enough to feel that the tiny body I had fallen backwards onto remained motionless beneath me.

I did not feel the pain from his last blow. Instead, I was anxious for him to strike me again to finish this. Broken in every place, I craved death. I knew I would not survive my injuries and I hoped he would grant death to me soon.

I could not hear him or see him, and for a moment I drifted. I thought I felt

Kimmy's little hand against my cheek and heard her calling me. Alarmed, I tried to open my eyes but could only manage to raise one lid.

I saw her floating above me. She wasn't hurt at all. Sweet relief flooded through my mangled skull and I tried to raise my arms to gather her to me but sharp agony stopped me and I was forced to remain still.

I wondered where he had gone, my husband, how long she had to escape. I tried to tell Kimmy to run but could not make the words come, and then he was back.

She was fading but it seemed only I could see her. Despite my broken mouth, I smiled. Kimmy had gotten away. She was gone now, my Kimmy. He could not hurt her again.

My husband grasped my ankle and pulled me roughly off my baby's bed. I hit the floor with a small exhale. He was panting by then, but whether from his exertions or fear at what he had wrought, I could not say.

"Are you still breathing, Colette? Jesus, Jesus." Breath whistled in his throat. He rolled me to the side and I felt a thick fabric envelope me, and then, with unusual gentleness, he lifted me, wrapped in this way, into his arms. My head fell forward, boneless against his chest.

> *"You say you fear I'll change my mind and I won't require you. Never my love."*

When he reached our bedroom, he dropped me to the floor and yanked the covering off me. I heard his knees crack as he knelt beside me, a final moment of intimacy as he leaned forward and put his mouth over mine. I watched through my one uninjured eye as he pulled back, his own lips slick with my blood.

He smiled at me. "Bye-bye, Colette."

He fumbled with something on the floor and raised his hand. The outdoor light caught the glint of steel. I did not close my eye. He sunk the knife into my neck with force. He stabbed me again and again, but I felt no pain from his strikes. Then I watched with fading vision as he stripped off his blood-soaked top and placed it onto my chest.

> *"What makes you think love will end when you know that my whole life depends on you?"*

Dead, or near enough for it not to matter, I observed distantly as his arm moved up and down, up and down, piercing me through the chest countless times until, seemingly exhausted, he dropped the weapon.

My spirit floated lightly above the two on the floor below, watching the final intimate acts of their marriage draw to a close. He noticed the small knife clutched tightly in the dead woman's hand, the knife she never got to use, and he grunted in anger, prying it from her non-resistant hand and flinging it a few feet away.

> *"How can you think love will end when I've asked you to spend your whole life with me?"*

The red man who had been my husband stood and began kicking my poor ruined body in the thigh and, seemingly inspired, he leaned forward and dipped his fingers in the quickly coagulating blood of my neck and chest, and began writing the word 'pig' on the headboard in my blood. A final note to me, a late Valentine, yes, but the color held true.

My heart blood sent the strongest message of all.

Chapter 49

Being a ghost is like every other new thing, it takes a while to adjust to, to become competent and comfortable with. I know that for my baby, for Kristy, she has remained at Castle Drive all these years, thus forcing me to remain as well because she has never understood that she is indeed dead. She was two years old. Death is not something a two year old is designed to understand.

I, on the other hand, understood immediately what had happened to me, or better I should say, what had been made to happen to me. The night my husband killed me I followed him around, watching his frantic perambulations. In the beginning I was as small as a speck of dust, looking on the carnage and searching for my girls, but observant dust, and these are the things I saw him do:

After he painted the word 'pig' onto the headboard in my blood, he stumbled down the hall to the living room and sat down, shaking frantically on the sofa. He turned on the lamp and held his head in his blood-soaked hands. I believe he was deciding, should he tell, should he run, was there another way out?

His decision process, whatever he was thinking, was of a short duration. Always a child, though a calculating angry child, it did not take him more than a few minutes to decide that no, he should not be punished for these crimes, that his life, a life which held so much in the way of accomplishment and future promise, must not be destroyed because he had destroyed us. I watched him grab the new issue of Esquire magazine off the table and thumb purposely through it until he found whatever he was looking for. He read quickly and placed it back on the coffee table. Standing, he pushed the coffee table over onto its side and moved back down the hall towards my body.

He knelt briefly beside me, yanked out the ice pick he had left in my chest and exited the bedroom towards Kristy's room. That was the first time I saw what he had done to my baby. She was laying face down on the bed under her covers, and when he pulled them back, I saw that her back was drenched with blood. She was not wearing her pajama top.

If he flinched, I didn't see it.

He pulled her onto his lap and laid her across his legs, facing him. If there was one bad moment for him, one moment of remorse, this might have been it. For, to his credit, he made retching noises as he put the ice pick into her tiny chest over a dozen times.

I could see she was beyond pain by then. Her little face was blue. Her opened eyes had strange red dots on their surfaces and her throat was discolored. There was a blackened bruise on her chin. I understood then that what had befallen us had started hours before, between my husband and Kristy.

I watched, sick at heart, as he reached under her pillow, pulling out her bloodied pajama top and redressing her, his tiny dead doll. Carefully he tucked her in and rolled her to her side, positioning a baby bottle near her mouth. I tried to make a noise but it was far too early in my death for speech, and if he felt my presence, he did not show any sign of it.

He then walked into the bathroom and grabbed up the white bathmat, before returning to the master bedroom and my cooling corpse. He placed the bathmat over my abdomen and laid the ice pick down upon it. He fussily straightened it and laid the sharp knife with which he had stabbed me neatly beside it. Straightening, he pulled the club from the floor beside me, and with an expression of resignation on his face, marched stolidly back out into the hallway and into Kimmy's room.

My first little girl was lying in her bed, flat on her back, with her arms beside her, still as a small statue. It was only as I drew closer that I could see the terrible damage he had inflicted to the left side of her face. Grunting in apparent distress, he turned her onto her side as he had her sister, and raised the slat and smashed in the right side of my dead child's face. Only then did he tenderly roll her towards her side and cover her up.

He headed towards the door and stopped.

I shuddered, fearing that he was returning to desecrate her further, but instead he reached down to the floor beside her and lifted her dropped security blanket, and placed it against her under the covers. He remained a moment, looking down at her, and once more headed towards the master bedroom. Still holding the club, he leaned down and retrieved the knife and the ice pick from my abdomen and I followed him into the utility room, and then outside, where, after wiping off the handles against his pajama bottoms, he carefully laid them under a bush.

He hurried back inside as it was still pouring rain and I think too he feared being spotted by the frequent patrols that were common at Fort Bragg. He left the door ajar, which I did not immediately understand but do now very well. Once back in the apartment, I watched him with appalled interest. He was utterly calm, a man with a job to do, and he was following his own orders.

He strode briskly into the hallway and removed a small disposable scalpel from the closet where he stored medical supplies. Walking into the bathroom, he stood silently in front of the sink, his blood-stained visage stoic. Then, with a grimace, and making the only cry of distress I had heard from him all night, he incised his chest with the scalpel and dropped it into the toilet beside him. I did not flinch watching him.

Without hesitating, he went to the kitchen and knelt at the cabinets. He reached inside and pulled out a pair of surgical gloves from the back. Returning to the master bedroom, he rubbed his gloved fingers hard against my neck to find wet blood. Once he had done so, he went over to his message on the headboard and wrote over the original word, erasing forever his fingerprints.

He made another circuit to the kitchen, where he picked up the phone and called for help.

I listened.

"Help! Send M.P.s.. Stabbing. There are some people who might be dead. I'm hurt." He panted dramatically then. "I think I'm dying. Help!"

I raised an invisible eyebrow. Deadened, both literally and by the horror around me, I found that he could still amaze me.

He left the phone dangling, walked down the hallway and stopped briefly in the bathroom where he peeled off his gloves and dropped them into the toilet on top of the scalpel, flushing the toilet afterward.

He returned yet again to our bedroom.

Using one end of the top bed sheet, he picked up the bedroom phone. Apparently the line was still open, because he said in a thready voice, "Five-forty-four Castle Drive, on post. Hurry. Dying."

He laid the receiver on the bed and moved over beside my body. To my disgust, he lay down beside my corpse, and put his head on my shoulder and his arm around my neck.

Chapter 50

For several days after our killings, the apartment was constantly filled with strange men who threaded through examining each piece of the detritus of our poor lives. I imagined that my husband must have been arrested shortly after they had removed him from the scene.

I did not accompany my own body, or those of my girls, when they took us away. I was busy searching for my little ones. Almost from the beginning, from the first cloudy dawn that broke a few hours after our murders, I could sense something different about the light that came through the windows. There was a force to it. I felt that if I merely inched my spirit towards it, I would be enveloped, so I avoided it assiduously. I needed to know about my girls first.

It took months before I began to understand, months of me existing as a vague haunting presence in my former home. After a short while all the noise and activity ceased, and no one came at all. I spent endless hours gazing out the front windows, hoping for a glimpse of my girls, but always ignoring the deeper light that hovered just beyond my vision. I was waiting for a sign telling me whether I should stay or attempt to go, but where I could go, or how, I didn't know.

Oddly I did not think about my husband much. Naïve in the ways of the world while I lived, death did not bring me a new sophistication. When I thought of him at all, it was with a kind of dark glee, imagining him in a real cage, imagining him realizing that maybe his life with us had not been nearly as terrible as he had thought when contrasted with his new reality.

Time passed slowly as the mud and light snow outside gave way to grass and spring, and then the heaviness of deep summer. As the days grew long, I existed in a quasi-somnolent state and might have become nothing more than another of the dust motes that drifted in the hot trapped air of my home.

But then Freddy came.

I was stunned, delirious with joy. Freddy, *father*, home. My joy was short-lived. He looked ancient, a stooped old man, his face scored by countless tears, and still it was indescribably wonderful to see him.

He was accompanied by two strangers and I did not understand their presence there. Before I could begin to try, the apartment was racked by desperate screams.

"Grandpa, Grandpa, Grandpa." A small, sweet-scented whirlwind brushed past me and I watched in despair as my baby flung her insubstantial form at Freddy's knees. Her screams, so excruciating to my ears, were noiseless to the living.

I was torn between joy that I could see her and horror that she was still here. I tried to reach for her, calling out to her. "Baby, Kristy, it's Mommy. Look angel, it's Mommy." She could hear me. I saw her tiny frantic fingers still against Freddy's leg and her bloodstained little back stiffen. She turned and stared at me with wide frightened blue eyes, raising her hands and backing away, disappearing.

She was afraid of me, my baby. My little tough one blamed me for her death. She didn't remember, or maybe she did. Her mommy had not saved her. She wanted her Grandpa to help her, but because of me, she had run away and hidden instead.

Ghosts can see each other much more clearly than the living can see us, but we are adept at hiding too. We can become, as I often was, a speck of dust or a shadow on the wall, and Kristy had gone again. I did not try to find her, fearing I would only frighten her more. I stayed by Freddy, my arm wrapped around his waist as he walked the apartment, my head against his chest as he listened to the two men tell him how they believed my husband had killed all of us. The men were very close to the truth, missing only that it had started with Kristy.

As I listened along with Freddy, I began to understand that my husband was not in a prison somewhere but was living out beyond me in the world, free and unfettered. Basking in my time with Freddy, I did not allow rage to darken those precious hours. Rage would come in time, come and remain with me through all of these years.

Freddy stayed until late that night. I don't think he felt me but he did speak of me, of me and the girls, with all the love which he had always shown us, and he whispered a prayer to me as he left us behind that night.

Chapter 51

Then there was nothing, a decade of nothing, a futile, hopeless time of lonely despair mixed with a growing hatred towards the monster that had sentenced me to this. I heard, and sometimes saw, my baby girl, but my entreaties to her were never returned and the days of my death were ones of ceaseless misery and regret.

One day our tomb was reopened and I understood that a trial was at last occurring. A dozen sad-faced strangers were admitted to our silent unchanged chamber, some in tears before they made it through the front door. These I quickly understood were the jurors, but they all faded because he had returned with them.

My husband had come back to Castle Drive.

I drank in the sight of him. Unlike Freddy, grief had not laid its dark hand on him. He looked young still, and handsomer than I remembered him being. His hair was longer, his suit was expensive and his eyes were like glaciers. He saw me too, I know he did. I watched his pupils expand in shock. I think he heard our child as well, her whispered 'Daddy'. She said his name in tones of shock and awe. Could he hear, as I did, the longing underneath? Maybe, for he suddenly began jostling people aside to escape from our former abattoir. He was leaving and I flew to the window to watch him.

Outside, despite the heat, he seemed to regain his balance, his endless confidence. I stared with my dead eyes as women and small children gathered around him, offering smiles and support. A little girl shyly handed him a flower.

From inside I offered up impious prayers for his death.

Death, but not here, not inside the only place I had. I wished him somewhere unimaginable but I did not know then if there was any other place. Castle Drive was my only point of reference, and as I turned away, unable to look at him any longer, I wondered if this was all there was to death, an endless life in the place where life had ended.

Years passed and I learned only that my husband had been convicted, then freed, then remanded back into custody, because one day the Army builders came and began to ready Five-forty-four Castle Drive for a new family and they gossiped as they worked.

The new and improved apartment was much nicer after the remodeling. I was not sorry to see the traces of our ruined lives removed. I did not mind the new families either. They had children, and it was the children whom I loved to watch and listen to that eventually brought my little girl back to me.

She was delighted by the children and she couldn't resist them. And they all saw her. They rolled balls to her and played hide-and-go-seek with her, and for the first time since the night of our deaths there were the sounds of children's voices raised in laughter and not screams.

It was the adult family members who helped to return her to me. She was still a very little girl and she would watch the living children so longingly as they were held by their parents. Eventually she wanted to be acknowledged by these strangers too.

But despite crawling onto their laps and surprising them at the side of their beds at night, they showed no response to her, except for the last family that lived in our old apartment.

There were four families altogether, the last a kind Latino Captain and his wife. I think they did see her, saw her and were afraid. Kristy was so hurt by their recoil of her tiny hands that for once she turned to my always-waiting, if insubstantial, arms. Once I could finally hold her, I found my own private heaven for a time. I had ached and prayed for nearly forty years, and at last I had my baby back in my arms.

I believe I could have existed then peacefully throughout time just that way, Kristy and I together, but one day the last good family moved away and what came in their place were the bulldozers.

Kristy and I huddled together in the falling corners of our only home until there was nothing left around us but rubble, and we stood exposed to the sky and to an outer world that we had forgotten existed. When the last wall fell, Kristy looked up at me trustingly and asked me. "Where we go, Mommy?"

I smiled with false confidence. I had no idea where we go, but I had my baby and the world seemed so incredibly beautiful to me that I swung her hand back and forth playfully. "Well, Kristy girl, we will go forward because we can't go back."

She nodded as though she understood me, and because I laughed, she joined me, flashing tiny white teeth.

In the end though it was Kristy and not I who seemed to know exactly where we were going.

"And a little child will lead them."

Suddenly, her face alight with joy, she disengaged her hand from mine and pulled away from me, her legs seeming to lengthen with every stride. I began running after her, so afraid that I would lose her again, until her excited shriek brought me to a stop.

"Kimmy, buddy. All my buddies is here. I is here too."

There she was, just as Kristy had said, my Kimmy, the same but forever changed. She still had the warm, wondering brown eyes of a child but they gazed at me from a woman's face. My girl had grown up. she shimmered with happiness and a palpable radiance. She was not alone. Kristy was right, they were all there.

My first father and Freddy and my mother and Kimmy, and standing beside her was a tall beautiful young man who had the face his father would have had if only he had possessed this boy's radiant heart. They were all there and they were waiting for me, hands outstretched and eyes filled with all the love and peace I had thought I had lost forever.

So this is the end of my story on earth, but in truth it was only my beginning.

Printed in Great Britain
by Amazon.co.uk, Ltd.,
Marston Gate.